Welcome
to the
Slipstream

Natalka Burian

Merit Press
New York   London   Toronto   Sydney   New Delhi

Merit Press
An Imprint of Simon & Schuster, Inc.
1230 Avenue of the Americas
New York, NY 10020

First Merit Press hardcover edition JUNE 2017

MERIT PRESS and colophon are trademarks of Simon and Schuster.

For information about special discounts for bulk purchases, please contact Simon & Schuster Special Sales at 1-866-506-1949 or business@simonandschuster.com.

The Simon & Schuster Speakers Bureau can bring authors to your live event. For more information or to book an event contact the Simon & Schuster Speakers Bureau at 1-866-248-3049 or visit our website at www.simonspeakers.com.

Interior design by Heather McKiel

Manufactured in the United States of America

10 9 8 7 6 5 4 3 2 1

Library of Congress Cataloging-in-Publication Data has been applied for.

ISBN 978-1-5072-0075-9
ISBN 978-1-5072-0076-6 (ebook)

Dedication

For Viola and Leo

Acknowledgments

Thank you to Kate Johnson, Jackie Mitchard, Stephanie Kasheta, Lisa Laing, Sylvia McArdle, Meredith O'Hayre, and everyone at Merit Press for bringing this book into your hands. I am also deeply grateful to Heather O'Neill, Nonie Brzyski, Rebecca Heyman, Neal Block, Dave Gooblar, and Sandy Hall for reading many different versions of this story. I would have given up writing entirely without the tireless support of the entire Table of Trust, particularly Erin Foster Hartley, Erin Latimer, and Megan Paasch. Thank you Margarita Montimore, for that really excellent and well-timed pep talk. I am also indebted to Julie Sondra Decker for her time and faith in my ability as a writer.

Thank you to Said Sayrafiezadeh for making all of this seem possible at a time when it seemed anything but.

Thank you to my siblings, Olesh Burian and Milya Burian; my mother, Irka Zazulak; and Nancy and Arnold Schneider. Thank you to my Ramona family for sustained awesomeness. Without the support of Scott Schneider and Elisabeth Schneider, I would never have had time to write a single page.

Thank you to the very first storyteller I ever knew, Daria Zazulak, and to the late empress of dramatic tension, Anna Dorosz.

Thank you Viola and Leonora, for making me see the world so differently—I am so grateful for every day I spend with you. Finally, all of my possible thanks to Jay Schneider, my best reader and best friend; I am perpetually overwhelmed by your love and support.

Chapter One

Twenty thousand feet above McCarran International, our plane looped in a holding pattern of repeating ovals. Mom had locked herself inside the onboard bathroom.

"Mrs. Lowell?" The flight attendant banged on the door. "We need all passengers seated immediately." She turned to me and gave me one of those *can't-you-do-something* looks.

"Mom?" I called. I moved until my shoulder touched the befuddled flight attendant's and tried knocking myself. The lavatory door rattled, and inside, something else made a grating, metallic sound. I knocked again, not sure if Mom could hear me over the clamor.

From her seat by the gold-rimmed, hard candy–shaped window, Ida stared at the woman and me like *we* were the ones delaying the plane's landing. Ida had been taking care of me since I was nine. She made sure that I could do long division, that I had clothes that fit, and taught me how to play guitar. She even showed me, under our twin grimaces, how to use a tampon.

I didn't really need a babysitter anymore, but I still needed Ida around. What I mean is, we all needed each other, Mom, Ida, and me. We were a frail, spare ecosystem, and I didn't want to think about what would happen if one of us disappeared. After I turned seventeen and could drive and nearly vote, I was positive Mom was going to let Ida go. When Mom told me that

Ida would be moving with us to Las Vegas, well, I was massively, perfectly relieved.

I was feeling less relieved by the second, though. With every bang on the narrow bathroom door, I looked over at the flight attendant, her brow bisected by a deep crease.

"Can we just kick it down or something?" I asked.

"I'm sorry?" The crease on her forehead multiplied into a neat row of lines, distinct as an empty staff on a piece of sheet music.

"I'm coming, I'm coming," Ida said as she heaved herself from her plush, leather upholstered seat.

"Mom!" I shouted as loud as I could.

"Van?" Mom's voice bled through the door. It sounded thin and wrong.

"Yeah, it's me. What's going on? Are you okay?"

"Of course I'm okay. I'm *fine*," Mom shouted.

"If she's having *digestive issues*," the flight attendant lowered her voice and raised her eyebrows, "I do have some medication in the first-aid kit."

"Mom!" I shouted. "Are you having any digestive issues?"

"What?" Her voice trickled back through the mottled gray plastic door. "Of course not! I'm just taking apart this sink."

All sympathy vanished from the flight attendant's face, and she reached for the phone built into the vestibule wall.

"Mom, we're landing in a minute—you need to come out!" My hands shook as I knocked again.

Mom mimicked my banging and struck the other side of the door. I tugged on the little recessed handle and tried to force it open. The flight attendant cleared her throat beside me, her sleek head bent over the phone.

The door slid open and revealed Mom, clutching part of the tiny sink's faucet in her fist. The little blue and red water taps jangled back and forth against one another. Her smile was triumphantly wide.

The flight attendant looked up, her mouth still open from speaking into the handset.

"My *goodness*," Mom said, offering the faucet to the furious flight attendant. "Your water pressure was terribly low. I removed and cleaned your aerator, so it's much better. Although," and here, Mom chuckled a bit, "I couldn't quite get the faucet back on—it wasn't installed correctly to begin with. Just popped right off." Mom brushed off the woman's sleeve. Her uniform was not one of the mass-produced polyester affairs on the attendants working our Uzbekistan Airways flight the night before. It looked like a dress the single young lawyer in a romantic comedy would wear on a date to a fancy restaurant. "You'll need to apply a touch of adhesive to it. Otherwise, good as new."

"Ma'am, I'm still not clear on your activity aboard our aircraft." The woman's voice had been trained to sound calm and even, but her expression—that was another cold, hard story. "I'm going to confer with our team on the ground."

"What's going on, ladies?" Ida asked. She'd been making her way up the aisle for a while. Ida moved slowly—arthritis in the knees.

"Mrs. Lowell just handed me this." The flight attendant brandished the petite faucet at us. "And I must inform you that tampering with the aircraft is a criminal offense."

"Since when is a loose plumbing fixture a criminal offense?" Ida looked between Mom and the flight attendant.

"And really, it just popped off," Mom said, wandering off down her own neural pathways. When her face got that closed-door look, I had no idea what she was thinking about, or who or what was minding the store back there behind her eyes.

"Please take your seats, ladies. We can attend to this matter once we land."

What would happen then? Surely Mom wouldn't be arrested—it was such a small thing. An arrest was the last thing Mom needed.

We packed up the Sirdaryo house, but left everything there. Things had not gone well. Mom had told her employers at the Uzbek Hospitality Group about her suspicions that the Russian government was intercepting and confiscating her e-mails. We had just the single day to leave. The only bags we brought were stored in a little closet-type space at the mouth of the plane. We had our clothes, Ida's special face creams, Mom's computer, and Ida's—well, mostly mine now—guitar. I didn't really care what got left behind, as long as Ida's guitar didn't. Playing guitar was the one thing I could do anywhere we went. It didn't matter what time zone we were in or what the word for Tuesday was—an E major barre chord was always the same.

"Mom," I whispered, while Ida murmured to the flight attendant.

"Hmm?"

"What were you *doing*? Getting sent to prison is not the way to start a new job."

"Prison?" Mom waved her hand in aristocratic dismissal. "Don't be dramatic, Van. I was just thinking about water pressure, you know, the things they have to do to control liquid flow in limited environments. And really, that aerator was filthy. I should bill *them*."

"Mom, I'm serious! After last time—you just—you need to settle down."

"Last time? It was nothing to do with me—in a government conspiracy like that I didn't have a chance. What is it the Americans like to say? With the eggs and the omelet? I was the eggs."

"Oh my God." I shivered as I watched Ida press a fold of cash into the flight attendant's hand, Mom's purse open in her lap.

Sometimes I wanted to say, *Why are you like this? I hate that you're like this.* But you can't say things like that to someone you used to dig apple peels out of the garbage with when you both got really, really hungry. Sometimes I did hate her, though. Not just in the usual teenage daughter way. I hated her because she was the one I'd had to come out of. There was no other option. I was stuck with everything because I started out in her uterus.

Back in my seat, I pulled my legs up against my chest and rested my face on my knees. I smelled the bony-smooth lumps of my kneecaps. The familiar, chalky seashell scent of my skin flooded the front of my face. Ida reached over and smoothed my shoulder, her head turned toward an oval slice of vibrant sunset over the desert. I lowered the shade.

A woman waited for us in the glowing square of window overlooking the runway. The sky had darkened to a dull navy by the time our small plane taxied to the gate. The narrow-eyed-but-placated flight attendant ushered me down the steel staircase pushed up against the plane.

"Oh good," Mom said, pulling her sunglasses from where they caught the lace of her shirt at the base of her throat. "Chantal is here."

Whenever we arrived at another one of Mom's consulting jobs, there was a Chantal waiting, although usually it was a Roderigo or Jonathan—women were rarely assigned to shepherd us through the far-flung places we travelled. Already, Las Vegas was different. Already, it felt wrong.

Ida passed the handle of her rolling suitcase to me and we filed into the airport.

Chantal met us at the gate. I'd never seen an older person stand so straight. She was almost as old as Ida, but Ida was always hunched over. She groaned and creaked any time she changed positions. Chantal appeared to be in perfect health. I wondered if she used to be an athlete. Her skin was a smooth and poreless light brown, and you could only see her age in the creases around her eyes and mouth. She held a green and white coffee cup in her hand and didn't smile.

"Mrs. Lowell, it's such a pleasure to finally meet you in person." Chantal juggled her coffee cup and a large envelope to get a hand free to offer Mom.

"Oh, Chantal, it's *my* pleasure," Mom said as they shook hands. "Please, call me Sofia. This is my daughter, Van, and our good friend Ida." We all shook hands, and Chantal finally put her paper cup on the floor.

"I know you ladies are probably tired after the long trip, so we'll just go straight to your apartment. Alex can handle your things."

Alex was a kid Chantal had brought along. He'd been lurking behind a framed luxury watch advertisement during the meet and greet. When Chantal called out to him, he ran over to us and started to pile our bags on top of one another. He was tall and had an eerily symmetrical face. A line of dark, straight hair kept falling into his evenly spaced eyes. Ida looked at him with a wide smile, and then looked at me. Ida was always doing this kind of thing.

"Thank you, young man. Boy, aren't you handsome," she said, poking me in the ribs. "Just like that Antonio Banderas."

Alex blushed, and looked slightly less handsome for it. "Thanks, ma'am."

I rolled my eyes at Ida.

"Alex is my intern," Chantal said. "He's a student at UNLV."

"Oh, an intern, my, my. A college boy." Ida tried to poke me in the ribs again, but I swatted her away. "What's your major?"

"Well, I'm only a sophomore, so I have some time to decide. But I'm leaning toward hospitality and hotel management, which is why I'm here." He smiled a little and hefted one of our suitcases at the same time.

I was alarmed by how young he looked, and then I wondered if I could possibly look that young, too.

Ida caught me staring and beamed her maximally lewd smile. And then *I* was the blushing one.

"That's a very good program. The third best in the world for hospitality management, I believe. Chantal," Mom said, once she was done checking her phone for messages. "What time is our first meeting tomorrow?"

"Early, at seven. Good thing you have the time change. It'll feel like you're sleeping in."

"Hmm," Mom said, in that little half-humming, half-chuckling sound she favored.

"Vanessa, I'm especially glad to meet you," Chantal said.

"It's just Van," Ida said.

"Excuse me, Van," Chantal continued, a little startled at the interruption. "I'm the one who selected your tutor. I hope you'll be happy."

"I'm sure it'll be great. I've been to a lot of weird school things, so I can pretty much get used to anything." I'd been to a learning center in Iceland located in a lady's basement, and a progressive school in Texas that was entirely outdoors. Mostly, though, I'd had tutors.

"Van, will you be needing a ride to class tomorrow? I bet college boy has a motorcycle."

I slung Ida a murderous look under the fluorescent lights.

"No ma'am," the stricken Alex said, in a very faint Southern accent.

"Don't worry, Van, we've got you covered," Chantal said. "You too, Ida," she added ominously.

• • •

There wasn't much talking in the car. The dark sky swamped around clusters of lighted advertisements: on billboards, on taxis, clinging to the sides of buildings. The blurred glow of the strip swam up out of the darkness like a living thing. The road we drove on circled the galaxy of neon lights at a distance, and the colors—electric pinks and golds and blues—all bled into one another as we sped by. Bright turrets and the blinking eye at a pyramid's peak climbed out of the darkness like giant beanstalks. And around all of this light, nothing, just an expanse of complete darkness. We drove out for a while, and I could feel the chill of the cooling desert through the window glass. The strip receded.

"Sofia, honey," Ida spoke softly, but her voice still punctured the car's thick silence. "Do you think maybe we should stop at a pharmacy on the way?"

Ida always knew when Mom was out of medication. I always knew, too. Mom had obviously been out of medication for a couple of weeks. I could see it in the way she kept opening and closing the cardboard flaps of boxes while we packed.

"No, I don't think there's time. I'm anxious to get there." Mom spoke quickly, but still not too fast, which was good. "I'm sure Van's tired."

"Alex can run errands for you," Chantal said.

"Fabulous, thank you," Ida answered. Only I could hear the forced lightness in her voice.

Every other move had started out this way, with a ride from the airport. Mom's last husband, William, had owned a consulting firm that fixed failing businesses all over the world. When William died, he left Mom the company. Mom had a way of looking at spaces, at getting them to make the most sense—she made them beautiful and useful, but she also made them special. Her unusual creative solutions led to frequent opportunities in the hospitality industry, but her unusual and creative qualities were what got her fired a lot, too. She'd never worked at a casino before—most of her experience had been in far-flung, emerging hospitality markets. I just hoped Mom would fix whatever needed fixing so we could get out of there. It already alarmed me, all of the light and the swarms of cars shuttling toward the thick, bright strip.

When we pulled into the circular drive of the Silver Saddle Casino, it was like arriving at a mirage. The building and the wide awning that stretched over the entryway were painted silver. Light splashed up the sides of the walls, illuminating the pocks and imperfections in the paint.

Alex pulled up to the door and a couple of bellmen packed our meager bags onto a rolling luggage cart. Two frosty *S*'s twined around each other in the center of each glass door. Chantal led us through the casino's gaming floor, a floor regrettably carpeted in skin-lesion peach. The machines around us thrummed incessantly. The people who sagged in front of the machines were older, and had definitely seen better days. A nearly bald woman seated closest to the entrance had a plastic cannula threaded through her nostrils.

It was so different from the silence of Sirdaryo. Our life there was loud only when a storm roared through, or when animals congregated behind the house. The noise inside of the casino physically hurt, like it was jolting something loose in my head. The lights blinked and flickered when Chantal pressed the button to call the elevator. She turned to us with a cheerless, flat face. "Welcome home," she said.

• • •

Our new place was about as different from our old home as anything can be. The house in Sirdaryo had been a six-bedroom, Soviet construction of the thirties. Mom said that, originally, several families had probably lived there. The windows were crap at insulating, so in the summer we were always hot. We hadn't stayed long enough to see what happened in winter. The house was so secluded that you couldn't walk to the next neighbor if you needed something, but, that wasn't really an issue since Ida and I didn't speak Uzbek or Russian, and very few people that far out in the province spoke English.

On the way up to the top floor, Chantal and Alex smiled these tight smiles at each other and at us in the mirrored elevator, so it was like all you could see for miles were these halfhearted smiles. They left us at the penthouse door. Alex actually came in to put the bags in the foyer, but Chantal waited just outside.

"I'll let you ladies get settled. If you need anything, you know who to call. Van," she said, turning toward me. "I'll send someone for you in the morning, about eight, all right?"

"Yeah, that's great, thank you," I told her.

When the door closed and we were alone again, Ida, Mom, and I fell into our normal domestic rhythm. We claimed our bedrooms. Mom's, of course, was the nicest, and Ida and I fought it out over the remaining two. The smaller rooms were equally lavish—we just liked to give each other a hard time.

The casino penthouse was much more well appointed than any place Mom or I had ever lived. The projects Mom worked on were almost always in progress, so we were lucky if our accommodations had indoor plumbing. It was thrilling to know there would always be enough towels.

Mom walked into my room and rubbed her hands across her face. "Is this okay, honey?" she asked.

"Very funny, Mom."

She smiled. "Yeah, well. Don't get too used to it. Who knows how this is going to go?"

I know, I wanted to say.

"I'm going to lie down, I think."

I didn't know how long she'd been up, but I hoped she would sleep through the night. It took a lot for Mom to look tired. Even on two nights without sleep she looked great. But that was because she was good-looking to begin with. Her skin was ridiculously perfect—no wrinkles, no pimples, just this golden honey color that looked its best in the sunshine. Even in the unflattering artificial light inside of the Silver Saddle, Mom glowed.

It didn't always bother me that Mom was so pretty. In fact, when I was younger, I loved having a pretty mom. People treated me differently, better, because of it. Everyone we met, clerks at the Federal Express, cab drivers, gas station attendants, and ticket agents, all of them were extra kind to me when I was with Mom. But it wasn't just her prettiness that did it. It was the money, too. The way Mom looked, you could tell she had money to spend. When the money started to come, she let it wash over her. As I got older, I watched people size her up. Their thoughts were painfully easy to read. They had no idea that Mom and I used to go through other people's garbage looking for shoes.

Mom got this smile every time someone underestimated her like that, thinking she was just an accessory for some anonymous old rich man. She told me once that when someone underestimated you, it was a gift. She told me it was like getting a head start in a race. People thought that Mom had always been rich, that she was born to it, and Mom let them think that. I have no idea who my dad was, but I was fairly sure I'd inherited what were mostly his looks—a sharp nose in an otherwise rounded face, medium brown hair, the same color as my eyebrows, medium brown eyes, and a thoroughly medium body. The only thing Mom ever told me about my dad was that he loved Van Morrison, and that's why she called me Van. In those moments when I thought about him, I imagined that he would be most impressed by how well I played guitar. Anyway, it's not like anything was wrong with me. I just wasn't like Mom. I wasn't like Mom in most ways, though.

I was generally grateful that the vortex of mysteries that worked inside of Mom hadn't yet appeared in me. But sometimes, I felt a stab of envy—what would it be like to be a genius, to be lifted away like that? Every day I wondered if that wildness was gathering strength inside of me.

I unpacked my bag and heard Ida shuffling around in the next room. I noticed Mom's door was cracked open, and I crept inside to check on her. I could tell she was in a deep sleep, which was good. She'd probably taken one of Ida's pills. Mom slept like a silent film actress, with her hair flowing all around her face and one hand up at her forehead. I closed the door with a little squeak and headed back to my room.

Ida called to me from her room in a whisper-shout.

"Van," she said, "is this really happening?"

"I think so," I answered, but in my normal voice. I knew Ida was excited to be around more people, and that made me nervous. We were used to open spaces and emptiness, where there was nothing but the special chemistry of our three minds. I didn't know if we would work correctly in Las Vegas. There were too many people already *inside of the building*, with different frequencies and snags to catch onto. I knew that we would have to change to survive here. I just wasn't sure how.

Chapter Two

The next morning, I opened the door to the most elaborate breakfast I'd seen in a long time. A gaunt, uniformed blond man with an acne-scarred complexion rolled in a table on wheels covered with silver trays of food. It was like a Fancy Feast commercial.

Mom poured herself a coffee as we started to eat. There were normal things, like pancakes and eggs, but there was also an array of heart-stoppingly gorgeous pastries—all burnished gold with some kind of invisible glaze. Ida and I kept eating and making faces at each other. I hadn't eaten at all during our thirty-six hours of travelling—I could never eat on planes—and was just trying to cover all of the ground that I could.

"I'm glad you two are impressed," was all Mom said. It was the first thing she'd said all morning.

"Can you blame us? If I could make love to this breakfast, I would," Ida said.

"Sick!" I laughed and gagged on my bite of pastry.

"Really, Ida," Mom said, seriously, but with a smirk.

In Sirdaryo, we'd eaten a steady diet of mutton shashliks, noodles, and lepeshkas. Occasionally, as a special treat, we'd had cottage cheese. It had been a long time since I'd seen a croissant. I noticed Mom hadn't touched any of the food. I waited for Ida to say something, to tempt Mom with a Danish or something, but she didn't.

"Are you sure you're not hungry?" I asked.

"No, sweetheart, I'll get something later. I can't be late to my first meeting." *Good,* I thought. *Reasonable.*

Mom slipped out to meet Chantal while I got dressed for class. I didn't bring a lot of clothes. I never did, when we moved. It seemed silly when I didn't know what I would be doing or even what the weather would be like. For Vegas, I'd brought some jeans and T-shirts, but nothing I cared about. I always left those kinds of things behind. It was easier to do that, to deliberately cast those things away, to choose what I was losing.

The doorbell to our new apartment—the suite even had a doorbell—rang at ten minutes to eight. My mouth stung with mint toothpaste and my hair was still wet from the shower. Ida lounged on the sofa in her pajamas.

When I opened the door and saw Alex, I tried to rush out—but I wasn't fast enough. Ida caught his eye from the living room and sashayed over to the doorway.

"Antonio! What a surprise," she trilled, delighted.

"Good morning, ma'am. Hey, Van," he said.

"Oh, you can call me Ida, sweetheart," she simpered. Ida adjusted the tie of the silky complimentary robe that had been waiting in our new bathroom.

"Oh God," I said, and pushed Alex out through the door, my hand just at the spot you'd put a name tag on your shirt. Once we were in the hall and the door closed behind us, I felt weird, maybe a little guilty for touching him.

"Sorry about Ida," I said. "She loves the fellas." I winced, immediately wishing I could unsay "fellas."

Alex laughed a little, like his smile was pushing up against a real laugh. I tried not to feel too relieved.

"No, I get it. Let's go," he said, and led me to the brass-plated elevator. "So, you came from Uzbekistan?" he asked, once we were inside.

I looked up at the mirrored ceiling. It was veined with gold paint, an unsuccessful attempt to mimic the pattern of natural marble.

"Yeah. Yes," I said.

I could almost feel him trying to make conversation, like all of his molecules were reaching out to me, but I kept my gaze on the elevator ceiling, and he stayed quiet.

My new classroom was called the Bill Pickett Room. All of the conference rooms at the Silver Saddle had names instead of conference room B, or whatever. Half of the light bulbs in the ceiling had burnt out, and you would think that the general gloom that coated the place would mask the worst of the wear and tear. It didn't. Instead, the ragged lighting drew attention to the burned and stained carpet, and the peeling, mildewed wallpaper.

"So, now you know where to go," Alex said, standing in the open door.

"Yep, thanks." I hated when I said things like *yep*.

Alex waved and left me alone. I hadn't brought anything with me; I was so desperate to get him away from Ida. I was lucky I'd put my shoes on, at least. I sat in a folding chair at one of the battered banquet tables and waited.

My tutor, Erica, was exactly what I'd expected. She rushed in, only a few minutes late, and got me started right away, asking me to explain what I'd studied before and how in-depth those studies had been. She seemed pretty impressed with my answers, which made me feel good. Erica was young, a graduate student at Nevada State studying chemistry. She was small and thin, with a severe, practical haircut. Her thick-framed glasses were so large that they looked like they had colonized her face in the name of eyewear. I liked her just fine. Erica was no great youth educator, but she was nice. She was really *interested* in math, and that was fine with me because I loved math almost as much as Ida loved the fellas.

Chapter Three

I saw Mom and Ida in the mornings and the evenings, but I was trying to leave them alone to do their own things. We all seemed to be giving each other room. Before, we'd had to cling together to weather our extreme and silent surroundings. We'd been like three astronauts in a spaceship—not in Vegas though. At the Silver Saddle, it was like we were back on Earth and it was time to re-enter the general population.

Ida, especially, seemed to have her own things going on. She strutted around the casino like she owned the place—she called out dozens of new names and laughed with people who were still strangers to me, while I just kept my head down and tried to weather this new, chaotic place. I was so distracted by doing my best to avoid human contact inside of the Silver Saddle that I almost succeeded in being unbothered. But, in that hive of human bodies and overbright light, it was hard to stay hidden.

• • •

I squinted down into the blur on my notebook that was supposed to be about antidifferentiation, so I didn't hear Alex when he knocked.

"Excuse me? Van?"

I looked up, and he took that as an invitation to stroll on in. He gave me a half-smile and looked down at my notebook.

"What are you working on?"

"Calculus. It's Erica's favorite."

Alex shuddered. "You'll never use it in real life," he said.

"How do you know that?" I asked him, my pencil still pressed into the notebook. "How much real life have you logged so far?" I heard how mean it sounded after I'd said it, but it was too late to take it back.

Alex laughed though. "Fair enough," he said. "Listen, I know you've been hanging out in here after class—"

"I've been doing *homework* in here after class."

"Right, well, whatever you've been doing, you're going to have to do it somewhere else. This room's booked pretty much every night for the next eight weeks."

I gaped out at him. "*This* room? People are paying *money* to use this room?"

Alex coughed out that same, surprised laugh again, and I was embarrassed by the satisfied warmth I felt deep under my rib cage.

"Yeah, well, you can thank your mom for that. I guess she convinced Chantal it was kitschy, and that we just had to market the space to people who can appreciate all of this." Alex swept his arms out, as though showcasing the splendor around us. "It's pretty amazing, actually."

"Yeah, she's pretty amazing." I meant what I said, but knew it sounded too sharp.

He looked at me; his eyes narrowed. "I'm sorry you're losing your calculus shrine."

"It's fine," I said, collecting my things.

And it would be. I probably could scale back on the homework. I needed to start practicing again.

Back in the suite, I opened Ida's guitar case and sat there on the bed with the golden-bellied instrument propped up on my lap. I couldn't get started. I hadn't really played since we arrived. The soundproofing in our suite was terrible—you could always hear shenanigans in the hall. I couldn't go anywhere in the casino without hearing a rumble, a ringing, or a roar of laughter. I drummed my fingers against the guitar's body. It was as familiar as a pet, and I felt just as guilty about neglecting it for so long. I really needed to find a quieter practice space.

I decided to ask Ida about it. I found her primping in our shared bathroom. She'd been flirting a lot with Ovid, this older, I guess kind-of-handsome blackjack dealer. She'd started sitting out at his table during his shifts. Sometimes she played and sometimes she didn't. Chantal didn't like her sitting out there, but she couldn't say anything since Ida was with Mom. I sided with Chantal on the matter, but only because Ida's coquetry made me nervous.

"Hey, honey," she said, applying a slick of gloss to her thin lips.

"Do you have a second?"

"Sure, pull up a chair," she said, waving the wand of lip gloss over the toilet.

I closed the lid and sat, watching as she adjusted the neckline of her glittery top.

"Well?" she asked.

"I need to find a place to practice," I said.

"What do you mean? You haven't been playing? Why not in here? You always play in your room."

"Yeah, well, my rooms have always been . . . quieter." Even as I said it, I knew I wasn't telling her the full truth. I'd avoided practicing because I didn't want to bring that private habit to the surface in this new life, where public exhibition seemed unavoidable. I looked at Ida's face in the mirror. She'd taken up a bright blue pick from the counter and winced with every pluck at her silver do.

"Hmm, I see what you mean."

I could tell she was only half listening to me. I sniffed the collar of my sweatshirt. It reeked of cigarettes. The smoke at the Silver Saddle was pernicious. It snuck into every fiber of clothing and every hair follicle. It was like a fourth roommate in our suite. Ida didn't mind at all. She said it was like the good old days.

"I mean it, Ida. I'm not going to remember anything if I don't practice."

Ida turned to face me, the pick still in her hand. She tilted her head and smoothed one of my eyebrows down with her thumb. "You're such a pretty girl, Van. Smart, too. Too smart."

"Oh my God, Ida," I let loose an embarrassed grunt of frustration. "I mean it! Seriously!"

"I got it, I got it!" Ida said, holding her hands up like a cartoon bank robber. "You know Ida always takes care of everything." She turned back to the mirror and traded the pick for an enormous cylinder of hairspray. She looked at me once more. "Better clear out. I know how the odors offend you."

"You don't have to tell me twice," I said, backing out of the brightly lit and already heavily scented bathroom.

"Don't worry," she called when I was nearly in the living room. "Tomorrow. I got it."

• • •

I believed Ida when she said she would figure it out for me. I felt kind of useless, though. I was nearly an adult—shouldn't I be able to solve my own problems? I went looking for a place to practice on my own, but most corners of the Silver Saddle were occupied. I finally found an empty linen closet on the third floor and squeezed inside, barely wedging Ida's guitar in after me. It wasn't perfect, but it was quieter. It was something. I dropped to the floor, my back against one wall and my stretched-out legs touching the closed door. I started to tune up and settled into the old feeling, that rush of doing something well, of doing something completely.

When I heard the scratching, though, I got nervous. What if it was an animal? Some giant rodent or feral cat?

Scratch, scratch, scratch.

I wondered whether I was losing my mind. And not in the casual way that expression gets thrown around. It scared me, sure, but it also thrilled me—I had watched Mom my whole life, and always wished I could know what went on inside of her. I thought, maybe, that the wild chaos of the Silver Saddle had loosened something in me. Maybe I was finally metamorphosing into what Mom was.

The door opened the tiniest bit, revealing a long, bright splinter of light.

"Van? Is that you?" It was Alex. I could tell by the tallness of the shadow in the crack of the door.

"Yeah, it is." I moved my legs.

Alex pushed the door open enough to ease his lanky body through, and closed it with his back.

"This is weird," he said.

"It's weird that you followed me here. Did Chantal ask you to keep an eye on me?"

"It's weird that *you're* in here."

"I just needed somewhere quiet."

"And you chose this microscopic murder closet?"

"It's the quietest place I could find," I said.

"What is that smell?" Alex tilted his head.

I shrugged and hugged Ida's guitar closer against my chest.

"Of course. A strangely scented murder closet is the perfect place for a girl new to Las Vegas. I think I can show you an alternative that's a little less crime-sceney."

"I don't know, I'm pretty happy with this."

"Van. Come on. I talked to Ida. If you want quiet, I know a better place."

"You talked to Ida? She said *she* would take care of it." I cringed at how juvenile and whiny I sounded.

"She did. She talked to me. Let's go." He waved his hand like he was trying to bring more of the closet odor toward his face.

"That's not how we usually do things," I muttered. It wasn't— normally, Ida kept everything between just us. Then I realized how creepy that sounded, even in my head.

"What was that?"

"Never mind. Is it bigger than this? The place you found?" I asked, before I stood up.

"It really is," Alex said.

I followed Alex so easily, even though I'd never followed a boy anywhere before.

"I didn't know you played guitar," Alex said. "Are you good?"

"What? I mean, I don't know. I practice a lot. Not as good as Ida, probably."

Alex stopped and I nearly collided with him.

"*What?*" he said, looking down at me. He was standing way too close, I thought. "*Ida? Ida* plays guitar?"

"Well yeah," I said. "She's the one who taught me."

"You're kidding!"

"Why would I kid about that? Ida can play every Neil Young song ever recorded, pretty much."

"*Really?*" Alex looked at me, all cowed and impressed. "That is so badass." He started moving again. I had to hurry to keep up with him.

"*Every* Neil Young song?"

"Yeah. She loves him." I said it matter-of-factly.

"Wow, you just made my whole day," Alex said.

We took the stairs down to the ground floor. It was four in the afternoon, and nobody was at the gaming tables or the machines except the regulars. The regulars, of course, now included Ida. She was perched on a stool at Ovid's table. She swiveled around and waved over at us. The front of her sequined sweatshirt caught the light in a glittery oil slick across her chest.

Alex seemed to know most of the dealers on the floor, and the cocktail waitresses, too. He threw up a lot of waves and gave out several head nods. An older waitress, wearing the silver cowgirl uniform, swatted him on the arm and said, "Hi there, handsome."

"So this is what you want to do? Manage casinos, like Chantal?" I asked.

"Don't sound so disgusted," Alex said. I could hear the remnants of that smile for the waitress in his voice. "I don't want to do this exactly. I want to open a hotel. Like a lodge."

"For camping, you mean?"

"Hmm, no. For someone so worldly, I'm surprised by how much you don't know."

"For someone studying hospitality, I'm surprised by how chivalrous you aren't. Are we there?" I crossed my arms over my chest.

"Basically," he said. Alex reached up and popped one of the foam ceiling tiles out of place. It made a grating, definitely not-foam-ceiling-tile noise as he slid it aside. He jumped up and his arm disappeared into the gap.

A rickety collapsible ladder dropped down with an unreliable-sounding clatter. Alex raised his eyebrows and pointed up.

"Oh no," I said. "After you." I felt like I'd just bumped into something, some ludicrous, mythical thing—a giant sea urchin, maybe. No, it was more than that; it felt like I'd just stuck my hand *inside* of a giant sea urchin, an intrusion that made my whole body prickle and thrum at the same time.

Alex laughed and leapt up the ladder, making short work of it with all of that tallness.

"Okay. You're going to follow me, though, right?" he called back.

"Maybe," I answered. My foot was already on the bottom rung.

I could feel the dust in the air around me, touching my skin and filling my lungs.

"So, will you make it up here before dinner?" Alex's voice floated down in echoing currents from a rectangle of light overhead. I couldn't see him because I was concentrating on not having a panic attack on the ladder. When I made it to the top, Alex gripped onto my forearms and pulled me up the last few rungs. After my eyes adjusted to the dim light, I saw a room twenty times the size of my old closet. I sniffed the air, expecting a nose full of dust at best, but discovered that it actually smelled pretty good. Lemony. Lemon-Pledgey.

"Did you dust in here?" I asked Alex.

"Is that really the question you want to ask? Not, what is this magnificent secret room?"

"All right, what is this magnificent secret room?"

"It used to be for surveillance," Alex said. "They stopped using it in the seventies, I think."

The floor was tiled with marble, but not the tacky super-shiny kind—the buttery, natural-looking kind. It looked like the floor of a cathedral, a place where thousands of people had stood and milled around for hundreds of years. The walls, shockingly, were paper-free. The Silver Saddle's most recent decorator's penchant for terrible wallpaper hadn't mangled this hidden place. The walls were painted not-quite-gray, but not-quite-silver, either.

"Whoa," I said. I nearly reached out and touched the wall. I couldn't help myself. "How did you find it?"

"I was organizing the blueprint archives for Chantal, and I noticed that this room was on some of the plans but not all of them. So I went looking for it."

Alex sat down on a long bench that had been stripped of upholstery. The bench was the only thing left in the surveillance room, apart from the bank of dead, old-fashioned monitor screens bunched against one wall.

"What do you think?" Alex gave me that raised double eyebrow again.

"Thanks for showing me."

"It's no problem. I think this'll be more comfortable than your murder closet. I know you'll take good care of it."

"If I don't die on my way up and down."

"Don't worry," Alex said. "I'll help you move whatever you want up here. You'll be making this climb by yourself in no time."

• • •

I started to spend every afternoon in the surveillance room after my lessons with Erica. Sometimes I just stretched out on that cool, milky floor and counted my breaths. But mostly I played. The acoustics were eerily grand—it was like playing music inside of a mausoleum. Getting that time, to move my fingers over the strings and hum along to the songs I loved, it was the best way for me to feel settled. I knew I should probably tell Mom about the surveillance room. It was exactly the kind of discovery she would have loved, but I kept it to, and for, myself.

Sometimes Alex left artifacts from the Silver Saddle there to surprise me, I guess, or as a joke. I couldn't really tell. I was never good at making those kinds of distinctions. I thought, at first, that maybe he was making fun of me. He left all kinds of things: an old blackjack horn, a plastic discard tray, a phonebook from 1988 with a leafy, plastic stem from an artificial flower nestled inside. It felt like what I imagined getting a postcard in the mail would feel like. Like someone was thinking about you.

Chapter Four

Our dinners were almost always room service. Sometimes we went down to the restaurant, but either way, the food was the same. I had already eaten everything on the menu, from the BLT to the chocolate fondue. So had Ida. So had Mom. Mom wasn't a big complainer, but Ida and I were pretty much over it. Even the glinting silver food covers and miniature ketchups had lost their allure.

The three of us sat at the coffee table in the living area of the suite. Mom and Ida perched on the couch, and I was on the floor.

"Dolls," Ida said, "my kingdom for some hot and sour soup."

I arranged my fries in a little log cabin foundation on my plate.

"Or sushi," I said.

"Or sushi," Ida agreed.

Despite the repetitive food selection, I was glad we were all eating together. Mom looked at us over her glass of sparkling water. I was glad Mom was only drinking water, too.

"Do you think we could go out to eat some night? Maybe to one of the casinos on the strip? You could write it off, Mom. Research," I said.

"Hmm, I don't know about that," she answered, chewing on a nail.

"Think about it, Sofia," Ida said. "It would be good for all of us to get out of here a little bit. Especially you. I could bring Ovid. I know he would *love* to show us around. Van, you could bring Antonio."

I threw one of my fries at Ida.

"Van, come on, don't do that," Mom said. "You two should go, if you want. I'm much too busy."

"Too busy to come out to dinner with us on one night?" I said, surprised by how hurt I felt.

"There's something you should know," Mom began.

Oh no, I thought. Dread pooled deep inside of my guts. Mom never offered up good news this way—these declarations were always followed by flares of warning.

"I won't leave this building for at least three months."

Ida and I looked at each other. We had a silent way of communicating when Mom started to get funny. Ida and I gave each other our clearest oh-shit looks. Ida raised her head just the tiniest bit, her sign that I should ask the next question.

"What do you mean, Mom?" I asked slowly.

Mom folded her napkin in a fan and then tucked and fluffed up parts of the fan shape and set a pale peach fabric swan on the table between us.

"Well," she said. "The Silver Saddle wanted someone who takes on-premises management very seriously. Also, this woman I consulted before we arrived confirmed that it would be beneficial to me. For my growth. Creatively and professionally. I decided to really commit to this."

"Huh?" Ida said.

"What woman?" I asked.

"A lady I hired for some guidance. It was a big decision, to take on this project."

"You mean you talked to a therapist? Where? When?" I asked, my heart on a freaking golden wing. God, if Mom was getting real treatment, maybe I'd be able to take really deep breaths and say all of the regular daughter things I had ever wanted to say.

"Yes," Mom answered, her face clear. "An astrotherapist. She's in Cleveland. We've been in touch on the phone. Really, she is so helpful. You both should talk to her," Mom said, looking first to me, then to Ida.

My heart sank to the inverse of golden wing. Of course I wanted Mom to be what she was, even if that meant she wasn't always perfectly all right. What I wanted more, though, was for Mom to be mostly perfectly all right *and* what she was. It was a balance she'd dabbled in every now and then, but, in the end, the medication and therapy appointments were flung aside to make room for all of her wild soaring.

"Sure, Mom," I said.

"But don't let me stop *you* from exploring the town." She rested a slim hand on her chest, over her heart. "I want you both to feel like you're getting something out of this experience, too. That's always what I want."

"That's sweet, Sof," Ida said as she sliced into her now-cold filet.

I didn't answer. I just folded my napkin into an identical peach swan and set it next to Mom's on the coffee table between our dinners.

I remembered one of our other, faraway meals together. There was a rug in one of our rooms outside of Chicago. It was the size of a bed, faded and balding, with once-blue curlicues swirling across a once-gold background. While we stayed there, when it got dark, Mom went out.

"Here, my little one, this spot." She pointed to a space between three blue spirals. "A protected place. Can you feel the magic here?" She held my hand over the invisible shape.

I nodded and looked right into her eyes. I'm not sure how old I was. Maybe four, maybe a little older. Old enough to remember.

"That's very good. Will you sit there and wait for Mama? Yes?"

I curled up in the spot, like she wanted, and she kissed me all over—on my forehead, on my eyes, on my chin. I giggled and pushed her away a little, but I loved the feeling of her lips on my eyelids. That light, ticklish pressure made me feel locked into what and where I was supposed to be.

"I won't be long at all, and when I get home, we'll have such a feast."

We hadn't eaten in two days. The rumbling of my stomach had mutated, first into a sharp, stabbing pain that made me cry, and finally a dull hollowness. I believed I would be safe, if I stayed in that magic spot. I knew that Mom would bring a feast.

"Muffins?" I asked.

"Muffins!" Mom laughed. "I promised you a feast, little one, and a feast it's going to be. Like kings and queens have."

"Really?" I rested my cheek on my folded arm.

"Of course." Mom smoothed an old sweatshirt over my curled-up body, and kissed me again, this time on my tiny shoulder.

I closed my eyes because I didn't like to watch Mom leave. The sun had set, and soon the room would be really dark. If I didn't see her leave, I could convince myself that she was still there with me, just being quiet, just sitting in some other corner.

Chapter Five

Ida had been staying out later and later. In the mornings, when I left to meet Erica, sometimes Ida was still in bed. Before, no matter where we lived, Ida was the first one up. Even when I saw her cooing at Ovid during his shifts, she seemed a little less electric, drooping over the green felt table. I thought that maybe I should talk to Mom about it, that maybe she could get Ida to give the late nights a rest.

I was thinking about Ida's recent sluggishness while lingering in the Bill Pickett Room. Erica had to proctor a midterm, so I was working through a timeline of Native American history on my own. The tables in the BPR were long and narrow, arranged in an enormous rectangle. The way I was seated, in the middle of the table at the front of the room, it was like I was running an invisible shareholders' meeting. I looked out at the imaginary shareholders and practiced a few authoritative hand gestures.

Of course, that's when Alex walked in.

I froze, with my hand in a squashed, Bill Clinton–style thumbs-up.

"Hey," I said, moving my fist up to my chin in what I hoped passed for I'm-just-thinking-here.

"Hi," Alex said. He sat in the chair directly across from me and put a fist under his own chin so that he mirrored me exactly. "Is this what we're doing now?"

"I'm just absorbing all of this," I said. "These timelines, you know, they get complicated."

He clasped his hands and set his elbows on the table, tilting his head at me, formally.

"So," Alex began. "Do you feel like playing hooky today?"

"I feel like playing hooky every day," I lied. I tried to push down the thrill I felt moving through this strange new friendship. *Don't get your hopes up*, I told myself. *Normal people don't get this excited.* "What about you? Won't you get in trouble? Or is Chantal proctoring a midterm, too?"

Alex let out a short laugh. "Nope. Sick!" He was as gleeful as though he'd been the one to spray streptococcus on her. "Seriously, let's get out of here."

"I promised Erica I would finish this."

"I'll finish it for you."

"Thanks, but no thanks," I said.

"Van," he said, lifting his clasped hands in supplication. "Consider this an intervention. Have you even left the building since you got here?"

The way he said it, and then the way I thought about it, seemed suddenly very creepy. Unhealthy at best. I liked to stay close, in case Mom needed me, but she'd be fine for a few hours. Ida was still around.

"You're right," I said, closing my American history textbook with a decisive thunk. "Let's go. Do I need a jacket?"

"Wow," he said. "You really haven't been outside."

• • •

I got what he meant once we were under the sun. Our walk to the employee parking lot was vacation-pleasant. I pulled off the green sweater I'd gotten used to wearing around the hyper–air-conditioned Silver Saddle.

"Is the fall always like this?" I asked.

"Pretty much, as far as I can tell," Alex said.

"That's right. I forgot. You're not from here."

"Is it that obvious?" Alex looked back at me with a small smile.

"I don't know. Would that be a good or a bad thing?"

Alex laughed again, one of those short, enthusiastic laughs. I didn't think it was a fake one. Although, I didn't think all of that laughter was for me, either. *It's just a free day off for him*, I told myself.

"Oh, hey!" Alex called out to a slim girl slouched over a cigarette beside the dumpster at the edge of the employee lot. She lifted her hand in a bored wave. "Let's go say hi," Alex said to me. "Have you met Joanna? You should definitely meet her. She's in a band—you guys should talk music shop."

He jogged a little up to where Joanna stood. She was pretty, Latina, all thin limbs and lush mouth, with a halo of short, wavy hair. She looked sexy even in her oversized Silver Saddle uniform.

"What's up, Joanna?"

"What's up," she said, as she nodded at me.

"This is Van. She's a musician, too," Alex said.

"Oh yeah?" Joanna lazily exhaled the last bit of her cigarette up into the sky. "What do you play?" She looked me over. "Clarinet?"

"Gui-*tar*," Alex interjected.

Joanna perked up a little as she stubbed out her cigarette. "Really? How long have you been playing?" She looked straight into my face, like she was watching the muscles move under my skin when I talked.

"A few years," I said, squirming under her examination.

"Huh," Joanna said, and then looked over at Alex. He opened his eyes extra wide and nodded at her a little. "Joanna's band is actually looking for a new guitarist," Alex said.

"What happened to the old one?" I asked.

Joanna flushed a little, and looked back at Alex. He looked down at his feet, and then so did she. When I realized I was the only person looking at anyone, I glanced at my own feet. Were we all standing in something gross? The dumpster *was* right there.

"You know," Joanna cleared her throat and looked back up at Alex, "you should bring her to band practice tomorrow. You should definitely come out," she said, staring at me again. There was something about her gaze right then that felt good—*keep looking at me,* I wanted to say.

"That's exactly what I was thinking," Alex said, clapping his hands with an abundance of enthusiasm. Joanna and I both looked at him, at how cheesy his excitement seemed, and smiled faintly at each other.

"Yeah, maybe," I said. My tone, the rise and fall of those two words—I felt sure I'd gotten that right.

"I have to get back to work," Joanna said, giving me a moderate but real smile. "Nice meeting you, Van. See you tomorrow?" She didn't wait for an answer and turned to walk back into the casino's employee entrance.

I stared after her.

"Ready?" Alex asked.

"How long have you known Joanna?" I asked as we walked to Alex's car.

"Not too long. What were we talking about again?"

"Where you're from," I said.

"Right. Texas."

"Why did you decide to move here?"

"UNLV has an incredible hospitality program. I really didn't think I was going to get in." Alex shrugged. "So, where do you want to go? You know Vegas has everything."

I knew the answer to this one.

"Italy." Italy was one place I'd never been.

"Are you sure? We could go to France or Egypt?"

"Definitely Italy," I said.

• • •

There was music in the car, but so soft I could barely hear it. Alex was a slow driver. He didn't chatter like Ida or get distracted and swerve around like Mom. It was barely noon, but the heat in the air filled the car quickly through the rolled-down windows. The dry dustiness of it made my throat and eyes itch, but the scent in that air was mysterious and powerful. It smelled ancient and metallic, but hauntingly organic at the same time, like you were breathing in the crushed bones of some lost civilization. I could see the strip in the distance, a dark smudge in the stretch of earth, mountain, and sky. As we got closer, I could see the strip start to bleed out; there were more cars, more roads, more low-rise motels, and garish gentlemen's clubs.

When we were inside of the buzzing wound, the buildings started to get taller and shinier. Even the sun seemed brighter. There were ads everywhere, mostly for table games with low buy-ins and strip club drink specials. Alex was focused, though, wary of gawking motorists who slowed down and sped up erratically as they took in the increasingly bizarre sights. We drove down the highway, along the outside edge of the casino skyline. I saw all of the landmarks I'd heard about: the long, bony giant's finger of the Stratosphere, Caesar's Palace, a squat, white wedding cake, and the faux statue of liberty watching over New York, New

York. Alex looped around, driving up Las Vegas Boulevard, the main street that split the strip in two.

Even in the early afternoon, the streets were crowded with sweaty throngs of people. Girls in bachelorette sashes and penis-bedecked tiaras sagged against one another and posed for pictures. Stoic dark-skinned men handed out flyers, flicking them out quickly, viciously, like reptilian tongues.

"We made it," Alex said. He looked over at me and then his face crumpled. "Are you okay?"

"Yeah, I'm fine." I shook my head a little. "You're right. I really haven't been out in a while."

"Do you want to go back?" Alex's eyes narrowed as he took in the way I had slumped down in the passenger seat.

It was my turn to laugh, but I don't know how convincing it was. "Definitely not," I said.

The Venetian's façade towered over the car. I could barely see where the bleached stone pillars of the hotel stopped. I peeked through a complex of swooping archways and saw a miniature courtyard rimmed with faux cloisters. An artificial river the color of aqua Listerine flowed through the center of it. Ornamental footbridges, coated with pedestrians, crossed the radioactive-looking water. A few gondolas floated listlessly by the bridges, manned by sweaty hotel employees festooned in polyester Italian outfits.

We parked about a million miles away in the garage.

"Ready?" Alex said, and led me toward a pair of heavy double doors.

• • •

The smell inside of the Venetian was not much better than the fume-riddled parking garage. Scented, violently conditioned air swirled around us. I imagined it smelled the way the radioactive, ersatz canal water might.

The floor of the lobby gleamed, polished to an Olympic ice-rink shine. Alex gave me a little nod, telling me to look up. I tilted my head back and scanned the array of cherubs and anonymous robed figures relaxing among enormous clouds.

"Pretty ridiculous, huh?" he said.

I nodded.

"It gets worse. Come on." Alex pulled at my elbow again, this time letting his hand slide down my forearm, holding lightly onto my wrist. I tried to keep my breathing calm and even. *It's not like we're holding hands exactly, is it? Be cool, Van.*

I gave the ceiling one more look and slid along the shining floor, trying not to smile too much.

"This is nothing like the Silver Saddle," I said.

"I know, this is so much worse."

"That's hilarious," I said.

"No, I mean it. Our hotel is something special. Not soulless, like this dump." Alex moved his arm like a weatherman demonstrating the movement of a storm system. I liked how he'd called it *our* hotel. "These big operations are all the same. If you've been to one, you've been to them all. So, Van," he said, nodding at me as he stepped on to the escalator, "now that you've been to every casino in Las Vegas, we should probably eat lunch."

A wide courtyard opened around us. The bright blue river that I'd seen outside swirled through the center of the square. Gondoliers ferried sweatshirt-clad tourists along its curves, past rows of shops and restaurants. There was music, too. The gondoliers sang different songs—"O Sole Mio," "My Way," "That's Amore"—all competing against one another and against the piped-in top forty thrumming through the speakers.

Alex and I, and all of the people around us, moved slowly. We stared into the windows of the shops selling porcelain figurines and signed baseball memorabilia, and gawked at the menus on display in the artificial cobblestone street.

"If you were wondering what to get me for my birthday next week, look no further," Alex said, tapping the glass over a throw pillow shaped like a slot machine.

"Is it really your birthday next week?"

"Yeah," he said.

"How old are you turning?"

"Nineteen."

"Well, you definitely have sophisticated taste," I said, tapping the glass where Alex had, in the same da-da-da rhythm. "Are you doing anything special?"

Alex shrugged. "I don't know yet. All plans hinge on my acquisition of this souvenir pillow, so, I'm still deciding."

I smiled into the glass, at the lumpy stuffed slot machine.

"Do you want to get pizza, since we're in Italy and all?"

"You have no idea. All I've been eating is room service," I said.

"Really?" Alex gave me that crumpled face again. "Are you serious?"

"Yeah," I said, and put my hands on my hips, just to do something with them. I didn't want him feeling sorry for me, so I said, "It's all been pretty glamorous, but I've definitely missed the lowbrow cuisine your kind seems to enjoy."

"My kind?" Alex said.

"Interns," I said, and then tried to smile, even though the joke hadn't covered over what I wanted it to. Or been funny.

"I'm just surprised by what's ordinary for you," Alex said, more to himself than to me, I thought.

"Nothing is ordinary to me." I said it harshly, and the funny thing was, I hadn't meant to say it at all. I'd only meant to think it.

Alex looked at me with his head tilted a little. "Well, something should be. Pizza? That's pretty ordinary."

• • •

I got home late, after-dinner late. Mom and Ida were both back in the suite, but Mom was on her phone in the little office off of her bedroom. Ida sat on the sofa with her feet up on the coffee table. Mom had laid out an array of tile samples there, and Ida's feet had pushed some to the floor.

"Look who decided to come home," she said, waving the remote at me like a sword. "It would have been nice if you told someone you wouldn't be back for dinner. Your mother and I were worried sick. And me, slaving over a hot stove for nothing!"

It was always hard to tell with Ida just how upset she was. She kept her real distress buried under a sarcastic, jokey layer. Her affection was the same way.

"There's a plate for you in the oven," Ida said as she crossed her arms in front of her chest and let her feet thud to the floor. I knew she wasn't really mad, then. There was no oven in our little kitchen.

"I just hope it's not lobsters again," I said, picking up the dropped tiles before plopping down beside her. "Anyway, I'm not hungry." It felt good to joke around with Ida, especially after my mangled attempt at humor in the faux Italian marketplace.

"Aha!" Ida said as she clicked the remote, stilling the screen. "I knew it! You were out to dinner with Antonio Banderas!"

"I was," I shrugged, "but not out-out. We didn't go for prime rib or anything."

"Oh no?"

"No, we had pizza."

"Pizza! You traitor. You could have brought me some."

"What? Ovid doesn't like going out for pizza?"

Ida smiled to herself and took my hand. "Van, honey," she began. "There comes a time in a young woman's life when she needs to learn when to say no and when to say yes. And I'm a little surprised that you didn't say yes to some take-out for poor Ida."

"Jesus, Ida!" I said as I pulled my hand away and smacked her on the shoulder.

"And now you're attacking old women. What's gotten into you, really? I'll just have to speak to your mother about this," she sniffed.

"About what?" Mom said, from right behind us.

"Jesus, Mom! You scared me," I managed to get out, mid-laugh.

"What have you two been doing out here?"

"Nothing, nothing at all," Ida said as she smoothed down the front of her appliquéd sweater.

"Did you just get home?"

"Yeah," I said, taking a few deep breaths and smoothing down the front of my T-shirt, too.

"Well, I'd like for you to be home for dinner tomorrow night," Mom said. "Both of you." She looked over at Ida. "We'll have a guest," she told us, biting her nails.

"I can't," I said, remembering Joanna's band practice, realizing that I really wanted to go.

"What do you mean, you can't?" Mom said, all stern and clipped.

"I have plans," I told her.

"*Plans*? Again? With *Antonio*?" Ida leaned over to me and waggled her eyebrows.

"No!" I looked down at my hands and could feel my face getting red. "Well, sort of."

"Why are my samples out of order?" Mom frowned down at the coffee table. "And who is Antonio?" she asked from around her fingers.

Ida and I both looked at her other hand, its fingertips bloodied, hanging by her side.

"He's a little friend of Van's," Ida said. "Nothing to worry about, Sof." She stood up and fished around in her purse.

"I don't really have plans with him, anyway. He's just taking me to band practice."

"*Band* practice? What?" Mom squinted a little and Ida froze where she stood, bandaging the wounds on Mom's hands. "Was this your idea, Ida?"

"My idea?" Ida let Mom's partially Band-Aid–covered hand flop back down to her side. "What band is this?" she asked.

"This girl, Joanna's." I shrugged. "I don't know. They just need a guitarist, is all."

"Well, I need you here. Tomorrow," Mom said firmly. "And I don't like this band stuff. I want you to be thinking about the SATs."

"Oh my God, Mom, not again with this."

"Not again with what? You're not wasting this opportunity, Van," she said.

"It's just a band, Sof. Maybe it's not so bad—" Ida began.

"Well I don't like it. Besides," she pointed at me, blood welling from the bitten-down finger she pointed, "you already have plans with your *family* tomorrow."

I sunk back into the sofa cushions and concentrated on the knot of anger in my gut.

"The family and a guest," Ida said, with that forced lightness she used when she was tiptoeing around Mom.

"That's right," Mom said, like it was her and Ida against me.

"What kind of guest?" Ida asked softly as she looked at me.

Mom thought for a minute, opened her mouth, and then closed it again. "The good kind." She turned and went back to her room, closing the door with a heavy click.

Understanding Mom was never easy, even at the best of times. Watching her, I felt like the person who makes predictions for the *Farmer's Almanac*—like my interpretations and expectations might be right but they might not. The way I counted on Mom, too, was the same way a person who works the earth counts on the weather; I was scared and grateful, all at the same time. I didn't expect her to be thrilled about my trying something new, but what else was I supposed to do?

Chapter Six

Mom was still there the next morning when I was getting ready to leave for class with Erica. She'd spread a stack of folders across the glass-topped dining table and was tapping a pen against its surface. *Plink-plink-plink-plink*, the exact sound you hear before someone makes a toast. Her eyes looked a little puffy, and her dark hair was pulled back in a ponytail.

Ida stumbled around the abbreviated kitchen counter, making coffee. "Sof, honey," she called. "You feeling all right today?"

Mom gave her shoulders a little shake, as if some invisible person had grabbed hold of her in a *get-yourself-together-woman* kind of way.

"I'm fine," she said, just shaking her head now. "I'm going to hang around here, for most of the day, anyway." Mom's accent was faint and ambiguous. She loved American figures of speech and throwaway words, like "anyway." I know she used them because they put people off of the scent of her accent. Sometimes, people thought she was from New Zealand; sometimes, they thought she was from Canada. They never suspected that she came from Belarus. I think her near-absence of accent came from her refusal to speak her own language. She'd never spoken to me in anything but English, and when I'd complained about it, she told me it was for my own good.

"Don't forget, you two. Family dinner tonight. With a special guest." She tapped her pen steadily and pointed back and forth, between Ida and me.

"Of course, how could we forget? So mysterious!" Ida teased as she set a ceramic mug of coffee in front of Mom's computer.

"Oh, Van," Mom began. "I want to schedule some of those college tours we discussed."

"Can we talk about it later? It's not like there's any rush." I couldn't even think about college. If I could barely carry on a single conversation with Alex, there was no way I'd be able to navigate hordes of other students. Anyway, I couldn't just abandon Mom and Ida.

"I don't want you to sell yourself short. Do you think everybody in the world gets to do this? I would have killed for this opportunity at your age. Ida, tell her I'm right," Mom said.

I looked over at Ida, but she was carefully studying the coffee can.

"Well, maybe you should take a couple of tours for yourself, Mom. It's not too late for you."

Mom snorted.

Ida handed me a cup of coffee. "Maybe just a visit, honey," she said.

"A visit would be totally unnecessary. How am I the only person who remembers that I'm taking a year off?" *Maybe two years, or five,* I thought.

I scooped a short pyramid of books into my arms.

"What, so you can be in this *band*? I won't let you waste this chance to better yourself," Mom said, her voice sharp.

"I'm not wasting anything. I don't even know what I want to *do*. It would be a waste to go *now.*"

"We're going to talk about this later." Then, Mom's brow smoothed and she practically chirped, "Maybe we can even discuss it with our special guest. Be back on time tonight, Van," Mom said. Her flash from angry to cheerful made me a little queasy.

"Sure. See you later, guys," I said, and let the door close behind me. I wondered if our special guest was Ovid. Maybe Mom thought it was time for us to get to know him better.

I thought about Mom's sentences. I replayed each one in my mind, counting every word. When Mom started to get wild, she lost control of her English. First she would drop her articles. *Go wait in car.* Mom was usually so careful with her second language. Even when she was losing control, it was the last thing to go—the point of no return. Ida and I had seen enough of Mom's cycles to recognize when she started to come apart. Ida would sneak Ambiens into Mom's drinks if she'd been awake too long. It almost always worked. Almost.

I preferred Mom's wildness to her expansive flats. Even though she was hard to subdue, there was a thrill, a kind of participation. Ida and I could get through to her at least. The flats, though, they were unbearable. There was nothing we could do then, just sit with her wherever she landed and wait for her medicine to work.

Low periods were easier to hide from Mom's clients. Ida usually just lied and told them that Mom had come down with mono, or something equally contagious. If they ever got curious or impatient and decided to come around and check up on her, all the Chantal-types would see that she couldn't get out of bed. Sometimes they were sympathetic, sometimes Mom came back enough to go back to work, but sometimes she got fired.

When it was just me and Mom, when I was really little—too little to help—things got bad. I remember, in some of my earliest memories, a flash of institutional lighting. An ambulance ride, Mom drooling in a hospital bed. A foster family, very religious. Jesus, Jesus, Jesus, spoken of so often and so casually it was like he was a member of the family, too. I didn't stay there too long. Just long enough to know what eating three meals a day and an afternoon snack felt like. After that, Mom was a lot more careful. She started to make a little money. She started to make *connections*, was what she called it. Even then, I understood that our life wasn't normal. I wasn't a complete idiot.

When she married William and hired Ida, everything got better, and we both tried not to look back.

When I got to the Bill Pickett Room, I found Alex loitering just outside.

"Are you ready for your big audition later?" He smiled out at me.

"Oh, I'm ready," I lied. "What time do we need to be there?" Maybe I could practice with Joanna's band and be home before dinner.

"Five. When Erica lets you go, meet me outside, okay?"

"Okay," I said, because how long could band practice be, really? Also Mom seemed kind of out of it, and maybe she wouldn't really care if I met the mystery guest or not.

"Great. Hey," Alex said, looking half at me and half at the god-awful wallpaper. "What are you doing next Friday? One of my friends is having a birthday party for me."

"Nice," I said, a little envious, wondering what it would be like to have a friend who would throw a party for you.

"No, I mean, do you want to come?"

I knew that all I could handle was this small sliver of a friendship, this outer edge, all weird gifts and juvenile secret hiding places. Thinking about Alex's smooth, normal, real life—away from the Silver Saddle—made me fully aware of the sickening jagged edges of my own. It was like I caved in on myself. I knew if I opened my mouth to talk, I would probably, accidentally, say something rude. So I bit the inside of my cheeks and waited for Alex to say something else.

"Van? Hello?"

"Yeah," I managed, and cleared my throat.

"Yeah, you can come?"

"No, I mean, I don't know," I said, and dropped my books. Alex bent down to pick them up. I stood over him and looked at the curl of his back beneath a pale blue shirt. I wondered what it would feel like to touch the place where his spine cut across the fabric plane. He stood up and I quickly looked to the side.

"Well, if you want to come, I can give you a ride."

I nodded and took my books, careful not to touch his hands.

"Are you sure you're all right?"

"I'm sure. I'll meet you outside when I'm done," I said as I walked backward into the Bill Pickett Room. I stood in the hallway a little longer than I should have, watching Alex shuffle off.

Chapter Seven

I was so nervous about the audition that I could barely hear Erica, let alone understand the chemistry problem she was breaking down in front of me. Eventually, she just sighed and circled a couple of proofs in my calculus book—proofs that I could have done in my sleep—and then opened her own textbook. I moved through the problems, getting that satisfied clicking feeling after solving each one. It felt good: balancing.

I texted Alex to meet me outside and tried not to think about Mom's dinner plans. *You'll make it back*, I told myself. *Maybe they'll hate you and kick you out after five minutes.*

When Alex pulled up to the front door, I was sweating.

"Nervous?"

I tried to give Alex a look like, *obviously*, but could barely scrape it together around my humming circulatory system.

"Just tell me if you're going to throw up so I can pull over," he said, smiling.

"I'm not going to throw up!"

Alex pulled into the parking lot of a squat, single-story brick building lit with an oversized rectangular sign that spelled RED'S.

"This is where they practice?" I asked.

"It's Carol's dad's place," Alex said with a shrug. "So it's free."

"Who's Carol?"

"You'll see." He held the door and I stumbled into the empty club. It smelled musty, but it actually looked cleaner than the Bill Pickett Room. I saw Joanna immediately—she was sitting on some kind of case with her head in her hands. She didn't see us.

"Uh-oh," Alex said. He strode ahead of me while I lagged, just staring. There was no stage, like I thought there would be—only an irregular section of floor cordoned off with blue painter's tape. A drum set—with a girl behind it—and a mélange of equipment I'd never seen littered the space like pieces of an abandoned board game. There, in the middle, was a glossy, mahogany-colored electric guitar. I glanced at Alex talking quietly to Joanna. I wondered if they'd notice if I picked it up. I just wanted to see what it would feel like to hold. I'd only ever played Ida's old acoustic.

"Don't touch that," the girl behind the drums snapped.

"What?"

"Jesus," she muttered and looked up at Red's dusty ceiling. "Is *that* her?" She shouted over at the half-collapsed Joanna. "Jo-an-na," she repeated, more loudly this time. "What is *that*?" She tossed her head in my direction. She was as full and plump as Joanna was wiry. She had a platinum blond pixie haircut, and her enormous boobs spilled so far out of her scoop-necked T-shirt, it was like she was shooing me away with them.

"I'm Van," I said.

"And I don't give a shit. Don't touch anything."

"Carol, calm down," Joanna said.

"Oh, I'm plenty calm," Carol said, glaring at everything in her line of vision. "Fucking Marcos," she muttered to herself. "*This* is the best we can do?"

"Who's Marcos?"

"Who *was* Marcos. And it's none of your damn business," she said. When I didn't say anything, she kept talking—maybe to herself, maybe to Marcos, definitely not to me.

"Fucking Marcos. The douchelord had to waltz in here and make a scene."

Alex pulled Joanna up and they shuffled over to the drum set. "Carol, did you meet Van?"

"Yes, I did." Carol looked down at me with disappointment.

"Van's great! She's been playing forever," Alex said.

I was confused by Alex's endorsement—he'd never heard me play. I cleared my throat. "Who's Marcos?"

"Fucking Marcos *was* our guitarist. *Was* Joanna's boyfriend, too—brilliant choice, by the way, Joanna. Fucking Marcos just showed up—*uninvited*—but we're over it now, right?"

Joanna gave a subdued nod.

"And I guess now fucking *you*," she pointed an accusing drumstick at me, "whoever you are—is going to be the new Marcos. Just don't fuck this one, J."

"Jesus, Carol," Alex said, kind of getting between us.

Joanna smiled and tamped down a giggle. I nearly laughed, too. Suddenly, I felt significantly less nervous. My palms tingled and sweated at the same time.

"Calm down, Princess," Carol said to Alex. "Let's give this a shot."

"So, can I touch this now?" I asked, pointing to the guitar.

"Well I guess you *have* to now, since you didn't bring your own. Which is *highly* irregular, I hope you realize. Better not be bad luck." Carol tapped one of the cymbals.

"It's not bad luck," Joanna said. "Let's walk Van through the first three songs in the set. We're not doing more than that right now."

"This is great!" Alex beamed at the three of us like the photographer at a baptism. "This is going to be legendary."

"Oh Jesus, get him out of here," Carol muttered to Joanna, before she snapped back to me. "Ready? I'm only going to tell you this once."

When I slung Marcos's guitar across my body and felt the dense weight of it, I knew I was going to like it. I waited for Joanna to adjust the amp and then slid my fingers across the frets, running through the chords Carol barked out at me. If playing my acoustic guitar was like walking, this was like skating. It was so much *easier* and looser. It was like I'd been given superpowers—I was faster, spinning out into a glossy wildness. Even when I misheard Carol, the wrong chords I played still sounded right.

Just the standing imbued me with unfamiliar power. I'd only ever played guitar sitting down, practicing in my room. Playing standing up made me feel like a lightning rod, and the chords that spilled out of the speakers and across the room just ran with heat.

The songs were easy—the hardest one was a basic one-four-five chord progression, and the strumming patterns were nearly all the same. I fumbled a little at first, but the songs were basic and repetitive. I got the hang of the first one after about ten minutes, and the others were so similar, they took even less time to get. We played through them all so quickly, and then we played through them again. I had no idea what time it was or even where I was, only that I was following these girls and it felt amazing.

Carol's drumming was bored, but angry. It dripped through every measure with a balance of contempt and laziness. I followed it, skating over the structure. I'd never played with anyone before—not even Ida. In our lessons, we'd always passed her guitar back and forth. She'd show me something and I'd copy it. I never imagined what it would feel like to play with someone else. I could feel Carol's eyes on me, on the slump in my back as I worked through the songs.

At first, when Joanna started to sing, I wasn't sure what was happening. Her voice was feral and rangy: powerful and dark. It sounded lonely, too, like one of those craggy, rocky islands in the middle of the sea where no one can go—waves crashing and salt stinging into stone. I followed her voice, too. It was like following a monster. I chased it, ran after it, over Carol's near-sleazy drumbeat. Joanna was good. I almost couldn't breathe, she was so good. Her bass playing was less good, but you almost didn't notice it beneath the wild stretch of her voice.

As I ran after her, I understood something else—I was really good, too.

I turned my back to Joanna and inched over to Carol—to that driving, sultry sound—and leaned into it. I closed my eyes, feeling all of the different waves come together. When I opened my eyes, I saw that Carol was still snarling, but not as much as before. Joanna thrashed her slimness against the sound we made, but I stood mostly still, wishing I could unlock my body like that.

I looked out into the empty club, and saw Alex on my right, beaming. It felt amazing; *this is what being high must be like*, I thought. And then I thought that maybe, maybe in the tiniest, most incremental of ways, I understood what my addict-dad had sought. What he had found.

When it was over, I realized I was even sweatier than before, but it was a good sweaty. Joanna looked as happy as I felt, and even Carol's leer seemed more festive than pissed.

"Not bad, Van," Joanna said to me.

"Not bad? That was amazing!" Alex shouted.

"Quiet, you," Carol shouted back.

"What do you think?" Joanna asked Carol. "Is she in?"

"I guess she'll do."

"That was really surprising," Joanna said, wiping her forehead with the back of her hand.

"Do you think she can play that party with us?" Carol asked.

"I don't see why not," Joanna said, lifting her shoulders.

"What party?" I asked.

"Alex's birthday. Next Friday." Joanna grinned out at Alex, and he returned the full wattage of her smile.

"Sure," I said, to all of them.

"You hear that? She says sure." Carol drummed a couple of measures and then threw her sticks to the floor. "Let's get out of here," she said. "I'm starving."

My guts lurched as I remembered my own dinner plans.

Chapter Eight

I was over an hour late. I expected Mom to be upset—maybe even to make a scene. But, when I walked through the door of our penthouse suite, Ida stood at the counter, calmly trimming a bouquet of multicolored roses down with a pair of nail scissors. She looked at me over the row of blossoms and nodded her head toward the sofa, where Mom and the mystery guest sat, giggling.

The guest was female, pretty. Maybe Mom's age, but probably a little younger. She and Mom laughed softly, their heads close. The woman's eyes were wide and dark, lovely beneath pale, coppery eyebrows. Her metallic-red hair was cut in a bob, and the formal black dress she wore was nicer than anything I owned. When she stood up, I realized how tall she was. She walked over to me, and Mom followed, scurrying behind her. I felt a stab of envy at her coolness, at her ability to make Mom giggle.

"You must be Van," the woman said. "I've heard wonderful things about you." She hugged me, hard, pulling me from where I stood almost three feet away with her long arms. I imagined being squeezed tight by an elephant at the zoo, its unwelcome trunk grasping my body in a hot, musky trap. It was her perfume, too, a dark tangy fragrance, that gave me that suffocating feeling. I froze, not sure if I should apologize for my lack of punctuality. It seemed a better bet not to bring it up—whoever this woman was, she sure made Mom cheerful. I wasn't about to meddle with that.

"What a lovely young lady you are," she said as she released me a little.

I turned my face away from her perfumed neck to take a breath of semi-fresh air.

"Van, this is the friend from Cleveland I told you about, Marine," Mom said.

Marine? Cleveland? I thought. *What?*

"You know, I've been working with your mother for some time," Marine began. "Remotely, of course. But she has such wonderful, vital energy, I couldn't resist coming for a visit to meet her in person."

Mom beamed at Marine, and then I realized who she was. The astrotherapist. I unthreaded myself from Marine's arms by ducking a little and stepping back.

"Oh sure, nice to meet you," I said. "I'm just going to wash my hands." I waved and retreated to the bathroom. Even when I closed the door, I could smell Marine's perfume.

Mom had ordered a special dinner—roasted chicken—and by the time I'd collected myself, she, Ida, and Marine were seated around the bird's carcass in the middle of the table. A bottle of wine stood at Marine's left. She lifted it and filled her glass, and Mom's, which was really, really not a good idea. I looked at Ida.

"Have a seat, honey," Ida said, tapping the chair beside her. "Marine was just telling me that she's from France."

"Oh really?" I said. I tried not to stare as Mom drank from her glass.

"I was born there, but I've lived here a very long time," Marine said.

Mom served herself from the bowl of potatoes on the room-service cart. Marine looked from Mom to me and reached across the table to grab my hand.

"You know, Van," she said, "I sense that you and your mother have a similar, powerful energy." Panic prickled at the back of my throat, the way it did whenever anyone compared me to Mom. Maybe that similar, powerful energy was exactly what I'd felt playing at Red's.

"Don't they, though?" Ida said, taking my other hand and turning it over in her own.

Marine nodded, her hair glinting under the track lighting.

"I would love it if we could use this opportunity to discuss anything bothering you. Perhaps your plans for the future." She gave Mom a quick but serious look. "I'd love to be able to help you, Van," Marine said. "I know Mercury is in retrograde right now and it's unwise to begin anything significant, but I feel I must offer."

I had no idea how to answer, but Ida quickly cut in. "That's a very good point, honey. You don't mess with Mercury in retrograde."

Mom gave Ida a look like a fly swatter. Mom was already protecting this woman. Already it was going to be something very difficult to undo.

"Um, no, nothing's really bothering me. At the moment," I told Marine, trying—and failing—to look into her eyes as I said it.

Marine took a deep breath, like she was inhaling the smell of the dinner.

"Of course, I respect that," she said. "But know that I'm here if you need me."

"That's so kind, Marine," Mom said. She smiled into Marine's face, one of her best smiles.

I went to bed early—Ida and I both did—to give Marine and Mom a chance to talk or astrotherapize or whatever. The next morning, though, it was clear Marine had not left. Her cheetah print purse still hung on the coat rack, and an unfamiliar cell phone was out on the counter, beeping erratically, advertising its languishing battery. The door to Mom's room was closed. *Great,* I thought. *Mom's a lesbian now.* Just when you think you understand all of the variables, you realize you know nothing at all.

I felt queasy, thinking about Mom with someone new. It was different when she got with William. We needed him, and he loved Mom. Also, there was something harmless about him. He didn't get in the way of what Mom and I were to each other. This woman, though. Mom already seemed too happy with her. Much happier than she'd been with William.

Ida was already waiting for me in the living room, along with a freshly ordered breakfast. "Well, how did it go?" she asked.

"How did what go?"

"Band practice," she stage-whispered.

I grinned and uncovered a plate of eggs and bacon. "It was great," I told her. I felt like I could have started crying, that's how good it felt to remember playing with Carol and Joanna.

"Ah, honey, I'm glad," she said.

Marine's phone beeped.

"Meanwhile," Ida said, giving the phone a grimace.

"Yeah, meanwhile is right. How long is she staying? Did she say? Before I came home?"

"Yes, about that—you owe me, young lady. I covered for your ass and I covered good."

"Do you want some bacon? Would that make us even?"

"Yes, I would, and no, it would not. I'm talking multiple-foot-rubs owe me."

"Sick, Ida!"

"I'm talking *ointment*-application owe me," she said gleefully.

"Eww!" I fixed Ida's breakfast plate and handed it over.

Marine's phone beeped again, and Ida and I both fell silent and looked over at it.

"She didn't say exactly how long," Ida began, "but she sure doesn't have plans to leave any time soon." Ida looked pale under the kitchenette light; the veins on her hands were raised and gruesomely blue. I felt a prickle of anxiety behind my ears, but I pushed it away. Ida was still in her prime.

"Why do you say that?" I pressed the space behind my ears, pretending to smooth down my hair.

"Did you see her suitcase? No, I guess you didn't because you were *late*. But that monstrosity she brought was the size of Delaware. Also, she said she's staying on as your mom's assistant, whatever that means."

"Jesus. Can we do anything?"

"Not yet, I don't think. Honey," Ida began, then paused, looking up at the ceiling. "Do you, I mean," she stopped and shook her head. "Has Chantal tried to speak to you about your mother?"

"What? No, why would she? Mom's been doing fine. Right?"

"Right. Well, for the most part," Ida said.

"Why? Has she talked to you?"

"She has." Ida paused again and squinted a little. Then her face relaxed, and she smiled. "She's talked to me so much, I'm starting to think Chantal has a thing for me." She smirked as she propped her bare feet on top of the coffee table. She wiggled her wrinkly toes. "Which one do you want to start with, left or right?"

"You are so gross," I said, smiling. "I'm going to class. You think she'll be gone by the time I get back?"

"That's rich," Ida mumbled.

Chapter Nine

On my way back from class the next day, I ran into Joanna. She was still in her uniform, but had her purse slung across her body.

"Oh hey, Van, it's you." She sounded relieved.

"Are you okay?" I asked.

"Basically." She nodded, worrying a red, glossed lip with her teeth. "It's my cx, Marcos. He keeps showing up."

"Like at Red's?"

"Yeah, and even at my house. My mom loves him, so she doesn't think it's a problem, but he's never come to my job."

"You mean he's *here*? Right now?" I asked.

"I've been seeing his car around. Which is fucked up, because if Chantal knew, I'd be fired."

"Do you think he'd do something crazy?" I felt genuine alarm, for Joanna, for myself, even, funnily, for the Silver Saddle.

"I don't even know. He's weird. Obsessive."

"Wow," I said. "Sorry you have to deal with this." I tried to sound sympathetic, but I was also curious. What would it be like to have someone around who was so *interested* in you? "Is there anything I can do?" I asked.

"Yeah," said Joanna. "If anyone asks, you never saw me, okay?" Then she gave me one of those easy, sly looks, a look that made me feel like I was part of something with her.

I tried to mirror her smile, pleased by how natural it felt. "On it," I said, and kept moving.

• • •

Back at the suite, I found that Marine had commandeered the dining room table and covered it with wide sheets of paper filled with different-sized discs. A woman's voice on a recording, deep and slow, filled the room. Marine's head was bent, her hands clasped demurely in her lap.

I stepped inside, trying to move as quietly as I could toward my room, but Marine perked up as I passed—suddenly, like she could smell me.

"Oh Van, perfect!" Her large eyes bulged like a frog's. "If you have a few moments, I'd love for you to join me this afternoon."

"Sorry, Marine. I have homework."

"Of course you do, of course. I just thought that you, my dear, would especially benefit from Laurel's wisdom."

"Who?" I was curious in spite of my desire to move away from Marine. The woman's voice washed over us. There was a quality and depth—a looseness, an ease—to the tone that reminded me of my favorite Nina Simone songs. *What makes it sound like that?* I wondered.

"Laurel is my teacher, and a great fount of wisdom. You might say she is like a mother to me."

"Oh, okay," I said, wincing at the contrast of my forced politeness and the sultry warmth in the recorded voice. I started to move away, but Marine's projects spanning the table caught my eye. They looked like pie charts, except the slices of pie were all uniform and annotated with strange pencil drawings.

Marine caught me looking and shouted, "Ah!" like she'd just killed a mosquito. "Yes, dear Van," she continued, "I thought you might be interested in what I'm working on."

"No, I was just getting some water." I turned into the kitchenette and reached for a glass. I didn't want Marine to think I was getting sucked into any of her New Age nonsense.

"How fortuitous, my dear water sign," she said. "It's like the universe wants us to have this conversation." She turned down the volume of the recording and the strange voice retreated to the corners of the room.

"Excuse me?"

"You're a water sign. A Pisces."

"Yes," I answered slowly, shifting from foot to foot.

"Have a seat," Marine said, and pulled out the chair beside her.

Marine moved the tools she'd been using into a pile in the center of the table: a silver protractor-looking thing, and an assortment of colored pencils.

"Now, Pisces," she said, "is one of my favorite signs. It's your mother's too, you know."

Of course I knew. I felt a flare of irritation as Marine scooted her chair closer to mine.

"And we are in the Age of Pisces." She pointed at a symbol that looked like a collapsing capital H. "The best thing, I think, and the reason I love Pisces, is you have a natural astral ability. More so, in my opinion, than any other sign."

"Sure," I said.

"The ability to access higher planes, to explore, psychically. It's been so eye-opening to work with your mother. She is more aware of the unseen than anyone I've ever met. She's a real virtuoso."

Even I could tell that this was getting weird. It didn't help that Marine's eyes were all glassy and that she kept gripping my hand.

"And you, dear Van. I suspect you have a gift like that."

"Yeah, maybe!" I said, with forced brightness. I pulled my hand out of Marine's and pretended I was just fixing my ponytail. I pulled apart two handfuls of hair until my scalp tingled.

"Just tell me when you're ready," Marine said, her ink-dark eyes locked on my face. "I know I will be able to help you tap into that great potential." Marine clasped her hand in a fist and held it close to her chest.

The glass tabletop rattled as I stood up and hurried away.

• • •

It bothered me the way Marine always seemed to be grasping—at me, at Mom, even at Ida. But, especially, at Mom. After those first tentative days, she and Mom closed all of the gaps between them. After that, if I saw Mom, I saw Marine. They were affectionate, too, which was really unlike Mom.

Their touching wasn't inappropriate—they weren't Frenching and groping or anything. It was more like they were making sure each other's bodies were still there: a hand on a shoulder, two hips touching as they leaned against the counter, their arms linked as they walked. I pushed back the fear that Marine would be able to get as close to Mom as I was.

It was easier to ignore the Marine-Mom development because I'd been to more band practices with Carol and Joanna. At the very least, Marine's arrival made my mind looser. That constant worry about Mom and her wildness, or her immobilizing sadness—the pressure was off a little, now that she had Marine. In a way, I appreciated the difficult job Marine had signed on for, partnering up with Mom. I had other things to worry about. Joanna and Carol and I were playing our first show at Alex's birthday party. I was nervous, sure, but mostly thrilled. I was even more thrilled that I hadn't had to explain it to Mom. *Thanks, Marine,* I thought.

I didn't sleep well the night before Alex's party. I woke up at five that morning having to pee really badly. When I opened my eyes, something didn't feel right. No, something didn't *sound* right. Laurel's disembodied voice oozed into my room. I cracked open my door and peeked down the hallway. Mom was sitting, straight and still on the sofa. The voice hovered between us. *"It is the charge of every sentient being to pull their white light to the fore. That white light is our great, divine gift and the source of all of our power. In some, it is stronger than in others. It is strongest in those who are made divine themselves. We must tend our own bright fires—and we must tend—and light—them in others."*

"Mom?" I said. "Are you still up?" I tried to cool the alarm I felt by counting my steps toward the living room.

"The white light she talks about," Mom said. Her voice was raw, like she'd been talking all night. Like she'd been howling all night. "Don't you feel it? Do you ever feel it?" Her gaze burned, not just with the ferocious intention of her question, but with something else. Mom had never asked me anything like that before. She'd never been so direct.

I shook my head, but of course I'd felt it. Laurel's white light coursed through me, its brightness streaked through my fingertips when I played. It filled my chest cavity with humming possibility. I'd pushed it out through my hands, practicing and learning. Ida had no idea what she'd done for me, when she showed me how to pour that light over the strings of her guitar. I was grateful and terrified, to play like I could.

I shook my head again. "No, Mom, I don't. You should really get some sleep." Mom tilted her head into the ripples of Laurel's voice, and I tried to go back to bed. I counted through the songs Carol and Joanna had settled on for our set that night, thinking it might help me get back to sleep for a little. It didn't. I wanted to pick up Ida's guitar and pace through some of the trickier songs, but I didn't want to think about white light, my own or Mom's.

When I got out of bed, I found Ida in the kitchen. She slammed the coffee maker lid closed. Mom was still up—she hadn't slept at all. The recording, thankfully, had been switched off—by Ida, probably.

"Oh Ida, you are so wonderful to make coffee every morning," Marine said. She was dressed, but still looked half asleep.

"Mmm-hmm," Ida said, and pulled four mugs down with a clatter.

Mom half stood over the dining table as she scanned a row of Post-it notes flapping across one of Marine's pie charts. Her lips moved silently. Marine bent down beside her, so close that they looked like a pair of quotation marks.

"Good Lord, Marine!" Ida said. "Let the woman breathe!" The irritation in her voice was as obvious to me as a neck tattoo across the pale sagging skin of her throat.

"Oh, Ida," Marine said, as she gave Ida an oblivious smile. "This is part of Sofia's treatment plan."

Ida spun around and my head snapped up. *Oh no*, I thought.

"What do you mean, hon?" Ida said, her voice carefully neutral.

"It's distance less than thirty-six," Marine said, looking down at the top of Mom's head tenderly. Mom didn't respond. She just pored over those Post-it notes, removing one at a time, tearing each one in half when she was finished with it.

"I'm sorry, could you repeat that, Marine?" Ida said.

"Distance less than thirty-*six*," Marine explained. She said it slowly, like it was a common combination of words, like Happy New Year, or Place All Hand Baggage Under The Seat In Front Of You. Ida and I looked at each other.

"I'm not familiar with what that is," Ida said, carefully.

"Of course," Marine nodded, as though she should have thought of that first. "In astro circles, it's very common. In fact, it was pioneered by my mentor, Laurel. The practitioner—*me*," she said, placing a hand on her chest, "stays physically close—no more than *thirty-six* inches from the client." Here she placed both hands on Mom's shoulders. "It opens the astral pathways, you see. Promoting the open flow of positive energy, of the brightest white light."

Mom finally looked up at us.

"Fascinating, right?" she said. She stared at Marine, unblinking. "Laurel's mind is one I need to know better." I tried to ignore the disjointed construction of Mom's sentence. *It doesn't mean anything,* I thought. *She's probably just tired.* I couldn't have her unraveling on the day of Alex's party. *Just let me have this one thing,* I begged.

"Fascinating," Ida replied, still looking right at me. If Ida was trying to get me to say something—*this is crazy,* or, *have you lost your mind*—she had the wrong girl. I wasn't about to stir anything up, not on the day of my first band playing its first show.

"Did I tell you?" Mom said suddenly, out of nowhere, mostly to Marine. "I located the old surveillance room. Good for private events, no? This is what we'll explain at the meeting."

I was stunned, not only by Mom's invasive discovery, but also by her irregular, semi-slurred speech. Had she taken something this morning? Had Marine given her something to take? *She's Marine's problem now,* I thought bitterly.

Marine and Mom left after finishing their coffee, hand in hand. Mom whispered close into the side of Marine's head. They really did seem to go to work together. At least, Marine went with Mom to all of her meetings. And if this thirty-six rule, or whatever, was really happening, surely Marine's involvement went beyond meeting attendance. I wanted to ask Alex what Chantal thought about it, but it seemed like Mom's private business. I thought it would be a jerk move, a betrayal, especially since I'd just joined a band behind her back and against her wishes. Not talking about it seemed like the least I could do.

I took the elevator down to the lobby. It was a shortcut to the Bill Pickett Room. I was sad—and a little irritated—to lose the surveillance room, but I realized with unprecedented relief that being in the band made up for that loss. I was running late after the morning's weirdness, and wasn't paying attention to my surroundings at all.

Basically, I walked into a guy.

"Whoa," he said, as we jumped apart. I rubbed my shoulder where I'd bumped him.

"Oh God, I'm so sorry," I said. "I'm just really late and rushing." I looked up, skimming over his face. He was smiling; that was good. He was young, maybe even my age. His eyes were a wide, warm brown, and his smile displayed a perfect braces-straight set of teeth. "I guess I need to slow down." I felt myself blushing.

He shrugged, his narrow shoulders sloping beneath a denim jacket. "Don't apologize," he said. "Any day you almost get knocked down by a pretty girl is a good day."

"I'm really, really sorry," I repeated. *Wow, Van, you're a brilliant conversationalist.* I shook myself a little. The guy bent his head lower toward me, like he could hear what I'd been thinking.

"If you weren't in such a hurry, I'd ask you to buy me a coffee."

"Yeah, sorry." I winced.

"Maybe next time you run into me."

"Yeah," I said. "I mean, sorry again." Oh God. *Leave. Leave now.*

"See you around, I hope." He waved, still smiling.

I was still smiling, too, as I turned toward the conference room annex, where I found Chantal and Alex waiting. Neither of them looked very happy. I wasn't surprised, especially since they'd seen me physically harm a guest.

"Good morning, Van," Chantal said, in a sonorous, principal-style voice.

"Oh, hi. Good morning."

Alex stood a little bit behind Chantal. The natural morning light changed the lobby so much it looked entirely different than it did at night. You could see every stain and scratch in the pilling carpet, and the sunlight streaming through the smudged windows caught the facets in the crystals that dangled from the ancient chandeliers. It was incongruous, all of that shabbiness pushed up against something that was once really special.

"Van?" Chantal's voice broke into my thought.

"Yes?" I was startled by how easily and how far I'd retreated into my own mind.

"I don't think you heard me. Would you mind sitting down with me for a few minutes before your lessons?"

"Well, I'm pretty late already. I'm sure Erica is waiting."

"No, she hasn't arrived yet. Alex will stay here to greet her and let her know you'll be along. Momentarily." Chantal overpronounced every syllable of the last word, like she was trying to force a steadiness into what she said.

Alex shifted to face me and nodded hello. I smiled, but looked away quickly. Chantal examined us, one at a time.

"Van? If you'll follow me?"

Before I registered her movement, Chantal stood in front of me, her arm out, waving me along.

She led me to her office, a small room off of the lobby. It felt like I was in trouble. I looked up at Chantal, waiting. The great wallpaper redecoration of the 1970s had had its way all over this little cube of the Silver Saddle. A variety of potted plants studded the office. They were lush and healthy—obviously very well cared for. None of them were from the desert.

"Please, have a seat."

There was a desk and chair-for-visitors arrangement at the center of the office and a small sofa in the corner. Instead of setting up what I was sure was a headmistress-student type discussion, Chantal sat on the sofa and motioned for me to sit beside her.

"I hope you're adjusting here," she began. "We're all very happy to have you. I'm sure Alex has been an ideal tour guide. I asked him especially to keep an eye out for you."

"Oh. Yes, everything has been great." It stung to think of Alex that way, and I think Chantal meant it to sting, that frank statement that Alex was paid to be part of my life.

"You're a very bright girl, and Erica tells me you've surpassed all of her expectations."

"Thanks," I said, feeling my face heat up. I suspected this was tactical, too. I'd also suspected that Erica was reporting to Chantal, but this straightforward declaration of Chantal's monitoring hurt. I was being watched everywhere, and now, with Mom's requisition of the old surveillance room, I had even fewer safe spaces under the Silver Saddle's roof.

"I don't want to put you in an awkward position." Chantal stopped for a moment and stared at the wall, as though willing the terrible pattern to morph into a lovelier one. "And we've enjoyed having your mother here," she added, so quickly I could barely make out the sentence. "Ida, too. Of course. She's *very* charming."

"She is."

"Your mother really has made some wonderful improvements. She's very good at thinking outside of the box." When Chantal said this, she drew an imaginary box in the air with her hands. "But, can you tell me, how much do you know about this Marine?"

I was already sitting as far away from Chantal as I could. I pressed my body against the armrest of the sofa, like I could open up some other dimensional tunnel and escape through it. This wasn't the first time someone had cornered me with questions about Mom, looking for some kind of explanation for her strange behavior.

"Not very much," I said, trying to make my voice cold and flat.

"Van," Chantal lowered her voice a little here. I could tell she was trying to be softer and less frightening. It wasn't working. "It must be difficult for you when your mom's personal life interferes with your family time." She paused and looked at me, waiting.

I let her wait. The breaths in our lungs whispered back and forth in the chill, still air of the office. Chantal wasn't going to squeeze anything out of me, I thought.

"Not really," I finally said.

"I see." Chantal wrung the softness out of her face. "Well, I'd like to share my thoughts on this matter, if you don't mind."

I was pretty sure Chantal would be sharing her thoughts no matter what.

"I am becoming concerned. I didn't approve Marine's hire, and I certainly can't condone the kind of . . . fraternization that's been going on. And frankly, Sofia seems to have lost quite a bit of focus since her arrival."

This, I'd heard before: loss of focus, general concern.

"I'm attributing this to Marine's entrance into the company," Chantal continued. "Let me be clear about that, Van. I hate to send you into any kind of awkward way, but I'm sure you appreciate that this situation is—well, it's unique."

I'd heard that before, too. Mom was a mystery to everyone. Chantal wasn't the first to try to use me to decode Mom.

"I've suggested to your mother that Marine isn't a good fit here, but I think the issue is *complicated* for her. Her personal feelings are in the way of what's best for the company. Do you see?"

I kept my face neutral, but all of the muscles in my body were tensed, even the smallest ones behind each toe. I just wanted it to be over; I wanted Chantal to kick us out of the Silver Saddle or just to send me off to class.

"I've discussed my concerns with Ida as well, but we seem to be getting nowhere." She shrugged. "I'm not entirely comfortable asking you this, but I don't know where else to turn in this delicate matter. And you, such a bright young woman, I thought you might have some unique insight for me."

I shook my head and looked at my hands. "I'm sorry. I don't think I can help you."

"Very well. But Van," Chantal said, while I was still moving. "If you ever *do* want to discuss this business with Marine, please know that I'm here for you." That artificial softness played through her voice again.

"Okay, thanks." I stood up and nearly ran out of her office. I had a feeling that this was only the first of my interrogations with Chantal. When I replayed what she said about Alex being my "tour guide," well, I was disappointed, angry even.

Alex waited in the lobby by the door to Chantal's office. "Hey," he said. He started to walk next to me when it was clear that I meant to keep going. I wanted to move away from Chantal, but I wanted to move away from Alex, too. I felt a metallic sweep of anger behind my eyes and in my throat. The heat that gathered there wasn't all Alex's fault. It was Marine's, and Mom's, too. I had to calm down. I stopped walking, and so did Alex. He just looked at me with that stupid, symmetrical face.

It was my fault that Alex's part in this upset me so much. I had known better. Why hadn't I kept myself safe and detached like always? *Those presents*, I thought. *I blame those presents.*

"Was it really that bad?" Alex asked.

An overwhelming feeling of being watched, of every corner of the Silver Saddle being bugged, propelled me toward the revolving doors. I had to get outside. The doors slung us out into the windy desert—me and Alex both. He'd scuttled into the compartment beside me before I could stop him.

I walked down the strip of sidewalk, doubled over a little, still holding my stomach. I felt Alex's hand on my back between my shoulder blades and wanted to shake it off. But I couldn't, for some reason. Even the illusion of another person giving a shit made me lose my head.

"Seriously, you need to get off," I said, and shivered away. I stepped onto the gravel of the drive and started walking. Alex followed, matching his steps to my steps, like we were doing a military drill. The bellmen, all smoking, watched us from where they lounged in a cluster on a bench.

The gravel crunched beneath our four feet and the desert air dried the tears in my eyes to a salty crust. I looked out at the fawn-colored flatness, at the huge, clear sky. I breathed in the dry morning air and turned toward Alex. All of his tallness leaned against the wind, leaned toward me.

"Chantal told me it was your job to keep an eye on me."

"What?" Alex squinted against the breeze.

"She was very frank. So you don't have to invite me to go anywhere or to do anything. And you don't have to leave me any more weird shit in the surveillance room. My mom found out about it anyway, so that's already over."

"What?" His voice was grainy, breaking up in the wind's shriek. "She said I've been spying on you? Van, she asked me to help you out, show you around. I was happy to do it at first, and then, I don't know, I thought we were friends."

I just shook my head. My hair whipped around my face. I felt the strands wind up in the air and plummet back down against my cheeks and forehead. *Stay out of my way*, is how I imagined I looked. Menacing.

Alex shoved his hands into his pockets and looked down, as though I'd pushed his head toward the sand with the power of my glare. It felt great. I mean, it felt terrible, too, but I felt a twinge of great. There was something about the set of his shoulders and the indent between his eyebrows that made him look really hurt. *Good*, I thought.

"Van, I'm a little confused, here," he said, muttering down to the earth. "I like you. I really believed that we were friends. None of this was about Chantal. You think Chantal made me ask you out? You think Chantal *paid* me to invite you to my birthday tonight?"

"Please stop it. Just stop. You're embarrassing us both for no reason. Just admit that the situation is what it actually is. You're a relatively nice person, and I'm not going to be rude if I don't have to be. Let's just be honest, here."

"A relatively nice person?" Alex nearly shouted. He turned and started pacing in a circle around where I stood. The air between us filled with dust, and I coughed into the sleeve of my sweater.

"I don't even know what to say." Alex paused to speak. "I guess you *are* just really young. Or really dim. If you didn't see what I saw, then I guess that's what's going on."

"What did you see?" I hated that I wanted to know.

Alex walked right up to me, as close as if we were facing off at a square dance. I saw, under the bright sunlight, that his eyes were more hazel, and not brown like I'd thought. I felt the heat of his body, and the strands of my hair caught up in the breeze whipped against the front of his shirt. That's how close we stood.

Alex took my hand, not like a hand-hold, hand-hold, with ten fingers all spliced together. He took it like you take the hand of a person getting off of a boat and onto a dock—a surrounding, reassuring grip.

"When I said I liked you, it was true. I like you. Do you know what I mean?"

I nodded, but really I didn't. Was it another trick, or something else? I wasn't sure which would be worse.

"I was never *spying*."

He didn't let go of my hand. I looked over his shoulder at the smudged pencil line of the horizon. I couldn't look at him, even though I wanted to try, to test myself, to make sure it didn't bother me to look him in the eye.

"It's fine," I told him, still looking out at the desert. "I get it."

"What does that mean?"

"It means it's fine. Friends, okay?" I wasn't completely sure if I meant it, but I just wanted this awkward standoff to be over, to look at it later, under the microscope of my own mind. When Alex wasn't touching me.

He gave my hand a quick little shake, like we had concluded a pretend interview.

"Friends," he said.

Then he hugged me, a big, tight, uninitiated-by-me hug. I couldn't remember the last time someone other than Ida or Mom—or Marine, that once against my will—had hugged me. I didn't think anyone ever had. I leaned into it for just a second and breathed in the smell of another person's closeness—all foreign-scented shampoo and rumpled, unwashed clothes. Before I could really sink into it, I pulled back and kept my head down.

"Let's go. I don't want to leave Erica just sitting there," I said.

"Hey," Alex said, suddenly.

"What?"

"You're coming tonight, right? To the party?"

I couldn't resist the rush of happiness that burbled up. It was my first time performing, and I was going to kill it. Chantal definitely wasn't paying Joanna and Carol to be my friends.

"Yeah, I can't miss our first show," I told Alex.

We walked back up the gravel path side by side, less than thirty-six inches between us.

Chapter Ten

I considered that terrible talk with Chantal. I replayed her voice in my mind, trying to get to the bottom of what she meant. To get to the bottom of her timeline, I guess. I'd been through enough jobs of Mom's to know the end was near. Thinking out of the box was right. Mom thought so far out of the box, she'd pack up the box and mail it to the International Space Station.

In similar situations—at other jobs—as Mom thought further and further outside of the box, the signals came, as clear as flares shot into the sky. Almost always there was a timeline. Sometimes they spelled it out: "You have three weeks to pull it together, Sofia." Sometimes, you had to read between the lines of their *concern.*

How much time was Chantal giving us? I wasn't ready to go. It had seemed urgent—bringing in a seventeen-year-old as a potential ally seemed especially last-resort. I went looking for Ida when Erica left for the day. She needed to know what Chantal was saying, I decided. If I passed the problem off to Ida, I could focus on the show.

Since it was Friday, the casino rang with thousands of slot machine plays and the energy of hundreds of bodies bussed in for the weekend. To compete with these new frequencies, everything was louder—the music, the voices from the throats of the waitresses and dealers, even the air conditioning whirred at its highest capacity.

"Hey, Van." A mellifluous voice interrupted my thoughts.

"Yeah?" I turned around to Joanna, stopped in the hallway with a stack of folded sheets in her arms. She smoldered at me over the pile of linen.

"Are you ready for tonight?"

"Yeah, I think. Probably."

"Don't sound so excited."

"No! I'm totally excited!" I winced when I heard how childish I sounded.

"Good. You're getting a ride with Alex, right?"

"Yeah, I am. Do you want us to stop at Red's to pick anything up?"

Joanna shook her head. "Nope, Carol's brother is bringing everything. Don't be late, okay? Get there at eight at least, so we can sound check."

"Yeah, okay, great," I said. "See you later."

She gave me the world's coolest-looking salute and sauntered off.

Eight—I had plenty of time to hunt down Ida and let her know about the Chantal shakedown. I walked into the heart of the casino, not wanting to risk wasting time waiting around in the suite for Ida to come back for one of her costume changes.

I could feel the swell of sound even in the relatively muted back hallways of the complex of conference rooms. Every atom that buzzed my body into being wanted to be away from the growling pit that I headed toward. Pushing myself into the thronged central room of the casino was like defying a law of physics. It *hurt* to be in there, somehow, like being burnt under the sun.

There were so many people, more young people than usual at the Silver Saddle. The cascades of laughter were raw and open. It was an inviting sound; *let in whatever wants to get in,* it seemed to say. Drinks slogged over the edges of their plastic cups and dribbled onto my arms. I knew I shouldn't be there. A few designated common paths cut through the center, and anyone could walk on those. Even me. On a Friday evening a minor on the floor was definitely not okay. I had to find Ida and I had to get out of there.

I scanned the room and spotted Ovid in the corner closest to me, a looming dark shadow over his green felt domain. I threaded through the stumbling bodies, careful to move my feet around the wobbling spikes of violently colored high-heeled shoes that shifted and stamped into the already beaten, stained carpet. As I inched closer to Ovid's table, I heard Ida's laugh, that familiar smoky chuckle, and my whole body slumped forward in relief. I practically dove forward into the flat of Ida's back, like I was a little kid again.

"Hey!" she shouted, turning around, brandishing her angriest face. When she saw that it was me, she pulled me under her arm. "Honey, what are you doing in here?" Ida had to practically shout in my ear.

I just turned into her and hugged her hard. Ida pulled me back by my shoulders a little, her forehead furrowed into a stack of creases.

"Are you okay? Van? What is it?"

I couldn't figure out where it came from, maybe the crowd, maybe Chantal, maybe Alex, maybe I was getting nervous about the show, but my vision went all funny, and the back of my throat felt hot. Ida knew my about-to-cry face better than anyone. Her hands gripped into the tops of my shoulders and she shook me a little.

"What is it? Is your mom okay?"

"She's fine," I smiled. "I just need to talk to you."

"Sure thing, honey." Ida pulled me close. "Let's go get some dinner."

The packs of bodies thinned when we got to the lobby hallway, and Ida wrapped an arm around my waist as we moved. We hadn't walked that way in a long time, and I was surprised by how different Ida's body felt next to mine since I had grown. She was much smaller, much thinner.

"Ida," I began, "Chantal talked to me today. About Mom."

"Ugh." Ida's voice snapped between us. "She threatened to bring it up to you, but I didn't think she'd actually go through with it. Boy, that's low." Ida tapped a finger against her exposed collar bone.

"She asked about Marine. She asked me what I know about Marine, I guess."

Ida snorted. "Marine. I don't know what your mom is thinking, bringing her in so close. Wouldn't we all like a little more information about Marine?"

"What are we supposed to do? Chantal's getting nervous. And I can't really tell what's going on with Mom since she's always with Marine. You know?"

"Oh I know, honey," Ida said. "Let's see if we can get your mom at least five feet away from that woman and get the lay of the land, okay?"

"Okay."

"It's going to be fine."

Except that it wasn't. Ida and I shambled through the lobby. I was surprised by how much she was leaning on me. I wanted to ask if I should be worried about *her*, but I couldn't even open that possibility in my mind. I just wanted things to be regular: Ida-steps-up-and-Van-steps-down.

I pushed the elevator call button. *Everything's fine,* I told myself. *Tonight's going to be great.* When the dented brass doors split in front of us, Mom and Marine barreled out. Mom had that look where she didn't see anything—she just blew forward and away.

• • •

I ran after them; I had no choice. I just hoped whatever was brewing would settle back down before eight o'clock. Ida couldn't keep up, and I left her behind. Because I knew that look on Mom's face, and I knew someone had to stop her, to slow her down at least. I had to do something while there was still a chance to prevent a full meltdown. Clots of guests in the lobby blocked my way, but I pushed into and against them, shoving their ridiculous beribboned rolling suitcases aside as I made a path to the revolving doors. I could see them, Mom and Marine, illuminated under the harsh brightness of the lights lining the carport.

The guests who waited outside clustered away from the two women. Marine's reedy tallness curled over my near-vibrating mother. I spun through the revolving doors and burst out into the chill night air. I hung back by a group of young women, and the smoke from their cigarettes poured across the line of my vision.

I could hear them, not the words, but the melody of their voices. Marine's voice was low and lilting, dipping and swaying in gentle, soothing waves. Mom's voice was rough, half screaming, half whispering. Her arms were moving and she was trying to pace, but Marine wouldn't let her; she kept skipping in front of Mom like a basketball player on the other team. *At least Marine has the right idea,* I thought. *Containment.*

The guests knew something was going on, even though the valets and bellmen were trying to smooth it over, making jokes and lighting cigarettes. Out of the corner of my eye, I saw Ida's face through the large plate glass lobby window.

I had to step in. *Just do this one thing, and then Ida can take over. Then you can leave.* I jumped forward, ready for the hit that was this blizzard of Mom. I ran up close, just short of touching her.

"Mom!" I shouted, trying to get her attention.

Marine turned to me, startled, like I had just woken her up. Mom shivered and chattered in the night air. It was like she was breaking up into little pieces, shaking all over the sidewalk. When she got like this, I imagined being trapped in a snowstorm, the wind and ice in my ears and eyes. Mom was all I could see or hear.

Marine grabbed my forearm.

"Van, my dear, you should go back inside. This isn't for you to see."

I looked at Marine, a you-have-no-idea-lady kind of look, but of course, she didn't get it. She put her body between my mother and me as Mom shuddered under the stars.

"All right, all right," Ida said, pushing her way through the groups of onlookers on the sidewalk. "Break it up, come on, come on," she said, her arms stretched out like a crossing guard.

"Let's go, ladies," Ida said, sweeping our group back into the pool of darkness behind a crescent of parked cars.

The three of us made a kind of wall behind Mom. Our feet scuffed through the gravel and I thought about the kind of tracks we must have made. Mom bounced along in front of us; if she tried to veer off, we'd reconfigure our human wall around her, like a cupped palm. It took a long time, but we finally made it to the employee parking lot out back, the place Alex had led me on what apparently had been a date. I still wasn't sure. And I felt like a real jackass thinking of it right in that moment. I shook myself, a faraway echo of Mom's shakes.

Our human wall broke apart past the second line of cars, and we let Mom loose. She roved and scampered across the sea of gravel, oblivious to the rest of us. Ida spun around and looked like she was about to slap Marine. She didn't, though, and I could see her practically sweating with the effort not to.

"What the hell is this, Marine?" Ida shouted, turning the other woman's name into an insult, putting all the emphasis on the -ine.

"Excuse me, but I'm not sure why you blame me for this," Marine shouted back. "You know her best, after all."

"Well I'm not the one who's been six inches away from her, twenty-four hours a day. How did you not see this coming?"

Ida yelled at Marine, but I felt like most of her yelling was directed at us, at herself, and at me. How did *we* not see this coming?

"Jesus, now where did she go?" Ida said.

We all pivoted where we stood, scanning the empty parking lot for Mom's oscillating figure. I strained to listen for the movement of the parking lot's tiny stones. If she disappeared onto the desert sand, in the dark, things would get really, really bad. I could forget about playing my first show, for a start. I pulled the sleeves of my sweater into my palms and pinned them down with my fingernails.

"Mom!" I shouted, as I turned and turned.

Ida crept along the rows of cars, stopping every once in a while to peer underneath their boxy metal bodies.

"Soh-of," she wheedled. "Sofia, honey," just like she was calling to a missing cat.

Marine sat cross-legged on the ground and started humming to herself. *Jesus*, I thought, *Just, Jesus*. I imagined having to identify

Mom's decomposing body on a table somewhere. I clenched my hands into fists and kept looking.

The three of us were out there a long time. I stopped checking my phone as the sky grew darker and the time inched closer and closer to eight. Marine meditated about Mom's coordinates, whatever that meant. Ida and I fanned out farther and farther until our footsteps pressed past the parking lot, beyond the off-brand landscaping and into the desert. I wondered if this was what it was like to be a bird, just circling and circling, looking and looking.

Loud staccato chattering broke up the search. I sprinted back to the poorly lit parking lot, where all of the noise was coming from.

"Oh Van, Van, my sweet, sweet Van!" I heard Mom's voice before I saw her, kneeling in the stony grit of the lot. Marine knelt beside her, cinching her close with both arms, murmuring something I couldn't hear.

Ida coughed out a string of curse words behind me as she made up the distance between us. Ida put her arm out, and, when I took it, she leaned into me trying to catch her breath.

"My Van," Mom said, rising from the ground. "I'm going for a mission, yes? But only a brief time." Mom's accent sliced out at us in the night.

"Sofia," Ida said slowly, "where are you thinking about going?"

"We've discussed it," Marine said. Her head popped up from where it had been resting against Mom's. "I'm taking Sofia on a mission. A spiritual mission."

"Oh my God," Ida growled, and then started to cough.

"What do you mean?" I asked.

Mom walked over to me, slipping out from under Marine's arms. She held my face between her hands. I wanted to pull away. I wanted to wrench Mom's own head into my arms and hold her down in one spot.

"Marine will transport me, and when I'm through, I come straight back to you. She needs me, this Laurel."

"What? Mom, *we* need you!" I yelled, even though I knew she couldn't really understand me when she was like this.

If we lost hold of Mom, if we lost track of her, she could do her worst. Ida steadied her breathing and put one hand on Mom's back and one hand on mine.

"Sure, of course you need to go on this mission, of course. But let's all just go inside, calm down, regroup—"

"No, no," Mom pulled away sharply. "This place needs me. I know I can help them."

"What place?" Ida asked.

"The Congregation of Blessed Light," Mom said.

Marine approached us and looked meaningfully at me and Ida.

"You see, Van, Ida," Marine said, "Laurel is a very skilled *healer*." She raised her eyebrows on the last word.

What is that supposed to mean, I wondered. *A doctor?*

"Okaaaay," Ida said. She drew out the word like she was trying to make more space between us and this healer, to figure out what was going on.

"Do you understand?" Marine asked, again with that eyebrow lift.

I lifted my own eyebrows back at her. Right then, I wanted to hit someone. I wanted to slap Mom, or Marine, maybe even knock myself unconscious so I didn't have to figure it out.

"What is she talking about?" I asked. I hated that I felt so jealous, on top of everything else.

"Laurel—she is practically my second mother," Marine directed this at Ida. "She runs a treatment facility of sorts. I was telling Sofia about it, that Laurel is a healer, not a business person, and that her facility is suffering as a result. Sofia believes that she can help." Marine reached out for Mom, but Mom had already stepped away, squinting out into the dark.

"I must go to her, to Laurel. Marine understands."

"Yes, Sofia." Marine turned to Ida and me. "I also believe my friend can help *her*. If you get my meaning. Now, I will just get your mother to my car, and we'll leave straightaway."

"Leave straightaway? Now just hold on a minute. No one needs to go anywhere," Ida said.

"It's not far at all. Only in Sedona. Believe me," Marine said, right at Ida and me. "This is the best option for Sofia."

Mom leaned over and kissed Marine. Ida and I stepped back, like we'd been cut out of the decision. I was stunned—I felt so physically pushed away. Ida leaned into me and said, "I don't know about this. I really don't know."

I looked at Ida, trying to pull myself together. The full force of the day fell on me and I said, "I think we have to let her go with Marine." Ida nudged me, hard. "What?" I said. "Marine's the one who got her all worked up about this Laurel, let *her* handle it." I *knew* how bad it would be for Mom to leave, and I still thought *I'm going to Alex's party. I'm going to play this show no matter what*—that was the selfish, sinister truth that bit through all of it. I was pissed that Mom had brought loopy, unnecessary Marine into our lives, I was angry that Mom had taken away my surveillance room safe haven, but mainly I was furious that she was trying to go off on some crackpot job without us. *Let her see how she does without Ida and me.* I felt chilled by what I'd said, but also charged by choosing something I wanted over dealing with Mom.

Besides, all of our normal ways seemed blocked. If we wrestled Mom back inside somehow to drug her, there would be a scene.

If we called an ambulance, it would be an even bigger mess. How would we smooth things over for Chantal, for Chantal who was already prepared to throw us out of the Silver Saddle? Of course I was selfish—I had plenty of selfish reasons. I wasn't ready to leave Vegas. I wasn't ready to leave the band and what it meant. I wanted Mom to the side for once, not to worry only about her.

"Are you sure about that?" Ida asked, squeezing my hand.

"I'm sure," I answered.

It didn't matter if I was sure or not, because while Ida and I whispered to each other, Mom and Marine had been walking. The silent, dark lot was punctured by the clip of a car door closing and the burst of an engine. I heard Mom's voice, streaming from an open window as they drove away.

"Well, Jesus," Ida said. She slapped her cheeks a few times and let out a long, creaky sigh. "We'll see. We can go after her, too, you know."

I froze, jerking Ida to a stop beside me.

"Ida, we can't. Chantal can't know she just left like that."

Ida wrinkled her forehead.

"Remember that little heart-to-heart she sat me down for?" I said, waving my arms up at the sky. "Mom can't get fired again. Not so fast." I thought of Alex, of Joanna and Carol. Of Ovid. "Are *you* ready to leave? Like this?"

We stared at the taillights of Marine's car as they retreated, the size of two glowing red thumbprints in the dark.

"Don't worry, honey," Ida said. "We got this. I got this." I wasn't sure if she was talking to herself or me. I snuck a glance at my phone: 7:15. I could still make it.

Chapter Eleven

I didn't realize how cold I was until we were back inside. The blast of air conditioning was balmy compared to the desert night air. My fingers tingled. It was hard not to rush Ida back up to the suite—I still had to change—but she was clearly having trouble walking. Ida's face was drained of color and her lips had purpled under her fuchsia lipstick.

Speed didn't matter, though, since Chantal was already there, waiting. She stood at the corner of the reception desk, poised to pounce on Mom, us, whoever made it back, once the terrible display was all over. If I thought I knew Chantal's angry face before, I was wrong. Her shoulders were tensed nearly to her ears, and her eyebrows were drawn low like two thunderbolts.

Ida and I held each other like a couple of orphans. I hoped she was going to do the talking, because I was finished. I had someplace to be. The possibility of the night ahead jolted through to the ends of my hair. It was probably compounded by Mom's terrifying but thrilling exit—with Mom gone and Ida distracted, I could probably do whatever I wanted. I might even stay out all night. The reception staff buzzed behind the desk, but quieted as we approached. Chantal stepped in front of us.

"Ladies, my office, please." The sentence barely escaped her clenched jaw.

It was my second time in Chantal's office in one day. Ida lagged behind me, and really took her time getting through the door. Chantal closed it behind us and nobody sat down. *Please don't let her call the police,* I silently begged. It would ruin everything for Mom, and there would definitely be no big night out for me.

"Will one of you please explain what is going on?" Chantal said, with that same, barely contained viciousness.

"Of course, of course," Ida said, waving her hand like, *What-this? This-is-no-big-thing.*

Chantal's eyes bugged out a little and she looked like she was going to throw something.

"Really cold out tonight," Ida continued. She gave a little burlesque shiver. Ida was stalling, trying to get her thoughts together.

I looked at the clock in Chantal's office.

"Yeah, you don't normally think of the desert as a cold place but . . ." I jumped in. I couldn't help myself—it was probably all the adrenaline.

"That's enough," Chantal said. "Where is Sofia?"

"You didn't see her?" Ida asked, her eyes wide with surprise.

"What?" Chantal banged a nearby shelf with her fist.

"We sent her up a while ago." Ida squinted toward Chantal in confusion. "She was so upset, poor thing. I mean, I don't know about you, Van, but I don't think I've ever seen her so broken up."

"Yeah, she was *really* devastated." I had no idea where Ida was going with this, but I tried to catch what she was throwing me. The faster we were out of Chantal's office, the better.

"To be honest, Chantal," Ida said as she picked a mint out of the bowl on Chantal's desk, "I don't think it was a hundred percent appropriate for Sofia to go off like that in front of Van here. I mean, personal is personal, right?" She pulled the striped candy from its cellophane wrapper and popped it in her mouth.

Chantal looked at us, back and forth. I could see her trying to replay, to rewind something in her mind.

"I mean, it's too bad about Marine. I know Sofia and she were very close, but I didn't see it going long-term. Did you?" she asked me from around the candy.

I still had no idea where Ida was going, but I shook my head.

"Yeah," Ida sighed, "I guess they'd been fighting for a while. I bet you noticed it, though, right?" She wagged a finger at Chantal, that you're-some-kind-of-sharp-cookie gesture that she had. "Poor Sof has been so distracted by that woman. Marine always seemed a little unstable, if you ask me."

I gaped at Ida, but fortunately, so did Chantal, so she wasn't watching my face.

"Yeah, Marine tore on out of here. They were having a really ugly fight. I'm sorry you all had to see that. I'm sorry *Van* had to see it. I tried to get them both to cool off, but there was no talking sense to Marine. I just sent Sofia up when it was obvious she was too upset to help the situation."

"She left you and *her daughter* to deal with her *girlfriend*?"

"No, no, no," Ida half chuckled. "It wasn't anything like that."

I stared at Ida like she was a loose tiger in the room.

"You know, she ended it with Marine, and Marine wasn't taking it well. Throwing things, screaming, getting violent." Ida looked down at her hand like she was inspecting a manicure. "I thought it would be better if Sofia was out of the picture. Just the sight of her was making that Marine come unglued."

Jesus, I thought. She wasn't the only one coming unglued. I didn't know who, if any of us, was still *glued*.

"Hmm," Chantal said. "I'm not surprised to hear that."

"Well," Ida said. "I got rid of her. I wanted Van nearby, for my *own* protection. Marine is nuts."

"I see," Chantal said. I could hear her temper coming down in the tone of her voice. "Maybe I should go up and have a talk with Sofia."

"Oh no, that's not necessary. I think she just needs to rest up. She wouldn't want you to see her all emotional like this. Sofia's nothing if not a real professional."

I started to laugh, a terrible, ugly bark, and clapped my hand over my mouth.

"Van, I need to get you to bed, too. Look at you, you're hysterical." Ida shuffled back around to me and stood so close I could practically taste the mint on her breath. "I know we'd all appreciate it, Chantal, if you could keep this matter quiet. I know how embarrassed Sofia is about all of this. She wouldn't want her colleagues thinking this is business as usual for her."

"Of course," Chantal said, finally leaning against her desk.

Ida and I started walking toward the door, but then she stopped and looked back at Chantal.

"I know she wouldn't dream of bringing this up," Ida began. "But I think it would be best if Sofia had a personal day or two, to get herself together."

"I'm not sure if that's necessary," Chantal answered. "I'll speak with her later and we'll sort it out."

Ida put her hands in the air. "Fair enough," she said. "You have a good night now, Chantal."

"Yes," Chantal said, slowly, looking out into the distance with that rewind face.

Ida elbowed me.

"Yeah, good night," I mumbled. We slipped out the door before Chantal could say anything else.

"Not a word until we get back upstairs," Ida hissed.

I still had to convince Ida to let me go out. Normally, I knew she would, she'd even help me get dressed. But, with Mom's running off, I wasn't so sure. Maybe it would be best to just slip out.

In the elevator, Ida held tight to me. She clutched my arm as we travelled the hallway to our room and held even tighter when we got inside. I couldn't shake the feeling that she was having trouble moving without my help.

"Ida, are you okay?" I asked as the door slammed shut behind us.

Ida fell onto the sofa.

"Jesus, Mary, and Joseph," she said, letting all the air out of her lungs. "What a night. I'm fine, honey. I'm just worn out. I don't think I can even make it to my bed. Just leave me here, all right?" She leaned back and closed her eyes.

"You did a great job down there."

"Oh, honey," she said. "I'm sorry you're in this mess. Get me my pills, will you?"

I hurried into the kitchenette and handed Ida a glass of water and a couple of her sleeping tablets.

"This was some night. Any plans we make now will be garbage. Let's just get a little sleep and talk about it with fresh heads, okay?"

I'd always loved that expression of Ida's: fresh heads. It made me think of pale green globes of lettuce in a garden.

"I love you, Ida," I said.

"I love you, too, kid," she said.

I willed her to sleep and to sleep hard.

Chapter Twelve

It was nearly eight o'clock and Ida was already snoring gently on the couch. I pressed myself into the corner of my room and bent my head over the phone. Four missed calls from Carol.

"Van?" Alex picked up on the third ring. "Where are you? I thought we were meeting downstairs."

"Yeah, I'm on my way now."

"I'm in the car. In the lot. I'll swing by and pick you up, okay?"

"No, no," I said, thinking of Chantal. "I'll just meet you out back."

"Okay, but hurry—something's going down over there. I guess there's an issue. Marcos is being crazy."

"What?" I asked.

"Joanna's boyfriend, remember? I guess he showed up, and now they're fighting. Joanna sounded pretty upset. So, you know, let's hurry."

"Oh, okay!" I said a little too brightly. "See you in a minute." I threw my phone on the bed.

Was Marcos there to repo his equipment? Then there would be no show for sure. No show for me, anyway.

My hands shook as I ran them through my hair, mussing it up a little. I hoped it looked cool and not like I didn't have time to shower. I didn't even have time to change, but figured that my sweater and jeans were innocuous enough. I stuck my phone in my back pocket and crept out into the living room, where Ida slept.

Mom's open purse sagged on the countertop. I could see the light blinking out from her silenced phone. I didn't think about who was calling. Instead, I reached inside and fished around for her wallet. In it were a few squashed hundred dollar bills. I took one out and smoothed it on the countertop. *Just take it*, I told myself. Ida snored behind me. *Ida would want you to go—under different circumstances she would* tell *you to go.* I shoved the money into my back pocket and left as quietly as I could.

I swooped into the front seat of Alex's car and could barely look at him, afraid my eyes were glowing with that same frenzy of Mom's.

"Let's go," I said.

"Wow, that was fast," he said, and we drove out into the night, just like Mom and Marine had only a little while before.

• • •

The university wasn't far. It was a lot closer to the strip than the Silver Saddle.

"There's the library," Alex said, pointing out the window to a sleek modern building topped with an arc of glass that curved into the sky. An up-lit row of palm trees stood by the entrance like sentinels. It looked nothing like the colleges that Mom had been looking at on the Internet for me. Those were all columns and white marble, some knockoffs of the ancient, and some truly old.

"Do you live here? On campus?" I asked Alex.

"Nope." He shook his head. "The dorms are pretty pricy. I live in an apartment. With roommates. My neighbor's the one throwing me the party."

"It's not at your place?"

"No, but that's for the best, for sure. My neighbor's place is much bigger. Besides, if Joanna's crazy ex showed up, I'd rather he trashed Mike's."

I tried to keep Marcos at the back of my mind, but my palms were all sweaty and I felt that low hum of anxiety as we walked up the steps to the third story. I turned to Alex, who looked a little nervous. His mouth was pressed closed in a tense line.

When the door opened, the intensity of volume hit like a wave of heat from an opened oven. There were *way* too many people crammed into the apartment. A heavily muscled but short dude in a tight T-shirt bounded over to us and wrapped Alex in an enthusiastic embrace. "Oh shit," he shouted over Alex's shoulder and into my face. "The birthday boy is he-ere!"

"Hey, man, thanks for doing this," Alex said, clapping Mike on the shoulder. "Oh, and this is Van," he said, clapping me on the shoulder with his other hand.

"Va-an," Mike bellowed. "Come get drinks!"

From what I could tell, it looked like all of these people had already hit the drinks pretty hard.

"I'm going to go look for Carol and Joanna," I shouted at Alex.

"Carol!" Mike snickered. "Don't look too hard for her. She is *pissed*!"

"Ugh, *there* you are." Someone grabbed my shoulder, and I spun around to Carol's glower. "Where the fuck have *you* been?" she asked. "Why are you covered in dirt?"

"What?" I said, looking down at my sweater and jeans. I was still dusty from the parking lot chase with Mom. *Mom,* I thought, and felt a twist of guilt in my stomach.

"Just, never mind. Come on, let's go help Joanna. Fucking Marcos *cannot* grasp the leaving gracefully concept."

"What, like we have to kick him out?" I asked, an upsurge of nerves sweeping through me.

"Yeah, killer," Carol said, giving me a once-over. "You're gonna have to escort him off the premises. You think you can handle it?"

"What?" I felt my entire head empty of blood.

"Oh my God, I'm *joking.* Calm down. And take off that obscenely bad sweater."

I automatically pulled the sweater over my head, while Carol regarded the plain black T-shirt I wore underneath.

"Hmm, maybe the sweater was better. At least the dirt was kind of badass."

"Guys!" I heard Joanna's voice thread through the noise of the building crowd. "Let's just play this before it gets too crazy for anyone to care."

"That's what I'm talking about," Carol answered. "Where's fucking Marcos?"

"He, uh, he's fine. He's going to stay to watch us play," Joanna said.

"Oh Jesus, J, you didn't get back together again, did you?"

Joanna shook her head and looked out into the crowd. "Let's go." She glanced over her shoulder at me. "He wants to talk to Van, though, after."

Me? What?

"*Fine,* let's do this before we all graduate," Carol said as she slogged through the room, pushing people out of our way.

Carol slipped back behind the drums and Joanna stepped up to the mic. She flashed a grin out into the crowd.

"Thanks for coming. We're the Terrors."

Carol counted us in so fast, I almost didn't realize we were starting. I fumbled the intro a little, but picked it back up. I felt exhilarated and powerful—like some creature of ancient Greek mythology—*like Mom*, I thought.

At first, the crowd didn't react much. They seemed kind of confused, actually. But Joanna whipped them up. Soon no one could take their eyes off of her. A clump of people gathered in front, close. I felt the heat from their bodies and the force from their feet as they stomped along with Joanna.

It was over too fast, and I couldn't stop smiling. Joanna staggered over to me and grabbed my arms. "Shit, Van!" She shouted into my face. "Don't you feel great? That was perfect! Carol, don't you feel great?"

Carol shrugged and ran a hand through her shimmering hair. I could see the sweat on their skin, and I could feel it on mine. My smile didn't go away.

"You wanna do one more?" Joanna asked.

I nodded and she bounded back to the microphone stand. "One more, okay?"

The kids in front of us roared and pushed against each other and clapped.

I'd never felt so great.

After the show, my vision wasn't quite right; it was all blurred, with the edges of things disappearing.

"Van!" Alex practically leapt into my arms. "You were amazing!"

"Carol and Joanna were amazing," I said, looking up at Joanna, who was already starting to move the equipment out of the way for the next band.

"You guys were so good!" Alex slapped me on the shoulder with every word.

"Ow!"

"Sorry, sorry," he said. Alex stiffened as a thin, familiar figure approached. "I'm going to make Carol say something nice to me. She's going to hate that *so much*. Best birthday present ever." He hopped over to where Carol was packing up her own things.

"Hey! It's the girl who owes me coffee." It was the spindly guy with long, dark hair I'd nearly decked in the Silver Saddle lobby. A worn T-shirt advertising the Cure was stretched across his narrow chest.

"So you're Van, huh? Marcos," he said, touching his hand to his chest.

"*You're* Marcos?"

He nodded. "I thought you were a guy, with a name like Van."

"What?"

He looked at his hands while his face reddened. "Sorry," he said, "that came out weird." He looked up at me and brought his eyes level with mine.

"You're really talented," he said. "You could be in a way better band than this."

"Thank you," I said, looking at him warily as I snapped his guitar into its case.

"I mean, if you ever want to play together sometime, just let me know," he said.

"Um, thanks, I guess. But how would we do that, considering we'd only have the one guitar?"

He laughed, an incongruous, high-pitched giggle.

"Yeah, you're right!"

Is this guy stoned? Is this what stoned people sound like? Oh my God, you are embarrassingly juvenile, I told myself. I shook my head.

"Thanks for lending me this," I said, rapping on the rectangular case. "But, it's yours, and you should take it back now. I've got to get my own, anyway." I thought about Mom again—I had to get home.

"Well, if you need any help, let me know."

"Uh, thank you," I answered. "I actually have to get going. I wasn't even supposed to go out."

"Wow," said Marcos.

"Wow," I agreed. "It was really nice meeting you. And thanks again," I said.

"Wait, can I give you a ride?" Marcos asked.

"No thanks. I think maybe Alex is going to."

"*Alex? That* asshole? Wait, are you with him, too?" Marcos snarled.

Too? My heart sank. Of course Alex was dating someone. "What? No, we're just friends."

The thought of meeting Alex's girlfriend made my throat feel tight.

"Uh, actually, Marcos, if you could give me a ride, I'd really appreciate it," I said.

"No problem," he mumbled, looking out over my shoulder.

I turned and saw Joanna with Alex and Carol. I could feel my pulse thrumming under the thin skin at my throat. I needed to get out of there—I'd left Ida alone, in the middle of a crisis.

Marcos drove an ancient minivan I'd seen parked outside the Silver Saddle. He didn't open the door for me or anything, like Alex had on our trip to the Venetian, but I kind of liked that. It made me less nervous, to maneuver myself in and out of the car free of scrutiny. I positioned my seatbelt carefully, just in case Marcos really was on drugs. He pressed a button and music, the Cure, filled the car. He looked up at me, grinning.

"Is that a tape, like a cassette?" I asked.

"Uh-huh," he said, delighted. "My parents still have a ton."

"Wow. Sounds like they have good taste. Are you close with them?"

"Yeah. They had us young, so we kind of like, grew up together. How about you? Your parents have good taste?"

"Not exactly," I said, picking at a curl of plastic—an old sticker—taped to the dashboard. I thought about Mom, and wondered whether she was still in Marine's passenger seat, maybe on the same highway.

"But you do. I can tell." He looked over at me longer than I thought wise.

"Maybe. So you're a big Cure fan," I said, looking out of the passenger side window, hoping he would turn back toward the windshield.

"Oh yeah." On the edge of my sightline, I saw him pluck at his T-shirt. "Whenever I'm into something, I try to surround myself with it, you know, swim around in it."

"Huh." I heard the surprise in my voice. "I like how you said that." I turned back to look at him, his profile handsome and dim in the night-filled van.

"What happened with you and Joanna?" I was embarrassed, surprised that I'd let the question out into the air between us. "I mean, you don't have to tell me. Not like it's any of my business."

"No, I don't mind telling you," he said. I could see his grimace in the dark. "It was a hard breakup. For me. I thought I loved her, but really I loved her talent. I really thought she was, like, this prodigy. Like John Lennon or something."

"She *is* really talented. You're not wrong about that." I pulled my hair back and held it in a twist at the nape of my neck.

"Yeah, she is. But not as talented as I thought." He looked right at me then, and I was flooded with embarrassment, like had there been a bathroom nearby, I'd have run to it. "I've never seen anyone play like you."

"Oh, well. You must not get out much." I wondered if Marcos could tell how red I was, even through the murk.

When we got back to the Silver Saddle, Marcos didn't try to hug me, and I registered faint disappointment.

"Well thanks, Marcos," I said, opening the silver passenger side door.

He smiled out at me, that same beatific grin. "I really liked talking to you. And I loved seeing you play. Do you want to meet up again? I mean it, about that coffee."

I felt a sudden, unwieldy rush of relief. "Yeah, that would be great. Thanks for the ride," I said, then shut the door and started waving like an idiot before I said anything weird.

Whatever happened now, I'd played a show. I may have been the world's worst and most selfish person, but I'd played a show. *Mom,* I thought, the guilt hot in the place behind my eyes. I took the elevator up to the suite and got into bed. I lay awake for a while. I thought about the audience, all of their shuffling sounds, their voices, the focus of all of those eyes. It was stabilizing and thrilling all at the same time.

Mom going missing blinked around at the perimeter of these thoughts, but I wasn't ready to let it in. Not right then. I held on to the power I'd felt performing, and I curled into a ball.

Chapter Thirteen

The second I opened my eyes, I found that all of my euphoria from the show the night before had disintegrated. My clothes smelled like the smoke from the party and were covered in the stubborn dust from the parking lot hunt.

I turned on the shower but I stood there, waiting. Like, if I didn't have to leave that bathroom, I wouldn't have to figure out what was waiting for me out there. Then I eventually did get in, and I just kept on lathering and lathering, comforted by the suds underneath my hands—it was like I was wrapping my body in a soapy, protective layer. I didn't think it was strange, until I stepped out, that Ida hadn't banged on the door during that whole long stretch of washing. I wondered if she knew that I'd left last night. I wrapped a towel around my hair and put on a robe emblazoned with the Silver Saddle logo.

Opening the bathroom door was like stepping out of a dragon's mouth. The steam floated out around me and into the freezing hallway.

"Ida?" I called.

There was no answer. I padded over to the living room, where I'd left her sleeping the night before. She was still there, asleep, in the exact position she'd dropped down in. I knelt down next to the sofa and looked closely at her face. I half expected her to be dead and half expected her to pop up and shout "Gotcha!" at me. I touched her dusty sleeve.

"Ida," I whispered.

She shifted and snorted and cracked open an eye.

"Hey there, sweetheart." She rolled over onto her side and put a hand to her forehead.

"Tell me I dreamed it," she said.

I shook my head.

She rolled over onto her stomach and groaned into the couch cushion. She lifted her head. "All right. Let's make some coffee and figure this out."

I nodded and headed for the kitchen.

"No, wait! We're going to order that coffee. We'll get room service to send up a big breakfast for three. I bet you Chantal is watching every move we make from that roost of hers. What time is it, honey? She's got a head start on us, that's for sure."

"Should one of us *call Chantal*?" I asked.

"Yeah!" Ida pointed at me like a game show contestant. "Wait no—let me just think for a second." She put her hand up to her mouth and bit down on her index finger.

I stood there, unmoving.

Ida clapped her hands together. "This is what we do. You call Antonio, sweet-talk him a little bit. You know, last night was tough, my mom's sleeping in. Maybe," Ida looked up, her eyes lit with frenzy. "This is what you say. You say, 'Look Antonio, baby, my mom was so upset, Ida had to put her to bed with a Scotch and a couple of sleeping pills, just so she could get some rest.' Okay?"

I just looked at her, not sure about any of this.

"Or something like that—you can improvise. I'm going to order breakfast and lay the same story on Marisol downstairs. She's got a big mouth on her, too, so it'll get around that Sof is just recovering up here."

"I don't know, Ida. Are you sure? Maybe we should just tell Chantal. And, maybe—do you think we should go look for Mom?"

"Honey, I think she's going to be okay. Physically, she'll be okay. I think."

"Why did I let this happen?"

"No, no. No, listen. We stabilize this situation here, and then I'll call Marine."

"Okay," I said. "I'll call Alex, you call the breakfast."

"Yes," Ida said. "Yes!"

I really didn't feel like calling Alex. I remembered Marcos's mention of Alex's girlfriend. I remembered Chantal's expression in her office the day before when she told me Alex was paid to show me around. She was positively flush with schadenfreude. I found my cell phone in the pocket of my jeans just as Alex's name flashed up out of my palm.

"Hello?" I said.

"Van? It's Alex."

"Yeah, I know. I was actually just about to call you."

"You were?" I could hear the smile in his voice.

"Yeah. I don't know if you heard—"

"Oh, I heard. Things got pretty weird, at least that's the story I'm getting from reception."

"Yeah, they were pretty much on the front lines." I rubbed my eyes, trying to focus on Ida's plan.

"I heard you and Ida were on the front lines. Why didn't you tell me last night?"

"I'm not sure," I lied. "It got overwhelming. I just didn't want to talk about it."

"Is that why you left like that?"

"Yep . . ."

"Do you want to talk about it now? Is your mom okay?"

"Oh, she's fine—just resting. I think Marine went kind of batshit on her, you know?" I closed my eyes, prepared to do a lot more dumping on Marine before it was all over.

"Um, Van?"

"What?"

"You were so, so great last night."

"You have to stop saying that!" I half shouted. I didn't want to be reminded of what I'd done last night. Or what I hadn't done. I'd do one good thing for Mom at least—I'd help her keep this job. "Thanks, though. I hope you had a good birthday." I tried to say it like Ida would: charming.

"Yeah, I did, actually," Alex said. I wondered if he knew about my ride home with Marcos.

"Great—um, one more thing? Could you let Erica know that I probably won't be in class for a couple of days? I think my mom needs more time. To process."

"Yeah, Chantal's been calling her."

"I know," I lied. "She's just really embarrassed. She needs to regroup. So she can focus on work again. Do you mind? Letting Erica know?" I asked.

"Sure. I'll let her know. Do *you* need anything?"

"No," I almost laughed. "I don't need anything. Mom just wants me to stay close, I guess."

"Okay, well if you get bored up there, let me know."

"Thanks, Alex."

I knew one thing—I sure wasn't going to get bored.

• • •

The rest of the day, Ida was on the phone or on Mom's computer. I tried to clean up a little since Ida wasn't letting anyone in—not even housekeeping.

"I'm sorry Rosalba, honey," she whispered to the apron-clad woman at the door. "Senora Lowell has a migraine, and we're trying to keep it quiet in here."

We ate the three breakfasts all day long. I made my bed and picked up the relatively clean clothes off of the floor and folded them. I gathered the dirty ones and threw them in the laundry bag.

"Hey, you putting that out?" Ida asked from where she hovered over Mom's computer.

"I was going to."

"Go get something from your mother's room for the bag, too."

"This is ridiculous. Chantal's not going through our laundry. She's not Columbo!"

"Wanna bet? Just do it. An extra wash never hurt anything. Would your mom sign an e-mail, sincerely, or thanks, comma?"

"What?"

"Best! Never mind, she uses best." She snapped her fingers a few times and kept working.

I dragged the laundry bag down the hall to Mom's room and opened the door. When I walked inside, I realized that I hadn't been in her room once since the night we arrived. Mom's smell hit me before anything else. That smell of Mom's—verdant, straight from the outdoors—concentrated in that small room, took me straight back to my very earliest memories. Memories where I was hungry or afraid. My whole self transformed into a hollow, growling stomach, just burrowing into that smell to feel better.

I looked around, not surprised that clothes and shoes were strewn all over the floor. When Mom cycled into one of her wild— or even her flat—periods, disarray followed her. The floor and the bed were covered in a colorful, glinting landscape of scarves and jewelry. Mounds of silk were piled around mismatched boots. An open compact shone like a landscaped pond under the afternoon sunlight flooding the room. I closed the drapes and shoved a few clumps of fabric into the laundry bag behind me.

I sat on the floor and wrapped my arms around the bulging bag. I breathed in Mom's smell.

And then I heard the crash.

"Ida?" I shouted.

I leapt up and the bag fell to the floor with a thud. I knew it was bad before I saw anything. A sound like that—heavy—a sound of breaking things, of reckless, rolling smashing—that's a sound that can only mean the worst. I ran toward Ida, who was face-down on the floor. She'd fallen onto the coffee table, and it had partly overturned on top of her. Blood welled up by her face and spread out in a dark, silky patch. I stared as it grew and couldn't move or speak. I didn't want to touch her—I didn't want to hurt her.

I felt my mouth opening. I called her name, louder and louder. My throat was open. Sounds were still coming out, but I had no idea what they were. I just stared at the blood, growing and growing out across the floor.

I was vaguely aware of a smattering of knocks on the door, knocks that built in intensity until they were banging. There was so much banging—I could tell, I noticed it, noted that it seemed important at the time—that more than one person was banging.

Good, I thought, *I'm going to need a lot of help.*

The door popped open with an electronic click. I didn't realize it, but my body was covering Ida's. It was like my arms and legs had curled into a giant talon and had just clamped on. I felt people prying me loose. I heard them yelling, a phone call in rapid Spanish. I couldn't pick out a single word. The room, the sounds, everything outside of Ida and me, was a wash of white noise.

"Is she alive? Is she alive?" was what I said, when I could hear myself making sense again. There were people all around me, holding me by the shoulders. The door banged open again and more figures poured inside. Alex was there, and Chantal, too.

Alex came over by me and put his arm around my shoulders, dispelling the pocket of soft, fragrant women who'd surrounded me.

"Did you call an ambulance?" I asked Alex, trying to calm the vicious breaths I was pulling into my lungs.

"They're coming. It's okay. She's going to be okay."

I leaned in and squashed my face into his chest. I didn't care about the snot and tear prints I left on his clothes. I just leaned in. It felt better to have someone, another body, right there when something this terrible was happening. I heard the scrapes and beeps of the EMTs who worked over Ida, but it wasn't until I heard someone repeating my name that I looked up, unfastened from the temporary shelter of Alex's shirt.

"Van, can you hear me?" It was Chantal.

I looked out at her, and all of the sounds and the heat from all of the bodies blared into my face.

"They're asking if you want to go with her to the hospital," she said.

I nodded and looked for Ida. She was strapped to a stretcher and covered in a blanket. The EMTs were heaving her toward the door. I held my hand out for Alex. He took it, but turned back to where Chantal's strong, clear voice floated in the air.

"Sofia isn't in here. I'll try to track her down," she said. "Call me when you have some news."

I let go of Alex's hand then. A very small part of me remembered that I was still angry about something, still torn, not sure what Alex was to me.

We spilled out of the emergency exit to the parking lot, where the uniformed men loaded the stretcher into the back of the ambulance. The lights flashed silently against the darkening sky. I jumped into the back of the ambulance when one of the EMTs reached a hand out to me. Alex followed. The young EMT—the one with a full, soft baby face—helped me buckle the strange seatbelt across my Silver Saddle robe.

"She's a tough lady. I can tell," the other EMT said. He was older and dark-skinned. He was tall, taller than Alex, and sinewy. He stooped over inside of the belly of the ambulance, even while sitting down.

The young one nodded.

"Will she be all right?" Alex asked. I could feel the sweat in my clasped hands.

"We're going to get her the help she needs, don't worry," the older EMT said.

The sirens crooned around us as we sped into the night.

Chapter Fourteen

At the hospital, no one talked to Alex or me for a long time. I wasn't sure how long we waited there, but it was long enough for other people waiting to ask us where the vending machines were. The sky had been completely black for a while—I'd been watching the night through the window across from the vinyl seat adhered to my terry cloth–covered butt.

"Should we call Ida's family?" Alex asked.

"I think maybe there's a cousin in Canada. I don't know. I'm sure Mom does."

"Do you want to call her?"

I had nothing. No money, no cell phone, no Ida, and no Mom.

I massaged my cheeks and forehead, trying to loosen the layers of tension. "Why haven't they told us anything? I'm just going to go back there," I said as I stood.

"No, no," Alex said. "I'll go ask." He turned away and walked toward the ultrafluorescently lit reception area.

I stared at a couple sitting across from me. The woman looked like she hadn't eaten in weeks. Her skin was mottled with abscesses. The man hunched over in her lap had a towel pressed against his mouth and nose that was half drenched with blood. The woman patted his arm and bit down on her lips a little. I was so lost, I seriously contemplated asking that hard-faced woman what to do.

Thank God Alex came back before I could. He carried a Styrofoam cup of coffee in one hand and a gold-wrapped Twix in the other. A can of Coke was clamped under his armpit. He sat down next to me and shuffled around the things he brought, handing me the Twix.

I took the coffee from him, too, worried when he didn't start talking right away. I could almost hear his brain working to fit together what to say, and I could tell by how long that was taking that it probably wasn't anything good.

"She's in serious condition. That's all they would tell me."

"Can we see her?"

"I don't know," Alex said. "I called Chantal," he said quietly, into the thumbprint opening of his soda can.

"What?" My voice was louder than was appropriate in a place like this. An orderly pushing a groaning man in a wheelchair looked over sharply. The man in the wheelchair turned his open-mouthed roar on me, displaying a mouthful of missing teeth.

"Please don't be mad. I'm just not sure what to do. I mean, your mom is the one who should be here, getting Ida's people on a plane."

"I *am* Ida's people!"

"I know, I know. You definitely are. I'm sorry." He looked down again.

"What did Chantal say?"

"Well, yeah. She didn't say much. Only . . ." He looked up at me then, with the full force of his perfectly symmetrical, concerned gaze. "Where is your mom, Van?"

I looked at him through the globs of tears forming in my eyes.

"Excuse me, you're the nephew of Ida Bouchard?" A too-young-looking doctor asked.

"That's me," Alex said, as he stood to shake hands with the doctor.

"If you'd like to follow me, I can give you an update on your aunt's condition."

Alex and I both nodded and stood to follow him.

"Is this your sister?" the doctor asked, finally looking at me, probably noticing my state of robe-wearing dishevelment.

"Yes," I nodded as I spoke.

"No," Alex said at the same time.

The doctor looked at us through narrowed eyes.

"Where are your parents?" he asked.

"Travelling," Alex smoothly replied.

The doctor looked over our shoulders, like he was willing someone more appropriate to materialize. When he realized he only had us, he shrugged and waved us over to a corner, where we sat down in a row: the doctor at the end, Alex in the middle, then me.

"Your aunt is in serious but stable condition. She's suffered a stroke."

"Oh my God," I said. I tilted my face into my hands.

"Was she experiencing any headaches or dizziness that you can recall? Any numbness or problems with her speech?"

"Is she awake?" I asked.

The doctor hesitated for a moment. "Well, no."

I felt his eyes on me—all of that silence and hesitation was focused *on me*. I lifted my head out of my hands and sat up as straight as I could and looked the doctor in the eye, the way Ida would have done if I were in the hospital.

"Look, when will your parents get here, do you think?"

"Actually," I said, "she was having some trouble walking earlier."

"Hmm. Well, as I said, she's unconscious, and she may be for quite some time."

"But she'll wake up, right? She's going to wake up." I leaned forward to get closer to the doctor. I wanted to pitch myself straight into his eyes and swim down into his brain to see what was really going on. *Just tell me!* I wanted to scream.

"If you'll give me a few minutes, I'd like to share what you've told me with my colleagues."

"When can we see her?" Alex asked.

"Not just yet," the young doctor said. "Let's wait for your parents."

I looked down into a dusty corner and thought about how completely screwed we were. Alex stood and watched the doctor walk away.

"Van," he started. "I know you don't want to talk about this, but we kind of have to. Your mom's not here, is she? She's not at the Silver Saddle, and she's probably not even in town."

I shook my head.

"Van, where is she?" Alex asked with all the gentleness he could scrape up under the circumstances. I could see how hard he was trying, and, somewhere in my mind, I appreciated it.

"I'm not really sure," I whispered.

"Okay, well. Okay," Alex said and stood up again. He paced back and forth in front of our row of vinyl seats. The waiting room had filled with people while we talked to the doctor. An entire extended family had come in together, clustered around a sweating woman in labor. More bodies meant more heat. This emergency room wasn't as lavishly air-conditioned as the city's casinos and hotels. I swept the back of my hand across my throat to wipe away a thin film of sweat. Alex stopped in front of me.

"I think I have to ask Chantal to come here."

As much as I hated to do it, I nodded.

• • •

Chantal swept in a half hour later, looking her poised, pulled-together self. She saw us and moved across the room with a wide, military stride.

"What's going on? Alex?"

"Well, we're not getting any real answers from the doctors here. And we don't know where Mrs. Lowell is, either. That is, Van doesn't exactly know."

"I see," Chantal said as she began to sink into one of the seats in our row. She turned her head a little and carefully inspected the seat. When she saw how cracked and sticky the vinyl looked, she thought better of sitting and stood back up. "I take it that she doesn't have her cell phone with her."

I shook my head.

"All right," she said. "First we see to Ida. Where's the doctor?"

I was surprised that Chantal gave two shits about Ida. Her concern, or maybe her natural human obligation, reached out to some important part of me.

"Chantal," I said.

"Yes, Van?" she said as she set her handbag on the chair next to mine. She squeezed a glob of hand sanitizer out of the tiny bottle she pulled from the side pocket of the bag.

"I think I may know where my mom went. I'll go and bring her back."

"I don't want you to think this is all your responsibility," Chantal said. I could tell by the way she couldn't look at me that it made her uncomfortable to say that. And, that she didn't believe it.

"No, it is. Or, it's my mom's. She needs to be here for Ida. We need to get in touch with Ida's family, and only my mom knows where they are. My responsibility is only a temporary thing."

"I understand your meaning, but I don't think it's as easy as finding your mother. I mean, is she entirely well herself?"

I didn't say anything.

"It's just that—if you find her or not, I'm not sure that you should go alone."

"It'll be okay. Marine was taking her somewhere in Sedona. I'll call her. Marine. And we'll figure out how to get my mom back here. I just want to see Ida before I go."

Chantal sighed and cleared her throat. "I suppose you will have Marine's help, and I can't think of any other clear course of action here. Other than notifying the authorities." I watched Chantal absorb my flash of panic. "But that will be a last resort."

"Thank you," I said.

We walked to the reception desk together and waited while the sleepy woman behind it paged the young doctor. Chantal drummed her fingers on the desk.

The doctor we'd seen earlier looked really terrible. He slouched, and his scrubs were suddenly filthy, but he mustered a professional smile as he approached us.

"Ida Bouchard's family, right?"

The three of us nodded in unison.

"This is your mom, guys?"

"Yes," Alex said, and slung an arm around Chantal's shoulders.

"What can you tell us about Ida?" Chantal said. I could see how hard she tried not to shake Alex off—every line of every muscle had tightened across her back.

"Well, a little good news, I'm happy to say. Since I spoke with your kids," he looked at Alex and me, and then back at Chantal.

"Our stepmother," Alex said.

The doctor shrugged. "There has been some improvement."

I smiled so hard that my eyes watered.

"That's great," Alex said.

"Can we see her?" Chantal asked, snapping the doctor's eyes back up to hers with that magnetic, principal-like control.

"She isn't conscious at the *moment*," he said. "Her vitals have stabilized, and that's really what we look for in the period directly following an event of this nature. We moved her up to the ICU on the fifth. But, please, visiting hours are over at eleven, so—"

"Eleven?" I said. "Is it that late already?"

The doctor didn't hear me. He had already scurried away to some other family in some other cell of the hospital.

• • •

The ICU was as different from the emergency room waiting area as the Venetian had been from the Silver Saddle. As soon as the elevator doors peeled open, I breathed a little easier. *Ida will be okay here,* I thought. *This is actually a really nice hospital.*

The floor was open; there were probably ten or fifteen little rooms that ringed the unit. A nurse's station was settled in the middle like the center of a flower.

"We're here to see Ida Bouchard," Chantal told the nurse at the desk. "They sent us up from the ER."

The woman leaned against the chest-high barrier. "Just a minute while I call for confirmation," she said, fiddling with an amber button on her cardigan sweater.

Chantal nodded and we milled around on a highly polished tiled floor as the nurse murmured into a phone. She hung it up with a clatter and turned back to us.

"Follow me. Sorry about that. We always have to check—you wouldn't believe the wackadoos we get in here sometimes."

"I'm sure," Chantal replied, dryly.

The nurse knocked on a door to our right. Ida's name was scrawled on a white eraser board in nearly illegible handwriting.

I only knew it was Ida's name because I knew those letters next to each other as well as I knew my own name. I'd recognize them anywhere, no matter how misshapen they might be.

The bed was enormous. Ida was tucked beneath a crisp white sheet. Her whole body appeared deflated—most of what made up Ida were her voice and eyes and laugh. Machines stood guard all around the room. Some of the hulking figures pumped and beeped away beside her, while others sulked in the corners.

I felt the heat from Chantal's body as she leaned over my shoulder.

"Van, Alex and I are going to step outside. Take all of the time you need in here, all right?"

It was the second time in half an hour that I felt this rush of relief over Chantal's presence. I couldn't believe how different things were since only the day before.

I was already beside Ida. I didn't remember moving, but there I was.

"Thanks. Thank you, Chantal."

Standing there with Ida, I let all of the fear and exhaustion and tension of the day pulse through me. I collapsed on the end of the bed. I lay across the bottom, over the lumps of Ida's legs, my own legs hanging off and my feet nearly touching the floor. For a while I timed each of my breaths with the rise and fall of her chest. I thought about how we were all breathing together: me, Ida, and the machines around her. Like backup singers. God, I was so selfish. If I hadn't let Mom run off like that, Ida wouldn't have worked herself up so much. She wouldn't have landed here.

I reached down and wrapped my hand around Ida's ankle underneath the covers and just held on for a little while.

"I'm going to make it right, Ida. I'll bring Mom back here, okay? Everything will be fine."

I rose from that spot on the bed. I walked the length of Ida's body and leaned over all of the blankets and tubes and tape and kissed her.

"I'll be back soon."

Okay, honey, I imagined her saying. Then I left to find Chantal and Alex.

They'd waited by the door the whole time. I felt another swell of gratitude for both of them.

"Chantal talked the nurse into letting us stay after visiting hours. She could probably convince them to let you stay over tonight with her if you want."

Chantal examined me in one efficient sweep of her eyes.

"I think Van needs to rest, Alex. She needs to put that call in to Marine. Let's get her home, and then we can regroup in the morning. We'll come back and see Ida then."

"No," I said.

"No?"

"No. I actually spoke with Marine. While I was in there with Ida." The lie was out of my mouth before I could stop it. "She told me to come to Sedona right away—I need to get going. Will you guys drop me off at the bus station?"

"The *bus* station?" Alex said.

"Marine's going to pick me up. We'll all come back here together. My mom needs to be here." I threw each sentence out with vicious force. The force was more for me than for Alex or Chantal. I needed to galvanize. The longer I had to think about resting beside Ida, maybe even sleeping there, the harder it would be to convince myself that I could make the trip to somewhere I'd never been, alone, to do something I'd never done.

"No one's going anywhere tonight. It almost two in the morning!" Chantal said.

"It'll be fine. I told you, Marine will be there waiting." I shivered under the lie.

Chantal and Alex looked at one another. Chantal sighed. "I'll drive you back to the hotel. You'll need to change at least."

I looked down at my soggy, wrinkled robe. *She's right there*, I thought.

Chapter Fifteen

I slept in the back of Chantal's car. I must have, because when we jolted to a stop and I heard the engine putter out, I lifted my head from Alex's shoulder.

"You two go pack up—Van, get changed. I'll get your ticket. Meet me back in my office when you're ready."

Alex and I unfolded ourselves out of the car, but Chantal stayed in the driver's seat looking out into the darkness.

A cluster of three figures by reception called out to us in unison as we walked by. "Is she okay?" they asked together, their faces all formed into the same expressions. *Like three backup singers;* I thought about the breathing machines in Ida's room.

Alex just nodded over my head, like I was already asleep.

When we got back to the suite, I was grateful almost to the point of tears when I saw that the housekeepers had cleared away all evidence of Ida's fall and the EMTs' trampling. They'd cleaned the room and left out handfuls of turndown chocolates on the dining room table beside a stack of Marine's astrological charts.

"I'm going to pack," I told Alex.

I went into Mom's room first, rifling through her drawers and closet. Looking for clues, I told myself. Clues about what she'd been thinking. And if I was honest with myself, clues about who she really was. It was the thing I was most curious about in the whole world, because if I knew who Mom really was, I'd know who I really was. I couldn't help feeling we were these composite people, that our lives were like a two-dimensional slide show. I'd get these vivid flashes from her every now and then. Sometimes, when Mom touched me, I remembered things. I felt things. Sometimes they were good things, like sleeping on the grass in Mom's arms. Sometimes they were terrible, memories of feeling so sick and weak it was like breaking in half. They weren't always my memories, though. It was like these flashes were the best and the worst in both of us, and that was all that existed. There was none of that sticky middle-ground stuff that made up most of the world's lives.

• • •

I don't know if I was just too tired and dull, or if there weren't any clues to find, but I uncovered nothing. I knew I was really going to have to call Marine.

But this wasn't Marine's job. It wasn't Marine's job to look after Mom. It was mine. I untied the filthy robe and peeled off my underwear. I hunted around for any clean clothes. I chose a striped navy dress from a pile on the bed and pulled it over my head. It fit pretty well, I thought, landing just above my knees. It felt right, somehow, to wear something of Mom's. Not comforting exactly—talismanic.

I hurried into my room and plucked out a pair of jeans and a couple of T-shirts and found a dirty sweater under a chair. My phone and charger still dangled from the wall where I'd had that last phone conversation with Alex. From when Ida was orchestrating the ruse from the living room.

I paced the room and called Marine, pressing the phone to my ear. I listened as it rang, the long tones like languid drops of water falling out into nowhere. Maybe she wouldn't answer, I thought. Maybe I could just leave a message.

"Allo?" I'd already forgotten what Marine's voice sounded like. *Right,* I thought, *she's from France.* God, I was really tired.

"Marine?" I said. "It's Van."

She sighed like she was letting a whole day's worth of air out of her lungs.

"Van," she said. "My dear, dear Van. I'm so glad you called. Your mom is doing great."

I felt a breeze of relief. "She is?"

"Yes. Great." Marine's words were too clipped and too small to encompass the miracle that was Mom-doing-great. "You know, I think we will be back in Las Vegas very soon."

"Actually," I began, "I'm coming to meet you in Sedona. You guys are still in Sedona, right?"

Marine was quiet for so long I thought she'd hung up on me. "We are here, yes."

"Great. At what address, exactly?"

"It's not important. I think it's best that you stay where you are."

"What? I can't—"

"Yes, definitely for the best. I repeat, *do not come.* It will be much too disruptive."

"But, you don't understand," I said.

"I understand, dear. Stay put, okay? It's best for you, believe me. *Bye-bye!*"

I heard a beep and then Marine was gone. I tried her again and was sent to voicemail. I called again and again—nothing. Marine had dismissed me. *Well too bad,* I thought as I slung my bag over my shoulder.

When I came out, I found Alex in the kitchen. Marine's astrological charts were spread out in front of him on the counter.

From a distance, they looked like pages from a child's coloring book.

"Hey," he said, squinting down at the charts. "I just talked to Carol."

"Yeah?"

He shook his head. "It's not important. Let's go find Chantal. I'm sure she's going to want to head home eventually."

Of course Chantal had better things to do than chase me and my mom around the southwestern United States. Alex probably wanted to go home, too. The sooner I was on my way, the better for everyone.

"Yeah, let's go." I grabbed Mom's wallet from the counter.

• • •

Chantal had her computer open and the light from the screen washed her face in a sickly blue.

"Okay," she said, while still looking at the screen. "I have your ticket here." She slid a single sheet of printer paper across the top of her desk. I took it and quietly folded it into thirds, like a business letter, the way Mom had shown me a long time ago.

"Your bus leaves at six A.M. It's—what is it? Almost four now? You should go."

"Thanks, Chantal."

"Listen," she said. "If you change your mind for any reason along the way—or once you get there—you can call us. Someone will come get you no matter where you are, all right? I hate to send you out there alone, but if you're sure Marine will be waiting there . . ." She sighed, a sigh for three people. "Maybe I should touch base with Marine."

"I *just* talked to her. She's going to pick me up." I didn't like lying to them, so I added something true. "You guys have done more than enough for us."

"Do you need any money?" Chantal asked.

"No, I'm good." I patted Mom's wallet where I'd zipped it into my bag.

"Well, please try to sleep. And Alex," she continued, "make sure this child gets something to eat before she gets on that bus. And make sure *you* sleep a full eight hours before I see you back here."

"Yes, ma'am."

"All right, Van," Chantal said, half standing over her chair.

Nobody standing in Chantal's office knew how this goodbye was supposed to go. Chantal didn't appear to be a natural hugger, and a handshake now seemed like going backward. She settled on a wave and I waved back.

• • •

The bus station was terrible. It was one of the more depressing bus stations I'd seen, and I'd seen quite a few. Maybe it had something to do with the hour. When that late night bleeds into early morning, nothing looks right. I was early. A few people slept on benches, but most people slouched underneath the smell of the room. Alex looked around and wrinkled his nose.

"You have some time. Let me take you out for a real breakfast," he said.

"I don't know," I began. "What if my bus leaves early?"

"Van, a bus has never left early, not once in the history of recorded time."

"Okay," I said over my growling stomach. "But only if I can take *you* out for a real breakfast. It's the least I can do."

"Sure." Alex smiled and looked down at his feet.

In Las Vegas, our dining options weren't as limited as four-thirty-in-the-morning-by-a-bus-station breakfast choices elsewhere. There were two diners and a donut shop, all open and doing a brisk business. I chose the less busy diner, because I was still worried about the time. Under the bright light of the diner, Alex's eyes looked puffy. I didn't want to know what I looked like. I smoothed my hair down, thought twice about it, and twisted it into a knot on top of my head. I could feel Alex looking at my neck and tried to push through the slush in my brain to think of something to say. Something not depressing or weird.

"Thank you so much, Alex, really," I said. "You didn't have to stay with me." I pulled over one of the steaming coffees our white-haired waitress had deposited on the table between us.

"It's no problem," he said, and grabbed hold of his own coffee cup.

"I know you're going to be busy with your classes and Chantal and everything, but . . . can I ask you for one more favor? I know this is incredibly selfish, but I hope you won't say no."

Alex forced his swollen eyelids open wide and nodded at me to continue.

"Will you check on Ida every day? Please? I can't believe I'm just leaving her alone like this. I need to know someone I trust is watching out for her."

"Of course I will." Alex smiled with half his mouth. He looked so tired. "Ida's important to me, too. She's important to a lot of the people she knows here."

I was overwhelmed by a terrible wave of nausea.

"Oh God," I said. "Did anyone tell Ovid?"

"Chantal told him last night. Don't worry. We'll all be checking on her." He reached a hand out across the table, palm up.

I slapped my own hand down on his, like some weirdo high-five. Even as I did it, I *knew* it wasn't the right thing to do and cringed into my coffee.

"So, when I talked to Carol, she told me you went home with Marcos," Alex said.

"Yeah, he gave me a ride." I watched him closely. The tension around his eyes loosened and he looked, suddenly, much less tired.

"Oh, I guess Carol was exaggerating. I told her it didn't sound like you, going home with someone like that." *He means sex,* I thought, mortified, but indignant. *What, I can't go home with someone and have sex with them if I want? It's not like he has any right to care.*

"Do you think you're going to see him again?" Alex continued, lightly.

"What? Maybe." *Who knows? Maybe I will,* I thought.

"So you like him? Even though he got all crazy with Joanna?"

"I think he's just enthusiastic, not crazy. He was really complimentary about my guitar playing," I said.

"Yeah, I bet he was," Alex mumbled.

We looked at the table until our aged server slid two plates in front of us, breaking up the awkwardness.

Alex and I devoured everything on our plates without talking, passing ketchup bottles and little discs of butter back and forth like people who'd been eating breakfast together for decades. As I ate, I realized much of my peevishness had been hunger related, and as the pinched irritation I felt eased under the enormous breakfast, I reminded myself that Alex really had done things an acquaintance didn't have to do. A renewed gratefulness to him and Chantal swelled through me as I leaned back into my side of the booth.

I paid for breakfast, and we walked out into the very early morning. I surprised myself and grabbed Alex's hand as we crossed the empty street to the station. A few people were already lining up for my bus when we got back.

"You should go," I said, adjusting the straps of my backpack. "This is no kind of place to wait around."

Alex looked at me, at my whole body, which made me feel a little weird.

"Do you have a jacket?" he asked.

"No, but I think it'll be fine."

"Just take this, please," he said, pulling the midnight blue sweatshirt over his neck. He shoved it into my arms. "If I thought there was time, I'd make you go buy a jacket right now."

"If there was time," I said, smiling. "Nothing's open!"

"You forget, Van," he said as he shook a finger at me. "This is Las Vegas we're talking about. The city that never sleeps."

"Pretty sure that's New York."

"Maybe. Well."

"Well," I said as I tried to reach out to him. With the clunky backpack behind me and Alex's sweatshirt in my arms, I couldn't really initiate any hugging. He drew me in close and wound his arms around me, even around my backpack.

"Be careful, Van," he said. "I'm really going to miss you. Call, okay?"

"I'm going to miss you, too. And thanks. Thanks for everything."

Chapter Sixteen

When I stood at the curb beside the enormous bulk of the bus, it seemed like everything was moving in slow motion. The driver heaved the bags into the guts of the bus with the urgency of a well-fed, old cat. His oversized rectangular nametag—GEORGE—was scuffed and chipped. It looked like George had been driving buses a long time. He'd probably seen it all. My anxiety to move was nothing to him. I kept standing up and sitting back down in my seat. I willed the others to hurry up and climb inside.

I slumped back on my seat and waited, drawing my knees up just as I had on the plane that had brought us to Vegas. I realized, then, that this was the first trip I'd be taking alone. When George started the bus and pulled out of the depot, it was definitely after our scheduled 6:00 A.M. departure time. The sky was already pinking, and I could nearly see that wall of desert heat strengthening and pushing against the air-conditioned window.

The bus wasn't even half full. There was me, an elderly couple from the Midwest, their accents climbing out of their mouths across the bus, two grown Boy Scouts at the back in dull olive uniforms, and a large Spanish-speaking family sprawled throughout the middle: a dad, a mom, four little kids, a grandma, and maybe an older auntie. The kids smiled and chattered. The mom held the one that was still a baby and rubbed her eye with her shoulder.

I pressed my forehead against the greasy glass and watched the desert open up around us. Thin streamers of cloud hung in the blue-pink sky. A hawk listed and dipped in the wind like a dark slip of paper. I didn't want to think about Mom, or Ida, or Alex. I wanted to pretend, for one minute, that it was just me in the whole world, me and that hawk.

I woke up a few hours later with a completely numb ear. I stretched my neck and pressed the tingling cartilage between my fingers. The bus smelled like other people's food and portable bathroom chemicals. The elderly couple and most of the kids and the dad were asleep. The mom still held the baby and looked at me where I stretched. Her gold-brown eyes pored out at me, like she knew why I was on the bus. Like she felt sorry for me.

"I'm going to make a stop at the next rest area. Ten minutes, please," George said, and cleared his throat over the PA.

A block of bathrooms and a vending machine jail were set at the precipice of an orange-gold canyon filled with afternoon light. Everyone got up to use the bathroom and loitered in the scenic viewing area. The kids stuck their hands in between the iron bars that caged in the vending machines. They slapped their little palms against the plastic, over the chocolate bars and bags of pretzels. The grandma shooed them away.

The view into the canyon made me sick, like a migraine might be coming on. I was getting scared, I think. Everything before this rest stop was what I *had* to do. I had to make sure Ida was as okay as she could be. I had to head out to find Mom. I had to get to the bus station and hand over my ticket. But that was as far as had-to-do got me. This next part was entirely what-to-do. What-the-fuck-to-do.

George walked back to the bus and we followed.

"Your stop's next, young lady," George told me as I climbed back into the dust-covered bus.

The panic and adrenaline were kicking in, stirring up the blood and keeping me awake. *I'm really going to have to sleep*, I thought.

The desert pooled in front of us, vast and golden-red. How would I find anyone here? The bus rumbled on until we reached what looked like an actual town. I hadn't known what to expect of Sedona. But there it was: a town, with parking meters and coffee-place chains. The bus heaved to a stop. I climbed out and took my backpack when George handed it to me.

I checked my phone—I had a missed call and a voicemail from Carol. The open-air bus depot wasn't entirely vacant, but the people who waited for their buses didn't look like people I wanted to open a conversational door to. There was one couple pressing up against each other as they leaned against a wall. A few scruffy, rumpled men roamed around.

I sat on a weathered bench outside of a convenience store and drank an entire bottle of water in long, cool gulps. I sat there, cracking the empty bottle between my hands. There wasn't any more to do. I had to get it over with. I had to hear whatever answers I was going to get.

The phone rang and rang. No Marine, not even her voicemail. Finally I texted: *In Sedona. Call me.*

Within a minute, the phone buzzed in my palm.

"Marine?"

"Yes, it is me. What have you done? I told you there was no reason for you to come. I think you should turn around. Go home, wait for us."

Real fury bubbled out of me.

"Are you fucking kidding me, Marine? I'm *here*. At the bus station. I'm going to wait until somebody picks me up. So, if I get raped or murdered in this sketchy, sketchy place, Marine, it is *on you*." I regretted that, even as I choked the words out into the phone. It was my fault we were all in Sedona, anyway. The bus station wasn't *that* sketchy. But I came for Mom and I was going to get her.

"Nobody asked you to come," Marine finally said. "In fact, I very clearly asked you *not* to. I don't think you can possibly understand what's going on here."

"What's going on *where*? Where, Marine?"

"At the Blessed Light Congregation, of course. Now really, I must ask you to simply turn around and go home. You are at the bus station, after all, so that is actually most convenient."

"What?"

"Have a nice trip, dear Van. Bye-bye!"

She hung up, and I waited for an idea to fall over me. I watched shadows stretch across the pavement and waves of people roll up and down the street while the cars flashed by.

I wondered if maybe I should call someone else, maybe Alex or Chantal, to confess Marine hadn't agreed to help, to let them know I was in Sedona, and to ask about Ida. But it had only been a few hours. Alex and Chantal were probably sleeping. I noticed the voicemail from Carol again, and tapped the tiny blue disc beside her name.

"Heeeyyy, Van. Well, I have good news and bad news for you, and if you actually answered the *phone*, I might have given you the option of good news first or bad news first. *But*, since you're an asshole and you didn't, I'm giving you the bad news first. Fucking Marcos took back all of his gear, and I do mean *all* of it. So you're going to have to dip into those money bags, Money Bags, and get some new stuff if you want to stay in the band.

"The *good* news is, if you stay in the band, we're going on tour. My cousin's touring next month with *his* band, *and* he saw our show, *and* he asked me and J if we would be into it, which obviously we are, so that's why I'm calling you. Hopefully you'll be into it too. Call me back. Seriously."

I was stunned. A tour was exactly what I needed; a place to go that wasn't college, to play music all the time. My first, own thing. And I knew I'd never go. I didn't deserve it—not even a little bit. I was a bad, selfish person, and I was going to do penance for however long it took me not to feel that way anymore. I would nurse Ida back to health—I would feed her and bathe her. I would take better care of Mom. I had to find her first, though.

The Blessed Light Congregation, that's what Marine had said. I Googled it on my phone and found an ancient website. There was no real information—only a P.O. Box address and phone number with an area code I didn't recognize. I tapped the number and called, because, really, what else was there to do?

"Blessed Light, Carapace speaking." A male voice answered, high and musical.

"Oh, hi. Glad I got a hold of you." *What would Mom say? What would Ida say?* "I just got to Sedona, and would you believe it, I lost the address of where we're supposed to meet."

"Address? May I ask who's speaking?" The man's voice sharpened.

"Carapace, it's you, right? Haven't we spoken before? I just know we had a whole conversation about how the recordings changed my life."

"Oh yes, the recordings," the voice singsonged. "Aren't they extraordinary?"

"Oh, absolutely." I felt him giving way.

"Did we meet at the conference in New Hampshire?"

"That's right! We did!" *Tone it down, Van.*

"Well of course you must join us. We're at the Wind Song, right off of 89A. You can't miss it. But call again if you get lost."

"Perfect, will do. Thanks, Carapace."

"My pleasure," he said, and hung up.

Well, I'd done something. Now I had to get there.

The taxi I climbed into smelled like an old tuna can, and I cracked the window to let the late afternoon air in. The driver was a quiet elderly man who only raised his eyebrows when I told him where to go. I caught on to the dry-sun smell of the desert and closed my eyes. I tried to recall the feeling of playing with Carol and Joanna. I put Alex's sweatshirt back on and smelled his comforting, oily boy scent. I imagined I was a person with a different life, that I had told Carol yes, I'd love to go on tour, that I was Alex's girlfriend.

"Excuse me," the driver called, over a thin thread of Spanish language radio. He pointed toward the passenger side window. There wasn't much to see—a row of sagging trailers and a barely lit sign that read: Wind Song Mobile Home Park. We pulled into a parking lot—not a paved one, just a wide square of bald earth. I paid the driver with one of Mom's hundreds, and as he counted the change back into my palm he said, "This is the right place?"

"Yeah. Thanks." I could see the doubt skating over his face. "Really. I'm visiting a relative."

"Okay." He rolled up the window and drove away.

I walked around the pressed-dirt lot, looking for signs of manic, spiritual activity. I hoped that didn't mean large groups of people dancing around naked. I took my phone from Alex's sweatshirt pocket and thought about calling the Blessed Light number again. I was chilled by the prospect of what Carapace might look like naked, and by how meager the reception was at the Wind Song. I put the phone back into my pocket.

In the murky twilight, I finally noticed a thin dirt path, a path no wider than a single footprint. The air was dusty and fragrant. Scents of desert plants—herbaceous, smoky smells—twisted in the breeze. I passed a row of mint green trailers and kept going toward some kind of campground.

I got close enough to see a circle of light—a chain of different-sized tents with small fires burning in front, and various-sized lanterns wobbling in the wind. I walked down into the shallow, lit basin. I had a delirious fantasy of waking up, running to Ida, running to Mom; *You guys won't even believe this dream I just had.*

There was music—no, not music. Drums. I let myself feel the downhillness of the whole situation. The narrow path widened until it wasn't a path at all, just a sandy circle. Shadowy figures dipped and turned under the darkening sky. There were so many people, I thought. What were they all doing here? What was Mom doing here? What was *I* doing there? *Ida, Ida, Ida.* I beat back my rising headache with the sound of her name in my mind. I kept moving toward the large fire at the center of the campsite. Even I, a stranger in this deranged, mystical setting, understood that this was its beating heart.

A dirty white tent, like the kind used at outdoor weddings, marked the end of the campsite. The sides were open. Tons of people—and all of that drumming—were jammed inside. I pushed toward one of the corners where all of the campers, wearing a variety of homemade knitwear, seemed to be focused on a small triangular clearing. The force of the bodies and the drum pounding was so violent just then, I thought I'd fall dead to the ground. *This is how a person's brain explodes*, I thought. *No sleep, all drumming.* I cut through the last row of people before bursting through to the corner of cleared space.

Mom and another woman huddled together there on the ground: the valves of that terrible, fevered heart. Mom's face was painted a bright magenta. The woman leaning over her was older than I expected, and very, very thin. Her hair was bright white—it looked like it had been dyed that way, and she wore a voluminous knit poncho in the same magenta that stained Mom's face.

"Van?" Marine said. Her enormous eyes glinted at me unmistakably.

I didn't answer. Marine cleared her throat and clasped my upper arm with her giant's hand. "Van, you didn't listen to me."

The thin woman lifted her head slowly like a predatory jungle cat and looked up at us. Her eyes were blue and clear. This woman wasn't dancing around naked at least, I told myself. And that was probably the best thing I had going for me here.

"This is Sofia's daughter, Van," Marine said.

"Van!" The woman said it like my name was an amen. She stood, leaving my mother kneeling in the dirt alone.

"Mom!" I shouted. "Please! We need to leave! It's an emergency." Mom held up her finger, and I was shocked by the normalcy of the just-give-me-a-minute gesture.

I wanted to run over to Mom, to pull her up by the arms and wrestle her away. Instead, I watched the older woman approach me, this little woodland-creature-looking person. She moved like an exotic dancer—all hips and loose joints—which was weird because her emaciated body was stripped of all sexuality. It was this silly, Peter Pan–looking mess of jaunty, spritely lines. I almost wanted to laugh. Almost.

When she was right up in front of me, she stopped and looked me over. Not with just her eyes, but with her whole face and head. She started at the top of my forehead, standing on her tiptoes, and hovered her face all over me, like it was one of those metal detectors old men use at the beach.

I felt the eyes of the other spectators all over me, too. Laurel finished her inspection and knelt at my feet.

"It is you, Van," she said softly, to my sneakers.

What?

"It is the prophet's daughter!" she shouted to the crowd.

What?

The knitwear-clad throng drummed even louder than they'd been drumming already, and they whooped and roared. And for just one fraction of a second, I got it. I got why they were all here. Maybe why Mom and Marine were here. To be part of this wild, ephemeral organism. It was a very little bit like playing with Carol and Joanna.

But then I remembered who I was and why I was there. I moved toward Mom.

"Mom?" I said, and knelt down in front of her. "Mom?" I repeated, louder. "It's me, Van."

Mom opened her eyes. "I see you," she said.

"Will you just get up? Please? I have to tell you—it's Ida. She had a stroke. She's in the hospital. We need to leave, right now." I said it softly. I didn't want any of these people to know about Ida.

Mom nodded, slowly.

"Mom! Did you hear me? It's an emergency!" I couldn't keep myself from yelling.

In a feat of frightening flexibility, Laurel turned her neck while keeping the rest of her body straight and still. "There is only one emergency here. Sofia is in the middle of a transition."

"Excuse me?"

"A transition. Perhaps *the* transition."

"What?" I was flooded with panic, delirious in an instant. Wasn't *the* transition death? "Is she going to die?" I don't know why I asked Laurel that, like she was a real doctor.

"No, she is not." Laurel's eyes shone in the firelight. She swept a spindly little cricket arm over the crowd. "Sofia is a being of great power. We've all seen it. We are, each of us, witnesses. Perhaps *you* are the most important witness of all."

She stood and walked toward Mom and me, where we knelt like a pair of salt and pepper shakers in the sandy soil.

"Now is your mother's time, Van. I'm sure of it. Not three hours ago, we watched her levitate. She was floating six inches above the ground, at minimum. I've never seen anything like it."

Well, that explained Marine's curt phone manners, at least. You couldn't drop everything to pick a person up at the bus station while someone was levitating. I looked into Mom's magenta-gold face. Over the course of my life, I'd watched her spin out into something dangerous and great dozens of times. I'd seen her rashness and unpredictability ebb and flow. I'd seen her retreat into almost nothing. But I'd never seen her wildness look like this—so still. Not without medication, anyway. I knew Mom was on something. I just didn't know what.

"Mom," I whispered, my face right in front of hers. I tried to block out all of the other sights. "Mom, please, I need you."

"Yes, the people here need me, too," she said. Her voice was much too even.

"This is crazy," I said, trying to match her even tone. "Ida, a person we actually know and love, needs us right now. These people are insane. They're nothing to us."

"They're everything," Mom said. "Each of these men and women is as dear to me as you, or as Ida."

"What? What are you even saying right now?" I stood up and sat back down. I was dizzy with fury.

"I am a part of all things. A part of you, but a part of them, too. They need me here."

"Jesus, Mom!" I grabbed her shoulders, my fingers sinking into the thin layer of flesh there. "This is not the time to fuck around!"

Mom slapped me. It was something that she'd never done before. A sting across the side of my face, and then it was over.

"You will be quiet," she said. "Either you stay and help me, or you will leave."

I tried to tell myself that it wasn't really Mom behind that magenta face paint, but it didn't matter. I felt myself crying. I felt the anger and injustice of the terrible evening with every breath I took.

"Van," Laurel said, again filling my name up with that amen sound. "The spirits sent you to us, to your mother, at the most crucial moment. Tomorrow, our sister and prophet, Sofia, will begin a journey unlike any other she has known. Unlike any journey *any* of us has known. Tomorrow night, we move as one into the canyon, where Sofia will receive a divine visitation from our cosmic masters."

"Oh my God," I said, and put my hands over my face.

"Yes, oh my God and oh my Goddess," Laurel shouted to the crowd. Their murmurs and whoops filled the air like confetti.

I felt a pair of hands on my shoulders—Marine's.

"Laurel, Sofia, I'm going to put Van to bed. She needs to rest." Marine lifted me up, and I tripped along beside her, out of the tent, through the sweating, whirling crowd, and into the cold, clear night.

I wondered if Mom really believed she was their prophet, I mean down inside who she really was underneath this wave of her wildness. Mom's faith in her abilities had always been maniacal. When I was five, I broke my arm. I fell down a crumbling staircase in a condemned house we stayed in for a few months. I remember the rush of pain, that I threw up. Mom wiped my mouth and looked straight into my eyes, like I was an adult, like she and I were the same.

"Be calm," she said, her voice low and even. "Mama will fix it."

I stared into the smooth skin of her cheek as she reset the bone, gripping my wrist tightly and pulling slowly, slowly out.

I imagined that when she was done pulling, my arm would be as long as hers. My face was hot, the tears still on my slack cheeks, but I was quiet as Mom pulled and pulled. I saw the click behind her eyes when she knew that she'd pulled long enough. She beamed a smile of triumph. "There's my brave girl. Hold still." I nodded and kept as still as I could while Mom bound my limb.

So much of my life with Mom had been just that—nodding and keeping still, waiting for her magic to take effect. If Mom's faith in her abilities was maniacal, mine matched, maybe even exceeded it. After all, my arm healed perfectly. I trusted her. I trusted that she knew what to do.

But something had changed—maybe I'd realized it in that slap—and I couldn't trust her anymore.

Marine guided me through the opening of a dark green camping tent and over to a sleeping bag stretched out against one side. Somehow, she'd found my backpack and carried it along as we wound through the campsite.

"Sit down," she said, her voice firm, like she was scolding a misbehaving pet. I was so empty and tired, that I did.

"What were you thinking, coming out here? I meant it when I said this is no place for you." In the close confines of the tent, I noticed her real smell, noticed that her usual, commanding perfume was missing.

"I was thinking, *Marine*, that Ida is sick, really, really sick. Mom needs to help her. To help me." I felt a horrible thickness in my throat.

"I understand how you might see it that way." She nodded, bobbing her head along. "But this is something Sofia needs to go through. I know Laurel seems a bit much. And I admit, she's much more . . . extreme now than when I first knew her."

"What does that even mean? This levitation stuff and prophet stuff, and, Jesus Christ, this *divine visitation* stuff? Are you telling me you think any of it is real?"

"That's a tricky question."

"It's not tricky at all! Do you think it's real or is it bullshit, Marine?"

"Let me say this another way." Marine looked away for a few breaths before she spoke again. "Do I believe in levitation and so on? No, I do not. But, do I think your mother is a tremendously powerful woman? Can she change things here for the better? Of course. Is she a prophet? Most likely, she is not. But I do believe this quest is good for her. It will calm her. You'll see, my dear."

"Marine," I half sighed, half growled. "There's something I need her to understand. I mean, normally, I'd be with you on this. I'm all about Mom 'calming down' *not* in a hospital, but this? And even if it worked—which who knows if it will—I need Mom to come back with me *now*, back to Vegas. Ida isn't just sick with the flu! She's in the hospital. A stroke. Unconscious."

Marine pulled back.

"I didn't realize it was so serious," she said, sounding genuinely shocked. "Will she be all right?"

"I don't know," I told Marine and looked straight at her. "I need Mom for this. I don't know what to do. If something happens to Ida . . ." I heard my voice breaking up, like I was floating far away in the air overhead. I cleared my throat. "If something happens to Ida," I repeated, "I'm not going to know what to do."

"Oh Van, of course you won't," Marine said, a little violently. "Ida shouldn't be alone."

"Exactly." Relief flooded through me. *God bless Marine,* I thought, *Goddess bless this crazy broad.*

"I'll just have a word with Laurel and your mother. Laurel will understand if it's coming from me."

"Can't I just try talking to my mom, one more time?"

Marine looked down. "I don't think it's a good idea. You're upset, and we don't need any more violence."

"Are you serious?" I yelled. "*She* hit *me*!"

"Well, we don't need anyone hitting anyone," Marine said. "I'll see if she can talk tomorrow. The first step is that I must advise Laurel. Get some rest, dear Van."

Marine ducked out of the tent and left me alone. I knew that if I followed her, I'd find Mom again. But I just sat there, because I felt something dark, something that *did* make me want to hit her. I imagined it was Mom in the hospital, unconscious, instead of Ida.

I crawled into Mom's night-chilled sleeping bag and took a deep breath, inhaling her smell. At least she still smelled the same. I wanted to close out what I'd just seen and end that horrible day. But I needed to do one last thing. I turned in the sleeping bag and felt the lump of my cell phone in the pocket of Alex's sweatshirt that I still wore.

With my very last millimeter of presence of mind, I thought *tell someone you're here*. I twisted around and scooted the phone out of the pocket. Alex answered in the middle of the second ring.

"Van?" he almost shouted. "Are you okay?"

"Yeah. How's Ida?" I wondered if he could hear how bad it was.

"She's the same. I went by there today and she's still asleep. I waited around to talk to a doctor, but nobody told me anything."

"Oh," my voice was flat and thin, a dotted line reaching out into the dark.

"Are you with your mom?" His voice crackled in and out.

"Yes." I paused, not sure of how much I wanted to tell Alex.

"Well, is she all right? Are you guys on your way back?"

"Not exactly," I said, forcing my voice into words when all my throat wanted was to be still. *Just tell him*, I thought. "Alex," I began.

"What?" He really shouted that time.

"It's not good. I'm going to try to get her back, but this whole situation is just . . ." I thought about how to explain what was going on, but I could barely explain it to myself.

"What? The whole situation is what?"

"It's *not good*. I'm going to do my best to get Mom out of here. I think Marine can help me, but—"

"Wait, get her out of where? Is she in the hospital, too?"

"No," I said, so quietly that I wondered if he'd heard me. "If I'm not back in three days, come get me. Or, please send someone to help us."

"What? Three days? Van, you're freaking me out. You want me to call the cops?"

"No, no—just anyone who can help. Just someone who can help us." I could feel my voice slurring. It didn't seem possible that I could still be awake.

"Did you say Marcos? What, seriously?"

"Sorry, sorry. I'm just really tired. Three days, though. I'm in Sedona still. We're at the Wind Song Trailer Park." I was shocked I'd plucked the name from my depleted mush of a brain.

"The Wind Song *Trailer* Park? Is that a *joke*?" His voice flickered in and out, the connection barely there.

"No. Bye Alex, I have to sleep now." I hung up and switched the phone off. I knew he'd call back, and all I wanted to do was close my eyes. I tucked the phone back into the sweatshirt pocket and dropped into a hard, empty sleep.

Chapter Seventeen

When I woke up, I pulled my phone out and switched it on. A tiny number four lit up, announcing the number of voicemails I'd received overnight. As I played them, I knew without hearing them all that each one was from Alex. I'd call him back when I had something new to tell him. I needed to find Marine. Outside the tent, I found her waiting for me.

"Here, sit down." She handed me something wrapped in a linen napkin, and a bottle of water. "Make sure you drink this. We are in the desert, you know." She sat down across from me.

"Did you tell Laurel it's an emergency?" I asked, and unwrapped the napkin to find a peanut butter sandwich and a banana.

"Van," a voice spoke behind me. When I turned, I saw that it was Laurel, still swimming in her oversized poncho. "I'm so happy you'll be joining our group tonight. Your presence will certainly amplify Sofia's response from the cosmic masters."

"What?" I said slowly. "I thought Marine told you—we're leaving now."

"Oh, you can't mean that." A cascade of laughter spilled out after the words. "There's no question of Sofia leaving." Laurel swept her arms out like a person miming what it was like to swim. "Tonight we travel with her into the canyon." Laurel raised a hand to the horizon line and indicated a dark, narrow gap in the mountains. "We'll travel through the pass, in procession. Our group will camp at a sacred place, and then, we will send our prophet out into the universe."

"Right, about that—I'm sure Marine didn't have a chance to tell you, but we have a family emergency back in Las Vegas, and we really do need to go."

Laurel's face fell. "That *is* awful. But, I hope you'll think of us as your family now, too, as your mother does. Right now we are in perhaps the most highly emergent time in our history."

"Uh," I began, but was interrupted by a buzz from my phone. It was a text from Carol.

Before I could even check it, Laurel plucked the phone from my hand. She wrinkled her nose and said, "I'm very sorry, but I can't allow *these* in our holy space. I thought Marine would have told you. They interfere with the vibrations."

"What? You can't just take my phone!"

Laurel smiled blandly. "Ulrike!" she barked out.

A towering, leathery-skinned blonde woman loped up to us. She bowed her head down to Laurel's, face-height.

"Please take care of this," she said, handing over the phone.

Ulrike nodded and scampered off to wherever they burned the phones of innocent girls looking for their mothers. I couldn't even call the cops now if I wanted to. What was I supposed to do?

"Please, ma'am," I begged.

"Call me Laurel, or, Your Eminence, if you prefer."

"Please, just let us leave. Just tell my mom to go. Tell her she isn't welcome to stay anymore."

"It's not a question of *letting*, Van. The service we are doing here to benefit humanity greatly exceeds any obligation to a single person. Your mother understands that, and I believe after speaking with Marine, that you will, too."

Marine said nothing and looked at a pile of stones by her feet.

"But you seem so compassionate," I added, desperately.

She looked up at the sky and took a deep breath, raising her hands above her head. "I'm moved to grant you a boon. Tonight, you will walk with us at the head of the procession. It will be a good opportunity to test your place beside your mother and me."

"I'm sorry?"

"Tonight we will sing and feast, preparing for our prophet's return with what is sure to be a glorious message."

"Right. That all sounds—really interesting, but did you hear anything I just said? Aren't you in charge here? You don't need my mom messing things up for you. Please, I mean, you really seem to know what you're doing—you can't possibly need my *mom* for anything."

"Ah," Laurel coughed out. "I'm afraid that I could never ask her to leave—we are one now."

Marine looked up, sharply, the first sign she'd been listening to any of Laurel's pontificating.

"Besides," Laurel continued, "she is already in the midst of deep preparation. She's fasting in isolation. It's best that we don't disturb her."

Fasting in isolation sounded ominous, like North Korean prison ominous. Part of me felt that Mom deserved it. But Ida, Ida didn't deserve to be forgotten like this.

"I need to speak with her again," I said, desperate.

"Of course! And you will, once we begin the procession," Laurel said as she rubbed her palms together. "If you're going to join us, we have some work to do. You'll definitely have to learn some mantras. Ready?"

"Marine? Is this okay?" I asked. I don't know why I appealed to Marine like that. Maybe it was because she was my only resource, or maybe because she seemed to be bending under what I'd told her about Ida.

"Yes, you should go, Van. I'll sit with your mother while you're busy," Marine said.

"Perfect! Let's get a move on." Laurel waved over my head to someone behind me.

Marine came up and stood at my side. She looked at me like she was trying to tell me something, but I had no idea what. I raised my eyebrows at her and she raised them back. Before I could figure it out, Laurel swept me away—back to a cleared space behind the tepee. Several followers sat in a circle, their heads bent over busy hands. Knitting needles flashed in and out of a dense, magenta sheet growing between them.

I recognized one of the women, the middle-aged Scandinavian one, *Ulrike*, who'd stolen my phone. Laurel squished me into the circle, between a girl who wasn't much older than I was, and a man who was at least Ida's age. Laurel walked around, slowly, like she was building up the suspense in a round of duck, duck, goose.

"Now, everyone," she called. "I want to run through some of our mantras for Van's benefit. It will help with the work. Ready?" Then, like some deranged Maria von Trapp, Laurel started them in a round of monotonous chanting: *"Om mane padme om, om mane padme om, om mane padme om."*

"Van!" Laurel chirped over the droning voices. "Come on, join in!"

I moved my mouth, but let no sound out. *This is definitely in the top five weirdest things that's ever happened to me*, I thought. It was a realization that made me even more certain I could never jump into a normal life—at college, or in a regular relationship with a human being. The white-haired man beside me handed me his set of knitting needles and motioned for me to take over.

"Oh," I said. "Uh, I don't know how to do this."

"Nonsense, Van, this is in your blood!" Laurel called. "Tell her, Lou!"

"No, I mean, I don't know how to knit," I told the old man.

"Just trust yourself," he said. "Here." He tore off a magenta thread from the bulk twist of yarn at his side. "Hold it. Listen. Feel your connection to all of us. To all things."

"Again, louder!" Laurel said. "From the diaphragm, Van, that's how it's done."

The chant moved through and around me, even though I didn't speak. I started to feel dizzy, like all of those sound waves were needling into my brain or inner ear or something. In that moment, I longed for Ida, for Alex, for Carol, or Joanna. Anyone outside of this place—anyone who could tell me I belonged with them, and not in this unhinged circle. Laurel was really feeling it. She swayed in my peripheral vision, and I wondered how such a wisp of a person had inspired something so large and strange.

She came over to where I sat and set her palms on my shoulders. "Oh, Van," she said. "We are so grateful to your mother, and to you."

"What do you mean?" I swallowed back my building nausea.

"Why, without your mother's generous financial gift we'd never be able to hold this meeting with the cosmic masters."

"What?" I swam up through the woozy aural haze and tried to focus on what Laurel had said. "How generous was she, exactly?" I didn't think I could feel any sicker. I was sure that whatever infusion of cash that had come our way from the Silver Saddle was now lining the pockets of Laurel's robes.

"Oh, that's not important now. And anyway, it's how we knew she was the chosen one—our savior, so to speak."

Oh boy, I thought.

Chapter Eighteen

When the chanting was over, I wobbled away from the others. I'd go back to the tent and use Marine's phone to call Vegas. I assumed she had it stashed in there. The fact that Marine was hiding her phone—and its vibrations—from Laurel reassured me, made me believe she would help. I wanted to check on Ida again. Then I would talk to Mom. The light in the sky was lush and warm. All of those spiny, fragrant plants released their scents under the heat of the sun.

After wandering around a little, I found the tent and heard shuffling inside.

"Hello?" I called into the green, waterproof material.

"Van? Is that you?" A man's voice called out.

The zipper slashed open and a figure tumbled out—a tall, familiar figure.

"Oh my God, Alex," I said, and fell right into him. "What are you doing here?" I was hysterical with relief.

"It sounded like you needed help," he said, smoothing the part of my back just under my rib cage.

I did need help. I needed help so much.

"And you weren't answering the phone, so I drove out here."

"How did you find all this?"

"Wind Song Trailer Park, remember? You don't forget something like that."

My initial relief was peppered with anger. "You promised me you'd stay with Ida!"

"Don't worry, Ida's fine. Ovid is there. He's barely left her side."

"Is she awake?" I pulled away.

"No." Alex looked down. "Not yet. But her doctors say she's doing better."

"Well, that's good," I said.

Alex nodded. "Van," he said, "we need to get out of here."

"Yeah, no shit. But it's not as easy as just walking out. My mom doesn't *want* to leave."

"Did you tell her about Ida?"

"Of course I did!" I let my anger pour out over Alex.

"And what did she say?"

"She said she didn't care, basically. She's crazy, Alex!"

"Why didn't you call me?"

"She stole my phone," I explained, trying to breathe through the waves of rage flooding my body.

"Your mom stole your phone?"

"No, Laurel! She confiscated it, because of the vibrations!" I was shouting now.

"I'm not sure what that means. Just, I think we should call somebody—the cops, something!" Alex was shouting, too.

Hours before, I'd been desperate to call the cops myself, but I didn't like Alex suggesting it. And now that he was here—now that I wasn't completely alone—Laurel and her followers, well, they seemed less threatening.

"What did Marine say to you about all this?" he asked.

"Oh Jesus, Marine," I muttered.

"She seems really close to these people, but, I don't know, like she doesn't trust them."

"You think?" A hopeful glow coursed through me. "You talked to her?"

"A little. She seems, I don't know, she seems kind of jealous." Alex raised an eyebrow.

"That's good. I think." I paced around Alex and let my thoughts overlap, folding down into condensed, real possibilities. "Maybe we let my mom go through with this thing tonight, and then tomorrow, when everyone is all celebrating, we sneak away. If I have to hit her over the head and put her in the trunk, I will." If Alex had a car—it would be fine.

Alex didn't say anything.

"What? We can't call the cops," I said. "Do you have any *idea* what would happen if you called the cops?"

"No, I don't." Alex's voice was soft. "Will you tell me?"

I turned away because I couldn't even look at him. I couldn't even *look* at a real person. Why had I felt so relieved, I wondered, when Alex's showing up just made me feel like more of a mutant. His presence made me feel, horribly, like this campsite was where I belonged.

"Please tell me why we can't call the cops."

I let my arms fall to my sides.

"Have *you* ever called the cops?" I began.

"No."

"That's what I figured. Cops and people like us, people like Mom, are a bad combination." I risked a look up into Alex's warm hazel eyes. "A *terrible* combination." I turned my gaze back to my feet.

"Okay, I still don't know what you mean exactly."

I sighed and looked out over the basin campsite. The sun was just beginning to set, and the layers of sediment in the stone were bright and distinct.

"This isn't an easy thing to say," I began, "but people have called the cops on us before. More than once."

"Okay," said Alex.

"She's been like this before. This was mostly before Ida, when I was small."

Alex nodded.

"When they show up, they'll restrain Mom. They'll hurt her, whatever it takes. Then they'll lock her up in a shitty hospital where they'll give her medicine she can't take. Medicine that makes her sick. Medicine that she's allergic to, because they won't listen to her. Meanwhile, I won't know anything about it, because they'll separate us and shuttle me off to some group home."

"A group home?"

"Foster care. I'm not eighteen yet, remember?"

What I didn't say was, *What if they do a psychiatric evaluation on me? What if they throw me—the girl who participates in mantra knitting circles—into the same mental hospital as Mom?* We'd be trapped there together forever. Who was going to come get us? Ida?

"Okay, I get it, but Van," his voice filled my ear. "This is so fucked up—you need to get out of here. We'll go back and let your mom and Marine figure it out here. Whatever it is. Do you think if Ida was awake, she'd let you go through with this *plan*?"

It was true. I turned around and took a deep breath, trying to smooth out the wild peaks of energy coming out of me.

"You're right. You're *so* right. This is so incredibly fucked up. But so am I, and so is my mom. I need to help her out of this. I'm the only one who can do it." I believed it, as I said it out loud. "Please help me come up with a better plan."

Alex sat up and looked at me in the waning sunlight. "Of course I'll help you," he said. "How could I not help you?"

• • •

All around, preparations were being made. Tents came down around where we sat, and the magenta-covered campers piled

162

bins and bags and jugs of water onto carts. There was chanting and singing, too. They weren't all singing the same song, but they definitely sang the same family of songs. Even when the songs bled out of their mouths and into each other, there was no dissonance. An eerie, unplanned harmony wove through the basin, one voice picking up a thread from another and binding a new song to it.

"You're sure you want to do this?" Alex asked. "It's not too late to change your mind. We could stay here and wait for them to come back tomorrow."

"I'm sure," I said, getting restless waiting for whoever was supposed to come for me. Eventually, Marine and Ulrike found us. The sun at their backs was low in the sky, and their features were shadowed. They looked like twin statues that had climbed down from an ancient temple—with their identically tall, strong bodies, it wouldn't be hard to believe they were both warriors.

"We have to go now. We're already very late. Young man," Marine said, without looking at Alex. "Please help Van with the tent. I have to check on Sofia."

"Can I come with you? Just for a minute?" I asked.

"I'm sorry, Van." Marine shook her head. "There's no time. But don't worry. Laurel tells me you'll be walking out with your mother. It's a very significant, private arrangement. You'll get the time with your mom that you need. Maybe you can get through to her."

"When does that happen?" Alex asked.

"Very soon. A few hours from now, only. When the full moon is up."

"Oh sure," Alex said. "That makes sense."

Marine rushed away before I could answer. Alex reached a hand out to me, but before I could take it, Ulrike pulled a cart between us. It was the size of a small horse-drawn wagon, except it was Ulrike who pulled the cart along. She slung in our packed belongings and handed over a gallon of water to me.

"Water," she said. "You follow me." She took up her place at the front of the cart and led us away to where the rest of the camp was gathering beyond the basin.

I pulled on my backpack and Alex picked up the jug of water. We followed Ulrike and joined the others to wait for Laurel and Mom. The group began to move. I didn't see Laurel, Mom, or Marine. After a while, I didn't even see Ulrike. But we followed the others. Would I have done the same if Alex hadn't been there? I wasn't sure. I really wasn't.

"Alex, do you have your phone?"

"Yeah, why? Do you need it?"

"No. Just checking." I felt the anxiety build in my body. Little rivulets of it skittered through me, and I choked on gulps of air that didn't feel right in my lungs. Bodies shifted and shuffled all around us. I took small, unnatural steps, trying not to touch anyone.

"Are you okay?" Alex asked.

I'd stopped moving without noticing. I wasn't okay, not at all. I felt like I was walking into something, walking past the point of no return. Alex took me by the arm and we drifted to the edge of the group, letting the stream of human heat pass by where we stood.

"Van, look at me," Alex said, gripping my shoulder. "What's wrong?"

"I need a minute, I think." I tried to pace my breaths by pushing down into my stomach in a rhythm of normal oxygen intake.

"It's okay, we'll just wait here. This is really—" Alex paused. I could see him wanting to yell for us to get out of there. I watched him tamp down that feeling. "This is really just an unusual situation."

I opened my eyes as wide as I could and laughed a cool, gorgeous, screen-siren laugh. I don't know where it came from, or who I was in that second, but I surely wasn't Van.

"You can say that again," I said, or whoever that not-Van was, who'd just taken over my body, had said. Maybe it was oxygen deprivation from all of the hyperventilating. "I'm fine," I said. "Thanks for stopping. Let's just go."

"If you're sure," was all Alex said.

We walked toward the canyon wall for almost an hour, and when we reached the narrow pass, the campers in front of us trickled through the gap in the stone. I tried to look into the shadows beyond that opening, but didn't see anything. Certainly not anyone or anything I recognized. We waited for all of the others to go ahead. I looked closely at the towering rock formations. They reached up to the sky like turrets of a decaying palace, the former seat of some great, forgotten civilization.

Then it was just me and Alex in the middle of nowhere—the stretch of empty earth behind us and this mountainous wall the color of the sun before us. I knew I had to go through that dark gap, and I knew something strange and wild was coming. I knew it was coming right at me.

"Let's go," I said, and nodded to Alex to go through.

He looked over his shoulder at me, hunched under the weight of the water jug. I waited until he disappeared into the shadows on the other side.

"You coming?" His voice floated out through the wall.

I finally stepped through.

Chapter Nineteen

The other side of the wall was not what I had imagined. It wasn't filled with shadows at all. It was a bowl of gold light—gold from the stones and from the exiting sun. The gap opened onto a small mesa. The others looked like ants as they wound down the path deep into the canyon. It was like nothing I'd ever seen, like some giant god had cupped its hands to capture something earthly and beautiful. *This Laurel knows what she's doing*, I thought.

"Whoa, right?" Alex said. His voice shook me out of the semitrance I'd been in.

I nodded.

We followed the others down and down. Shivers of loose stones fell around our feet. I was the last one in line, my eyes on the back of Alex's neck.

The path ahead of us cut through a dense mass of trees. The other stragglers pushed through the piney branches, and Alex helped me through, holding back the fragrant boughs as we broke out into a clearing. Laurel's team had been busy. Their work was evident in that basketball court–sized space. There was some low brush bursting up along the edges, but the ground was mostly clear. An enormous tepee had been set up in the center.

Others had begun to set up their small tents around the vividly embellished conical structure. The fawn flaps of the tepee had been painted with feathers and birds and faces. Under the very last light of the sun the magenta on the tepee looked especially sinister, like an incurable wound.

"Van! There you are!" Laurel had found me. She was dressed in billowing white robes. "We've been waiting for you. You'll need to hurry now. The ceremony is about to start. Leave your things with your friend and come with me."

"Is this okay with you, Van?" he asked.

I nodded, remembering that if I was about to see Mom, it would be better if Alex wasn't there. I didn't want him to see her like that, to see that genetic potential in me. I didn't want him to see what I was going to say to her.

"Well, I'll be close." He pointed to a spot next to the tepee. "Within yelling distance," he added.

Laurel put her hand on my back as a light breeze filled the canyon. Her robes billowed out and around us both. She guided me to the entrance of the conical tent.

"Now," she said. "Do you have any crystals with you?"

"Um, no," I said.

"Well, this *is* a problem. Crystals are an integral part of tonight's ceremony. Perhaps Carapace can lend you one of his. Carapace!" Laurel called, like she was summoning an animal.

A thin, bearded man, maybe Mom's age, scuttled up to us. *Carapace,* I thought, the man with the singsong voice.

"Please lend us the use of one of your crystals. Just for a moment—Van's forgotten hers."

I shrugged, trying to convey my generally sincere apologies to Carapace.

"Oh, of course," he gushed, displaying a set of yellowed teeth. "It would be my honor." He had a kind of utility belt wound around his bony hips, and unclipped a leather pouch from it. He poured the contents into one palm. Crystals clacked together like dice in his open hand.

"Well," Laurel said. "Choose. You know, pick each one up, touch it, see if it speaks to your energy." She paused a moment. "Have you seen *Harry Potter*?"

I nodded.

"Pretend you're selecting a wand. Pick up each stone and give it a wave. See if you can make magic."

Carapace let his hand hover a few inches from my face. I made a pincer with my fingers and picked up a small piece, probably the most gruesome-looking one, about the size of my pinkie nail. I pressed it between my thumb and forefinger, because I figured that was the way to test a crystal. I felt a sharp shiver up my arm, like a static shock. The weird thing was, I kind of expected it before it happened. I knew something was coming out of the hideous ruby scab for me. I tried it again, just to make sure I hadn't imagined it, and felt that same little shiver. It wasn't unlike the thrilling, near-discomfort that I felt holding down a power chord. I held my arm out in a somebody-take-this gesture.

"Ah," Carapace and Laurel sighed together as though my choice had answered an important question.

"No, Van. You hold on to it. I want you to focus on the vibration of that stone and the vibrations of your own energy. I'll do a quick cleansing before we begin the ceremony. Just hold still."

Carapace held out a large breakfast-in-bed tray filled with all kinds of grubby odds and ends. Laurel floated her hands over it and chose a short, fat wand of dried plants tied together with string. Carapace set the tray on the ground, flipping out its little legs so that it was slightly elevated off of the sand. He pulled a miniature blowtorch from his utility belt, the kind that the Silver Saddle kitchen used on crème brûlées. Laurel held up the wand between them and Carapace lit it like a comically large cigarette. The end of the twist of dried leaves caught fire. Laurel spoke over it, softly, and blew out the flame, leaving the wand trailing plumes of fragrant, musky smoke as she moved it around.

She waved it over my head, around my shoulders, even down to my knees and feet. The smoke stung my eyes, and when I took a deep breath, I started to cough.

"That's right," Laurel said. "Reject the negative energy within." She circled me a few more times and handed Carapace the smoking wand. "Now," she said. "Inside."

I pushed open the tepee flap slowly. Mom sat cross-legged in the center, underneath the point of the cone. She wore white robes that matched Laurel's, and her face was still painted magenta and gold. Her eyes were sealed shut. Marine sat in the sand behind her. She looked right at me, her dark eyes pouring out a message. I stared back at her, but couldn't decipher it.

Ida would never have let things go this far. She would have come with me and whisked Mom from Laurel's campsite before anyone knew what was happening.

Laurel closed the flap and stepped in behind me. A few others were planted around the tent—drummers mostly, and two or three people holding some kind of maracas. Laurel stood directly in front of Mom and raised her arms. She began to chant, rhythmically and repetitively. I assumed it was another language, but really I had no idea.

The tempo and cadence were like the sound of a train— chug-a-chug-a, chug-a-chug-a, chug-a-chug-a. The drums began to beat and the maracas rattled along to the same rhythm. The sound was so thick, I felt as if I could see it floating in the air, like I could slice one of my hands through its layers and feel something there. Laurel waved her arms, conducting the swells and dips of the chant until she cut it off with a series of handclaps. In the silence, she reached down and lightly touched the top of Mom's head.

"Here we go," I heard someone say. And then a sharp intake of breath from somewhere inside of the tepee, like a person had been burned. Mom opened her eyes. Her gaze was ferocious; it was beyond. My vision blurred and my throat hurt, but I didn't cry.

Laurel helped Mom stand and held her hands. Marine stood with them, a palm at Mom's back. It was clear that they were leading her outside. I stepped out of the way. The drummers filed out next and took up the beat again. I went after them: last.

Outside, all traces of the sun were gone and the full moon glowed in the clear, dark sky. Millions of stars cast a milky light all around, and a bonfire blazed nearby. More drummers surrounded the tepee and the fire, banging along as the campers sang in a rising and falling rhythm, the sound wrapping us all around. I closed my eyes for a second, and it was like being in a little boat on the ocean.

Laurel led Mom to the front of the fire and waved out to the others. The music and chanting dropped off, and Laurel began to speak, holding Mom's hand up to the sky.

"My brothers and sisters," Laurel shouted out into the night. "My sons and daughters, my friends and my lovers," she continued.

Eww, I thought.

"We have come to this sacred space on *this* night for a reason. Perhaps *the* reason. To learn why we are here. To learn from where we have come and where we will go." I could tell she was going for a Southern Baptist preacher kind of delivery, but she wasn't quite pulling it off. "All around us, in this canyon, there was once an ocean." A swirl of chatter wound through the crowd as the others looked around. "In this very place we stand, creatures of the deep once splashed and swerved, lived and died. Millennia of pulses and billions of heartbeats fill the air! Can you feel it?"

A few shouts popped up out of the crowd.

"This is the sacred place we have chosen to send our prophet, Sofia. This is where she will receive a message from our Cosmic Masters, from the Spirits of the Earth and Seas." Laurel let go of Mom's hand and began to circle around her. "She is ready! She has fasted and meditated for three days and three nights. Our blessed committee will accompany her to the center of the Thousand Seas Energy Vortex, and there she will wait, under the light of this bountiful full moon, until the light of the sun is at its peak tomorrow. Our message, *the* message, will be delivered to her there."

The beginning of a cheer stirred through the onlookers.

"When the prophet returns, we shall rejoice and feast, for the message will save all of mankind! Come!" Laurel raised her arms and the others raised theirs. I definitely did not raise mine.

"Come!" Laurel reached for my hand and for Mom's and started to walk, setting an awkward, jerky pace. A pack of people broke off from the crowd and followed us. Of course, there were plenty of drummers drumming, but there were also a few peripheral figures carrying lanterns and flashlights and bundles. The small pools of roving lights distracted my eyes from the lights in the sky. I snuck a look at Mom. Her eyelids were heavy, and she kept stumbling. She was definitely drugged, but I had no idea how, or what to do to snap her out of it. Or if I even wanted to snap her out of it. Drugged Mom would be a lot easier to abduct from Laurel's production than fully sentient, wild Mom. We just needed to get through tonight, and with help from Alex and, hopefully, Marine, we'd get out of there.

The drumming was disorienting—it was as bad as the slot machines at the Silver Saddle. I couldn't feel the shape of the night around me, couldn't feel the way the wind was blowing.

"Here!" Laurel bellowed. She stopped abruptly and everyone slowed around her. "The vortex! It's just ahead! Do you feel it?" she shouted into the wind. She dropped my hand and Mom's and started to twist around and sweep her hands over her body and through the air. I was beginning to wonder if Laurel was on something, too. She hadn't seemed this deranged earlier.

Carapace darted ahead and started to mimic Laurel's bizarre dance. The drummers began that first beat I remembered, the chug-a-chug-a, chug-a-chug-a, and a woman's voice spun out from the darkness.

Laurel danced a little farther off the path. Into the vortex, presumably. Mom and Marine stood beside me, the three of us still and quiet while the others roiled and shouted. Laurel hopped up onto a wide, flat rock and shot her arms into the air. One of the campers holding a flashlight pointed it toward her. The light was weak, so I could only make out bits and pieces of Laurel—a white curl of hair, a swish of robes.

"We are here, spirits!" she shouted, over all of the drumming and whooping. "We are here! Sofia!" She reached an arm out to Mom.

Carapace and a few others surrounded her, like a human raft, and jostled her forward to Laurel, who pulled her up onto the ledge. Laurel motioned to Carapace, who climbed up beside them carrying a jug of water and a rolled-up bundle. He put them down where the wide ledge met the canyon wall, and then he and Laurel settled Mom into a seated position on the rock. Two more campers started a fire in a ring of stones they'd made.

Carapace and Laurel climbed down, with surprising agility, and started to dance around again. This time, though, they began to move along the trail as they danced. Marine and I waited until the celebratory parade had snaked a little further away. We stood side by side and looked up at Mom, perched on the ledge.

"We're just leaving her here?" I asked.

"She will be all right, Van. It's only one night."

"But what about bears?" I shouted.

"There are no bears. Your mother can handle it."

"Even when she's on drugs?" I stepped a little closer to Marine, trying to intimidate her, to get in her face, but she was much too tall.

"She is not *on drugs*," she said, slicing delicate air quotes into the space between us.

"Well, she's on something," I muttered, feeling more helpless than ever.

"Nothing that will cause her harm. Honestly, this is the safest place she could be right now. Maybe this will really help. Come now, let's go. It'll all be over tomorrow."

I couldn't leave on my own. Marine had to steer me down the path. We followed the echoes of singing and drumming back to the campsite. I realized I still held Carapace's crystal in my clenched fist. I thought about throwing it down into the sand, about running back to Vegas with Alex. I slipped the crystal into my back pocket and moved along with Marine.

• • •

The camp was overflowing with celebration when we returned. The smoke from a dozen fires mixed with all kinds of music in the air. Someone had decorated the site with garlands of paper flowers and woven branches. A long line of folding tables had been assembled in front of the bonfire. Laurel and most of our procession, including Carapace, were already sitting.

"I'm going to talk to Laurel. Make sure you drink some water," Marine said, her brow furrowed. "There isn't a spot for me at the head of the table." She wandered away, toward the rejoicing.

174

"I guess I'll try to find Alex so we can check on Ida." I said this out loud to myself, like a real weirdo. Everything looked different in the dark. I could barely remember what color tent Ulrike had selected for me. Then I thought about how Alex and I would be sharing that tent. I didn't know if it was because Marine had just mentioned it, but my throat was suddenly dry as torture. I turned back and found another small folding table draped in cloth and covered with drinks. There were jugs of wine and plastic pitchers filled with vibrantly colored liquids, but no cups. Unopened gallons of water were lined up at the table's base. I took one, hauling it back to the edge of the campsite. I cracked it open and hefted it to my mouth, sloshing water down the front of my sweater.

"Good, the water," a voice said.

I jumped and spilled more water onto the sand. Ulrike stepped into the light, a terrifying vision of Viking blondness.

"Jesus, Ulrike, you scared me!" I wiped my mouth with my sleeve and screwed the cap back on.

"You drink water!"

"Okay, I hear you," I said, wondering if everybody in the camp was high. "Um, have you seen my friend? Alex?"

"Ah-lex," she said and then waited out a long pause. "No."

"Do you remember seeing my tent?"

"There." She pointed to the left of the fire.

"Thanks." I walked away as fast as I could while carrying the enormous plastic jug of water.

Nobody noticed me, but then, I didn't ask any questions, and I tried to keep my gaze down.

Out of the corner of my eye, I saw a sphere of blue light, about the size of a palm. I squinted into the darkness and saw someone doubled over a cell phone. It was a stoop I could have picked out of a lineup of hundreds. Part of me wanted to run over and tell Alex everything I'd just seen, about the dancing, about the vortex, about just leaving Mom in the middle of nowhere. But another part felt suddenly very shy, like I didn't want to go over there at all. I shuffled where I stood, trying to decide which way to go. Alex looked up and straightened to his full height.

"Van?" he shouted, just a little too loudly. "Is that you?"

"Yeah," I said as I walked over to him.

"What happened?"

"I'm not really sure," I said, and stepped a little closer. He squinted down at me.

"I think you should sit down. You don't look so good."

"Thanks a lot," I said.

"That's not what I mean." He shook his head. "Just come sit down for a minute, okay? Have you eaten anything?"

"No."

"Come on. You rest in the tent and I'll get you something."

Alex bounded around the improvised avenues between tents and fires to a tent that looked like many of the others.

"Did you hear from Ovid at all? Or Chantal?"

Alex slowed his pace but didn't look at me. "No," he said. "I tried to call, but the reception out here is terrible. I was going to walk around a little to see if I'd have better luck higher up, but I wanted to wait until you got back."

"Thanks," I said. "That would be great."

We walked a little more, huddled together.

"This is the spot. Here you go," he said, zipping open the front door flap. "I'll be right back."

I thought, again, about being alone, inside, with Alex. I flushed, hoping it would be invisible in the dark.

"Are you sure you're okay? Do you want me to stay with you?"

"No, no. I'm just going to sit down in here," I said, waving at the tent.

"I'll try to find a signal somewhere out here." He gave me a half-serious, stern look. "Don't go anywhere."

I nodded and slid inside. Two sleeping bags were rolled out on the ground side by side. Two jugs of water and my backpack were squashed up against the opposite wall. I thought I would lie down for just a minute, just until Alex came back. I turned onto my side and then nothing, only sleep.

Chapter Twenty

When I woke up, I was surprised to feel so warm. I remembered thinking, just before I fell asleep, that I should have climbed into the sleeping bag, that it was getting cold. I tried to turn onto my back but couldn't quite flip over. I shook myself a little, trying to break fully into being awake. When I did, I realized Alex was the reason I couldn't turn over.

Because he was asleep right next to me. Because his arm was settled over my body. Because I was pulled close against all of that tallness—his stomach to my back and the fronts of his legs to the backs of mine.

I didn't know what to do. *Should I pretend to be asleep again? Should I just sneak out?* What I did know, though, was that it felt great. It felt great and warm and exciting. It felt the opposite of everything I'd just experienced out in the vortex. I let go of the tension in my back and neck and let myself sink back into Alex's arms and body.

As I considered the new, thrilling closeness, I wondered what it was going to mean—in the space of our friendship, in this bizarre Mom-retrieval mission, in the return to Vegas, but especially, I wondered what it was going to mean in the tent. Right then. Alex was the first real friend I'd ever made, apart from Mom and Ida. How was that going to change with so much of my body touching so much of his body?

I wondered if there was any way I could stop myself from liking it. Maybe it was a mistake. Maybe Alex hadn't meant to pull me in like this—he was sleeping, after all. Maybe when he finally dozed off he started dreaming about his real girlfriend. *What about the girlfriend Marcos was talking about? Maybe it would be best to just remove yourself from the whole situation,* I told myself.

I flipped over so that Alex and I were face to face. I don't know what possessed me to do *that*. He was so pretty, even prettier up close, with those long eyelashes that fluttered on his cheeks. *Oh shit!* I thought. *His eyelashes are fluttering!* I quickly pulled back from under his arm and wriggled over onto the farthest edge of my sleeping bag and curled up, resting my head on my arms, and pretended to be asleep.

I tried not to squeeze my eyelids too tightly and kept my breathing even, and from my stomach. Ida told me that was how you could spot a fake sleeper—if your breathing was coming from your chest and not your stomach, you weren't fooling anybody. I listened to Alex shifting and heard the swish of his clothes over the slippery top of the sleeping bag. I felt the heat of his body move away and stretched out my arms and legs as I pretended to wake up. I cracked an eye open and saw that he had turned away.

I looked up at the roof of the tent. I imagined that ours was the only tent in the clearing, that the camp was empty. Would I know how to get out of there if it really had been abandoned? More importantly, would I know how to find Mom again? I didn't think so. It struck me that now would have been the perfect time to extract Mom from the camp, since she was alone and everyone was asleep.

I remembered the singing and drumming and Carapace's breakfast-in-bed tray, but I didn't remember anything about the walk to Mom's energy vortex ledge. The turns, the way the rock wall looked, whether or not we walked up an incline—all of those details eluded me. I thought about heading out in some general direction I could recall while everyone was asleep, but decided against it.

"Don't make things worse than they already are," I said to myself, out loud.

"What?" Alex's voice rumbled.

I shook my head, wondering if my stay in the camp was making me lose my mind. I hoped Alex's phone had worked last night. Suddenly I was anxious to ask about Ida. He *must* have gotten in touch with someone. Chantal at least.

"Alex?" I whispered.

Nothing. I moved closer, hovering over the space where his throat met his ear. More than anything, I wanted this to be my only problem: liking a boy, being in a tent with him, not knowing what to do about it. "Alex." I said it a little louder, and then I touched his ear, like a real weirdo. I couldn't help myself. His eyelids opened and I pulled away.

"Hey," he said.

"Sorry I woke you up."

"Did you sleep okay?"

"Actually, I did," I said, surprised by the honesty of the answer. "Do you know what time it is? How's Ida? Did you ever find a signal?"

Alex's face fell a little as he shook his head. "I didn't. And my phone died, so . . ." He trailed off and shrugged his shoulders. "Is anyone awake out there yet?"

"Doesn't sound like it." I sat up and pulled my knees to my chest.

Alex plucked at a loose thread on his sleeping bag and kept looking down at the thread and up at me, and back down again. The pale morning light bled through the walls of the tent, giving the impression that we were inside of some kind of giant egg. I don't know why I did it—it didn't feel like me, it felt like not-Van—but I reached out and held both of Alex's hands.

"Alex," I started, looking down at all of our gripping fingers, realizing then that he was holding my hands as tightly as I was holding his. "Thanks for helping me. I guess." I looked up and found Alex's hazel eyes staring at me. "I guess what I want to say is, thanks for being my friend. I don't think I've ever really had a friend before."

When I looked up again, this time he was looking down. We were both quiet for a minute and listened to the first birds moving and chirping in the trees around the camp. Alex cleared his throat.

"Van, how have you never had a friend?"

"Jesus, I know, I'm such a weirdo! Why did I even tell you that?" I said, pulling my hands out of his grasp and putting them up to my face.

Alex gently pulled at my wrists, opening my face back up to our conversation. This time, he let my hands go.

"No," he said. "That's not what I meant. I mean, you *are* weird, but that's what I like."

That's what he likes? What is that supposed to mean? I thought.

"I mean," he continued, "what about your life made it so that you never had any friends? I just want to know more about you."

I shrugged and tried to get more comfortable on the sleeping bag, but only managed to contort myself more. "Um, well, my mom and I have always been travelling. Usually to places where there weren't other kids or families. Sometimes to places where there weren't many other people in general."

"Like, where? Was your mom doing the same kind of work?"

"We lived in Iceland, and in Texas." I looked away, at the wall of the tent. "Thanks, by the way, for setting up the tent."

"You're welcome—please don't change the subject. I really want to know."

"We lived all over South America, mostly."

"Is your mom from there?"

"No, she's Belarusian."

"What?" Alex said. "I was definitely not expecting that. Did she come here for college or something?"

I paused. Mom had never been to college for anything. I thought about how much I should explain to Alex, and, flushing with embarrassment, decided that if we were friends, he should know everything.

"Mom came over in the nineties. To marry my dad."

"Like a mail-order bride kind of thing?"

"Exactly like a mail-order bride kind of thing."

"This is crazy!" Alex threw his arms up in the air, like he'd never heard anything more outrageous.

"Yeah, it *is* crazy. Mom married my dad, the big Van Morrison fan."

"No shit, that's why your name is Van!"

"Very good," I said dryly.

"Don't make fun of me—I'm just trying to keep up here."

"She married my dad, and was really young, like eighteen or nineteen."

"What's your dad's deal? Is he a musician, like you?"

"What *was* my dad's deal," I corrected. "He's dead. And I don't know. He lived in Seattle. I know that because that's where I was born. But he OD'ed when I was a baby."

"No shit," Alex said. "I'm really sorry."

"It's okay, I didn't know him."

"So what did your mom do?" Alex asked, his growing interest as vivid as face paint.

"Well, at first, I'm not really sure. Things weren't good. I only remember a little bit about it," I said and shivered. "Mom doesn't like to talk about it. And honestly, I don't either, but . . ."

Alex looked at me expectantly, like he wanted all of the dirt.

"I'm pretty sure we lived on the street for most of that time. Or, I guess we were vagrants, or whatever."

Alex's expectant look flickered into a horrified one, and I was really satisfied by the change for some reason. It was like, *Ha! This is not some lighthearted anecdote. This is a real, terrible thing that happened to us. This is why I am the way I am.*

"Oh my God, Van," he said. "I'm so incredibly sorry."

"It all turned out okay."

"So what happened?" Alex cautiously asked.

"Mom got married again, to a guy named William. I'm not sure how she met him." But I did know, or had an idea anyway. She wasn't exactly working the corner, but she did what she had to do to keep us alive. It was the only way she could make any money—her English back then was still pretty bad. It wasn't like my dad had left us anything or had any family who cared about what happened to us.

"How old were you?"

"Eight maybe." We weren't keeping very good track of the years at that point. "Anyway, she married William—Lowell was his last name, that's why it's ours, obviously. William had this business. He would analyze companies and figure out where they were losing money and tell them how to stop losing money. He mostly worked with South American companies, which is why we travelled there so much."

"What was he like?" Alex asked.

"He was really nice. He loved my mom. But he died. Heart attack. He was a lot older. Anyway, he taught my mom everything he knew, and she picked it all up really fast and took over the business. That's when she hired Ida, by the way."

"Anyone can see that your mom is smart, Van."

"Yeah, she is. I wish I'd inherited some of her better qualities." *But not any of the ones she's displaying right now*, I thought.

"What? You're *so* smart!" Alex said the word "so" like dunking a basketball.

"Thanks," I muttered.

"You're frighteningly smart." He looked down and started to fiddle with that thread on his sleeping bag again. "And you're really cute, too."

"Cute?" I half shouted in horror. "Like a baby?"

"No! No, no, not like that. Pretty, you're really pretty. I'm sorry. Did I make you uncomfortable?"

"You just compared me to a baby!" I said, and gave his arm a thwack. Although, I was so contorted, I almost fell over when I did it. I tried to dispel the awkwardness, but it clung to us like the smell from the campfires.

"Can I ask you something?" I said.

"Of course."

"Do you have a girlfriend? Sorry if that's too personal or whatever, I just . . ." I looked down so I wouldn't have to see Alex's expression.

"No, it's not too personal, and no, I don't."

I still couldn't look at him. "It's just that Marcos said something about it. At your birthday party."

"Yeah, I bet he did." Alex sighed, and then he was the one looking down. "There was a minute there, with Joanna."

"With Joanna?" I felt a little sick.

"Not anymore, though. We weren't really dating or anything—and I think Joanna and I both know that we're better off as friends. What about you and Marcos? Anything going on there?"

"No." I shook my head and shifted awkwardly. "What do you think's happening out there?" I asked, nodding toward the tent's door.

"I'm not sure. But I did hear last night that they're doing a big morning thing and then going back to get your mom."

"A big morning thing?"

"Like last night—a big party. I guess it's a brunch?"

Alex and I looked at each other and then laughter just poured out of us—hysterical, tension-dissipating laughter. It felt great—really warm and fluid, like bathwater. I fell back onto the sleeping bag and let the good feeling run over me.

I knew I shouldn't be laughing, but I couldn't stop. Alex climbed into his own sleeping bag, but the whole side, the side closest to me, was unzipped, and I could see his long body stretched out along the gap. He flipped onto his side and looked at me, with his head on his hand.

Alex reached out to me for an awkward lying down hug, but then didn't let go. He pulled me closer, underneath the top layer of his sleeping bag, so that there was basically no room between us. It didn't feel friendly; it felt tingly. I was nervous. I knew that whatever it was that Alex and I were doing here was brand new to me. I'd never kissed anyone or anything. And I was seventeen, practically voting age. *So pathetic*, I thought. *Stop now before you irreparably embarrass yourself.* I knew that I probably should, for lots of reasons: Ida, Mom, being in the middle of nowhere with a bunch of lunatics. But all of that fell away with the only nonlunatic for miles all snuggled up with me. *Listen to yourself—snuggled up!* I thought. *Could you be any more juvenile?*

But, pressed into Alex like that, I didn't feel juvenile at all. It was like my body was filled with radio signals, like all of these secret messages were being sent—messages to open up. So I did. I opened my arms and my legs and wrapped them around Alex. He sort of shifted me up so that our faces were almost as close as the rest of our bodies.

He put his hand on my cheek and then his mouth on mine. And then I just unlocked, letting my body send these silent messages to Alex's body, messages that I didn't seem to control at all. It was so easy, the opening and warming. After a few tentative seconds, I wanted more of it. I wanted all of it, this reaching up and into another body. It felt like magic. *How did I not know about this?* I thought. If I'd thought the noise at the Silver Saddle was shaking me loose, kissing Alex was like a car accident— turning something over that shouldn't be turned over and knocking something down that should never be knocked down. Everywhere Alex touched me—on my face and on my arms and then under my shirt across my back—I felt the warmth and the opening rushing up to his hands, like my cells were flinging open the doors. I couldn't help but touch him, too.

I reached under his shirt and felt the solid, smooth warmth there. It was thrillingly different from my own softness. And as I turned into him I was giddy from his tallness, his non-girly smell, the rough sound of his breathing. All of it was so different from me. *He* was so different from me. And then I realized there was something beyond the radio signals and the touching—it was the reaching into another person who wasn't me. Who was a vacation from me. I pulled back my head from all of the kissing and looked at Alex's lovely face. I could tell that he wanted to say something.

Maybe he wanted to talk more. But I didn't. I really, really didn't. I only wanted that beyond-verbal diving. Only feeling. I wanted to climb back into Alex and feel those normal thrills of the body. I wanted to confirm that even though my mind was running off, my body still worked, could still be normal, could still feel good.

While it was happening, it was great. I felt that tingling—but better, more—and a joyful ferocity that I could never generate on my own. I was grateful for Alex and all of his skin against all of my skin. But I also knew that it wasn't normal, that it wasn't supposed to happen that way—under the darkness of a disaster, with a person you're only partly sure of, only minutes after kissing another human for the first time. I knew it wasn't normal, but I didn't care, and that made me feel guilty. I knew it wasn't fair to Alex, what had happened. I had been trying to do something very different from what he'd been trying to do. I should have pulled back. I should have said, "It's best that you leave." A good person would have said it.

But I didn't. I wanted to feel everything. I didn't know when I'd get another chance.

"Allo?" A voice called from outside of the tent.

Alex and I raised our eyebrows in unison. I rolled away from him a little. "Yes?" I asked.

Alex started to laugh again, but then clapped a hand over his mouth.

"Good morning. Ulrike speaking. Please to come with me."

"Just a second," I called.

Ulrike was silent. Alex and I stood up and tried to make each other presentable. Alex straightened my shirt and kissed me on the forehead. We walked out holding hands, and Ulrike didn't say anything about it.

While Alex and I had been trying to climb into each other, the camp had fully awakened. Some people were already bent over their cook fires, roaring under the morning sun. Others were still getting ready for the day, spot washing themselves with scraps of cloth and water from the large plastic jugs. We weren't the best smelling group, that was for sure.

"Are we meeting with Laurel?" Alex asked.

"*Van* and Laurel," Ulrike corrected. "Then ceremony and get the prophet."

"Sounds good," Alex said as we rounded a cluster of tents and approached the tepee. It looked a lot less ceremonious in the daytime—the paintings along the side that had seemed relatively authentic the night before were embarrassingly crude under the sun. Alex held the flap open for us, and Ulrike stretched her arm across the opening, like human caution tape to keep Alex out.

"Okay, I get it. I'm going to find Marine, I guess," Alex called over Ulrike's shoulder.

I nodded and headed deeper into the smoke-filled tent. Laurel was sprawled across the floor of the tepee. It looked very much like she'd slept there, and not alone, either. Half-open sleeping bags and tons of clothing were strewn across the floor. There was nothing spiritual about it—it looked no more glamorous than the squats Mom and I had slept in a long time ago. And Laurel looked no better than the average squatter herself. Divested of her ceremonial garb, she appeared incredibly puny. An oversized pair of sweatpants and a ratty T-shirt with Goddess Bless This Mess printed across the front made her body look almost concave. Her white hair had been mussed in the night into an Andy Warholesque do. She half reclined against a large blue cooler and held a hand over her eyes.

"Good morning, Van." Her voice was gravel-rough—nothing close to the Nina Simone–like recording Marine had played on loop at the Silver Saddle. She waved Ulrike out, so that we were alone together. I thought about how crazy it was that I could feel so different alone-in-a-tent with Laurel than I had alone-in-a-tent with Alex.

"Did you get some rest?" she asked.

I nodded.

"That's good. You're going to need your stamina today. We'll have another ceremony, and, when the sun is at its highest," here, she pointed up to the sky, revealing her reddened eyes, "we'll retrieve Sofia."

"Okay."

"Just you, Ulrike, and me."

"Oh," I said. "I thought it would be everybody."

"No," she replied, and sprang to her feet. "They will stay here, preparing to rejoice."

"Sure," I said, nodding. "What about Marine? Is she coming?"

"I wanted to have a brief word with you, too, about Marine, and about Sofia's role here once she returns with our message." She moved so close that I could taste her smell in my mouth. It was not good.

"I wanted to talk about *your* role here, too, from now on."

"I'm sorry?"

"You *belong* to us now—that is, you belong to Sofia, and she is of the greatest importance to us. She's our prophet."

"Your bank, you mean," I muttered.

"Now, Van. Stop teasing. We'll work together, to bring this message to any who will hear us. You and Sofia will work hardest of all."

"What message, exactly, is that?" I asked.

Laurel cackled, the broken hysterical laugh of a vaudeville crone. "Oh!" she said, slapping my arm. "You're such a hoot! It's going to be wonderful to have you around. Why, you'll be the very first to know the message when we round up Sofia."

"Oh, right," I said, but *Jesus, dear Jesus, help me,* was what I thought. I'd talked myself into believing that Laurel was loopy but not dangerous, a temporary sidetrack in our lives. Not my long-term life planner. *What could I say?* I wondered. *You're insane and I'm leaving?* I needed Laurel to show me where we'd left Mom, and I had a feeling she wasn't going to react well to any kind of defiance.

Get out of here slowly; don't let her suspect a thing. The element of surprise is all you have going for you right now, I told myself.

"Well, I'm pretty hungry, Laurel." It was true. The first rule of lying, Mom always said, was tell the truth whenever you can.

"Of course." Laurel brushed off my shoulder fondly. "One more thing I wanted to discuss this morning." She paused. "Marine. And your friend."

"Alex?"

"How long can we expect him to stay with us?"

"Oh, not long. He has to go back for classes. He's in college."

"I see," she said. "Well, we are always looking to add to our family. If he decides to stay on, we have a wonderful purification committee that can help him transition to life here."

"Purification committee?"

Laurel nodded with such vigor, it seemed a danger to her twig-like neck. "They are spectacular. Of course, most of our cases are simple, but every once in a while you get a stubborn one. Like Marine," Laurel sighed. "We've had to tolerate her—because Sofia was so fond of her—but, now that the prophet is truly one of us, we can dispose of Marine."

"I thought you were old friends." I tried to say it casually, lightly.

"Yes, and it was my great wish that Marine would join us, but she's been," Laurel paused, squinting up at me, "*challenging* me.

You know—*resistant*. Even the purification committee couldn't make progress with her. Although, I suppose we could give it one more shot, right?" Laurel smacked my arm with a tiny karate chop. "They've been doing wonderful things with hair removal."

"Excuse me?" I wasn't sure if I was hallucinating, or what. I probably hadn't been drinking enough water.

"You know, where they extract the hairs of the body, one by one. They can be quite persuasive, and so *creatively*."

I kind of doubled over, there was such sudden fear in my gut.

"Well that's good to hear," I said. "But, I'm sure Alex is leaving, so, he probably won't be needing any purification." I thought I might vomit from the panic. *Were they going to try to purify* me*? Is that what they'd done to Mom?* My legs twitched with the need to move away from Laurel. I had to find Alex and Marine and send them to get help.

"I'm going to get some food, but I'm sure I'll see you later," I told Laurel.

"Undoubtedly." Laurel bared her teeth in what was not exactly a smile.

I ducked out of the tent and tried not to run while I scanned the camp for Alex and Marine. I was walking at a normal pace, but my brain was like a pinball—my neural pathways were going to disintegrate at the rate and volume my thoughts barreled down them.

I spotted Marine first, hanging her washing on a communal line. It was that bright bob of hair, the artificial red glinting under the sun as it turned back and forth, that caught my eye.

"Mar*ine*," I said, trying to moderate the level of my voice so that I wasn't shouting. But I still wanted to convey my fury with her, for introducing us to Laurel in the first place.

She looked up, her silt-dark eyes narrowed in confusion. I hustled over, and, as I approached, I realized she was already talking to Alex.

"What the *hell*?" I hissed. I reached out to both her and Alex, taking hold of fistfuls of their shirts and pulling them toward me.

"What?" Marine asked.

"Seriously? *What?*" I angry-whispered. I looked over my shoulder and out over Marine's, just to make sure none of Laurel's followers were within hearing distance.

"I thought you'd be pleased. I convinced Laurel that you should be part of the group going to bring back Sofia. She didn't tell you?"

"Oh, she told me. She told me a lot of things. Marine, just—" I turned my eyes to the sky, bright blue cracked through with wisps of cloud. I wondered how much to tell or ask her. I still couldn't figure out if she was really on our side or not, although I figured she kind of had to be now, since Laurel had torture plans for her and all.

"Please, just be straight with me. How could you bring my mom here? What do you think the deal with all of these *people* is?" I wiggled my fingers at my temple to connote loose-brained nonsense.

"First of all, your mother *wanted* to come here. She *insisted*. Surely you know that when Sofia wants something it's impossible to say no. And well, I trust Laurel," Marine whispered cautiously. "She's been my friend since we were very young."

"Okay, and when you met her, was it in a mental hospital?" I felt the slap in each word as I said it.

"No," Marine said. "A rehab facility."

Wow. I hadn't actually expected it to be anything like that.

"Laurel and I were in recovery together, and we both decided to become healers at about the same time. Laurel was good, very nuanced—her instincts were never wrong. If someone had a problem, she was so sensitive. She made them forget they had this problem at the same time she made them improve." Marine's voice was back at normal speaking level. "So I brought Sofia to her—"

"Shh-shh-shh," I parroted the way Ida had hushed me for years.

"I brought Sofia to her," Marine repeated in a whisper, "because I thought she could help. But . . . Laurel is not quite . . . the same."

"Well, you probably won't be too surprised to hear that Laurel has big plans for Mom and me. Big *long-term* plans."

"What do you mean?" Alex asked.

"I mean that she said to me, just now, that she expects Mom *and me* to stay on with the organization. Permanently."

"Are you sure that's what she meant?" Alex asked.

"Oh I'm sure. And she definitely wanted to make sure you'd be out of the way, Marine." I pointed toward her throat.

"She did?" Marine looked genuinely shocked.

"I'm sorry, but yeah," I answered. "I know our plan was to roll on out of here when my mom, I don't know—" I hunted for the right word, but fell short. "Came to. But I don't think it's going to work out like that. I think you both need to get out of here. I mean it—Laurel is fixing to harm you guys!"

"Fixing to harm us?" Alex smiled.

"It's not funny! She's talking about *torture*, and *purification committees*." I whispered it as fiercely as I could.

"Well, yeah, that's disturbing," Alex said, all humor gone. "But, all the more reason we need to stay and help you."

"No offense, guys, but I think we're going to need more help than just the two of you. Serious, *serious* help." I shook my head, trying to clear things up in there.

"You mean the police?" Marine said.

"I don't know." I felt my face crumple the way Alex's did. "Maybe Chantal, or someone from the Silver Saddle? This seems like something she would know how to fix."

"Do you want me to call her?" Alex asked. We had dropped the whispering, but still kept our voices low. I flicked my gaze to the outermost corners of my vision, to make sure we were still alone.

"No, I want you to go *get* her. Or *someone.* I want you to check on Ida. I need to know what's going on," I said, my voice crackling with urgency. I realized how bossy it all sounded after it was out in the air between our three faces. But I didn't care. "And Marine," I said, equally bossily. "You need to go with Alex, and show him how to get out of here." I sounded like Mom on the phone, I thought. I felt kind of pleased about it until I saw how miserable Marine looked. "Look, I really don't think it's safe for either of you to be here on your own. You have to do this, Marine. Please. I don't know what you feel like you owe us right now, but please, I'm begging you. I *cannot* live here!" My voice had climbed into the screech zone. Alex and Marine both shushed me and Alex rubbed my back.

"Of course I'll go with Alex, if that's what you want," Marine began. "But I think someone should stay and help you here. Don't you think I should do that?" she asked Alex.

"Please, go with Alex. I told you, Laurel is trying to *get rid of* you. There's no way you'd be able to help here. At least in Vegas you can check on Ida while he explains to Chantal. It'll be so much faster. Please, please?" I could feel full-fledged, hysterical crying swell underneath the skin of my face.

"All right, Van."

"You guys have to leave right now. Like this instant." I grabbed both of their arms and practically swung between them like a little kid between her parents.

"What? Van, no. Not when you're this upset," Alex said. "Right?" He directed this last word to Marine. I looked into Marine's enormous eyes and tried one of mine and Ida's mind melds: *this-is-serious-come-on-come-on-come-on-get-out-of-here-now-bring-help*. I wanted them gone before I drew more attention from the camp. I could feel myself unraveling. I must have looked pretty desperate, or maybe the mind meld worked. Marine nodded at me.

"Take my phone," she said. "It has a little battery left. I don't know if you can get reception anywhere, but keep it turned off unless it's really an emergency."

I fought the urge to roll my eyes.

"I don't want to leave you like this," Alex said, holding my hand.

"I'll be fine. Please, we need more help. And I need to know how Ida's doing." I wanted them to leave so I could get to raving and crying already.

"It's a long walk," Marine said. "Do you have any water?"

Alex shook his head, but looked at me the whole time Marine spoke.

"I'm going to go get some," she said. "And then we'll go. Maybe we can make it back here before tomorrow morning." As she walked away, I noticed that her movements were all tense and jerky.

"I really hope so," I said.

"We'll be quick," Alex replied, looking down at my throat, and I looked at his chin. It's hard to look into someone's eyes when you're standing so close. It was all so awkward and terrible.

I wanted to remember that morning in the tent with Alex, but I also just couldn't stand to think about it. I knew how strange that was. Any sane, normal girl wouldn't have been able to *stop* obsessing over that morning with him.

Alex ran his hands up my arms and set one lightly on each side of my neck.

"Van?"

"Yeah?" My eyes were still on the squared-off end of Alex's chin.

"I just think you're great. And that you can do anything." He leaned in and kissed me, but less intensely. It wasn't a climbing-into-you kiss, but it was still warm and made me feel like what he'd said was true.

"Thanks," I said as we hugged. "You too."

"Call if you and your mom escape first, okay? If I never have to come back here, that would be great."

"No pressure or anything," I said. Every word hummed with hysteria. I was shocked that I was making sense. *Is this how it feels for Mom?* I wondered.

I heard Marine shuffling her feet behind me. At least I hoped it was Marine.

"Ready?" she asked.

"Yes," Alex and I said at the same time.

Chapter Twenty-One

I didn't move from the spot they left me standing in until they—and the trail—twisted out of my sight. I took a deep breath. *You can do this*, I thought. *You're smarter than all of these people here.* I was surprised and a little embarrassed when the thought came to me, but also immediately soothed by how true it seemed.

I just hoped the Mom I found with Laurel in a couple of hours was the right Mom, and not the monster I'd met my first night in the camp. I hid Marine's phone in the waistband of my pants—it was invisible under my sweatshirt. Laurel wouldn't know I had it unless she had some kind of communal bath planned. I wandered back toward the middle of camp. The central bonfire had already been built back up, and so had Laurel. She looked washed and brushed since our earlier discussion, and her billowing white robes were back on. They were dingier, though, and freckled with red dust.

Laurel strode around, pointing at people, with Carapace and Ulrike on her heels. Again, Carapace carried his breakfast-in-bed tray, and Laurel grabbed something from it every once in a while to hand off to someone around the fire. There were braided vines, hanging down like beads at a fortuneteller's, that separated a small area from the rest. Behind the curtain of vines there was some kind of altar. One of the tablecloths had been draped over a boulder, and candles of various heights burned on the magenta and black surface. A few items were laid out, but casually, like they'd been thrown there: a cell phone, the thin chain of a gold necklace in a little lumpy pile, and a ring of braided *hair* rested in the middle. The necklace looked very familiar—the pendant on it was not actually a pendant but a wedding ring. It was Mom's wedding ring. *It was an altar to Mom.*

I stopped walking; I couldn't move any farther without feeling dizzy. *Jesus, is that her actual hair?* I didn't want to get any closer to find out. *Just get through whatever this is.* If talking to myself before had been comforting and even motivating, here, beside Mom's shrine, it was the reverse. *I'm going insane,* I thought. *Maybe they gave me some kind of hallucinogen while I was in the tepee. Maybe I didn't even notice it. And if so, this isn't any fun at all. It's the complete opposite of fun.*

The entire camp had gathered around the altar in a dense, stinking clot. I heard a tambourine somewhere, over the drums and the chanting. I tried to focus on that one sound, to zero in on the least sinister thing in the realm of my senses. *It's just a tambourine. You can do this.*

Laurel climbed up onto the altar; Carapace and Ulrike boosted her up. The chanting stopped but the drumming continued—so did the tambourine, thank God. I tried to breathe along with its benign rattle while Laurel waved her arms.

"Spirits!" she shouted up into the hot blue sky.

"Spirits!" repeated the campers all around me.

"Ancestors!"

"Ancestors!" Laurel's followers did not have a lot of call-and-response experience. Their repetition of her invocations was sloppy and ragged, almost like they were blurring the words instead of strengthening them.

"Masters of the cosmos!"

"Masters of the cosmos!"

I'd been pushed up close to the fire, and my throat hurt from the smoke.

"We seek your blessings and guidance as we strike out into the wilderness to greet our prophet! Carapace!" Laurel shouted this practically into Carapace's face. "Bring the offering!"

Oh God, I thought, *she's going to slaughter a lamb.*

Mercifully, Carapace did not bring Laurel any living creature. His breakfast-in-bed tray was filled with polished copper bowls, and, by the way he carried it low against his thighs, you could tell it was heavy. Ulrike handed up the first bowl.

"Honey!" Laurel shouted.

"Honey!" repeated her campers.

Laurel turned the bowl over and a thin amber stream fell into the sand below the altar. Ulrike traded her a fresh bowl for the empty one.

"Wine!" Laurel called.

"Wine!-ine! Wi!" shouted the others.

She poured the wine over the honey—it was red wine, and not quite purple enough *not* to look like blood. Ulrike passed her a third bowl, then a fourth—milk in one and saffron threads in the other. The empty bowls were stacked at Ulrike's feet in a woozy-looking, sticky copper tower.

The rank puddle at the altar's base looked a little less like vomit thanks to the saffron. It looked like a pile of delicate autumn leaves covering a pool of vomit.

"We invoke the blessing of fire," Laurel called out to us. "We work under the guidance of the sun and the moon. Sofia has received our message in their light. Now," she said, bending over to retrieve the ring of hair. "We pay tribute to fire!"

Carapace procured the crème brûlée blowtorch from his ceremonial tool belt and handed it to Ulrike, who passed it to Laurel. She flicked the cap of the torch open and pressed the button to ignite it, but nothing happened. She banged the base of the torch against the heel of her hand and tried again; still nothing. She turned to Carapace in a huff, speaking to him in a low voice the rest of us couldn't hear. Already-tan Carapace flushed a dangerous, hypertensive red. He shook the torch, fiddled with something on the side, and then had it burning.

Laurel touched the ring of hair to the flame, and it blazed up immediately. She dropped it onto the puddle of honey, wine, milk, and saffron. I pinched my nose shut and breathed through my mouth, willing the wind to take the smell of burning hair, to take Laurel, to take all of these people, somewhere else.

The chanting had devolved into a kind of roaring. A breeze moved around some of the stench from things-that-should-not-be-burning. I closed my eyes and let the clean air wash over me. I hadn't realized how sweaty I was. I reached under my shirt and felt my skin slick with it. No wonder I was so dizzy.

Part of me wanted to run after Alex and Marine, to cut my losses with Mom. Maybe I'd live with Ida, maybe I'd try something normal with Alex. Mom could find her way back alone, eventually. But, as I broke free from the massive, sweating group, I knew where my place was—and it wasn't anywhere normal.

I'd have to get back to Laurel and walk with her. I'd have to talk to her and not betray my plan to escape. The campers broke into a series of loose knots around the altar. I found Ulrike's cool blonde head in the crowd and decided to hover near her.

From where I stood, I watched Laurel and Carapace ladle out oatmeal at the head of a long, cloth-covered table. Hundreds of hands passed around bright blue paper bowls of mush. Since I was still on the outermost edge, I had no one to pass to when the man in front of me held out a bowl. So I took it and actually ate it. Despite the lingering acrid smell of burning hair—and despite the psychological ramifications of watching some lunatic cult leader light your mom's hair on fire—I was incredibly hungry. It had been days since I'd eaten properly. I thought about Carol and Joanna, about how I really missed them. It was embarrassing, how much I missed them. I wondered what Carol would have said to these people.

After all of the pouring and burning, I was surprised by how unceremoniously Ulrike, Laurel, and I left. Ulrike gathered me up while I was still hanging around the others, trying to figure out where they were throwing away their garbage.

"Now we go," she said, her accent chopping each word off at its last letter. She wore a small backpack and carried one of the ubiquitous jugs of water. She smacked me on the back and steered me toward the tepee where Laurel stood, surrounded by hangers-on. Carapace held the tent flap open, worrying the dirt with his foot, dejected.

Laurel smoothed her bleached-white hair down as she nodded and smiled at her campers. They flurried around her, kissing her cheeks and pressing her hands to their hearts. Watching Laurel preen under their attention really drove home the appeal of cult leadership. Sure there had to be a lot of nonsense and drama, but there was also this other part: being widely, fiercely beloved. For a second I imagined it was me under the attention of all of these campers, and then I realized, if Mom and I stayed on here, it *could* be me—prophet's daughter and all. *Have you lost your mind? Knock it off!* I told myself.

Laurel gathered her robes around her and lifted them out of the sand, delicately, like some merchant's wife in a renaissance painting. Without saying anything, Ulrike and I flanked her and we set off down the trail. When we were out of sight of the camp, Laurel slung the bulk of her robes over her shoulder, revealing a pair of purple running shorts and painfully skinny legs.

"How long do you think, Ulrike?" Laurel asked.

Ulrike squinted up at the sky, tilting back her golden head. "Forty minutes?" she replied. She looked at me doubtfully.

"What?" I said.

"Nothing, nothing. Ulrike just wants to make sure we are on time. It's a delicate process."

I stepped into Laurel's yielding footprints on the path where the trail narrowed. The path moved up, and there were a few difficult places where jagged rock formations clambered out of the ground into the middle of the track. Ulrike stood at the base of each of these obstacles and gave Laurel, then me, a hand climbing over. We waited for her on the other side, watching as she practically leapt over them and took her spot back at the head of our triad.

"Van," Laurel interrupted, "I didn't see your friend this morning."

"Who, Alex?"

"Yes, that handsome tall boy."

I shrugged, trying to convey no-big-deal-he's-not-that-handsome-whatever.

"Yeah, he went back for classes."

"Well, that's a relief," she said.

I just shrugged again. I was beginning to understand the beauty of shrugging—it was a really effective way not to communicate something you were trying to hide.

The trunks of the juniper trees we passed began to look twisted, a sign, Laurel noted, that we were approaching the vortex.

"It's there," Ulrike said, and pointed through a blur of leaves at the ring of stones that had contained last night's fire. As we pushed through a bit of brush, I saw the ledge we'd left Mom on. I saw a scrap of her white robes caught in a tree branch. I saw her still-full jug of water. What I didn't see, was her.

"Sofia!" Laurel called, at first playfully, but when she noticed the fear on Ulrike's tanned face, she began to call with more urgency. "Sofia! If you can hear me, call back! Sofia!"

Ulrike immediately pounced onto the ledge and shook her head. She started to climb up the rock face, hopping on to whichever narrow footholds she could find. She looked out over us, over the trees, and shook her head again.

"Do you?" Laurel cleared her throat and looked at me. "Do you think it's the vortex?"

Ulrike jumped down from the five-foot drop and landed like a superhero, in a crouch but with her head up, looking right at us.

"Not vortex," she said. "We look. Or we call rangers."

"No, we're not calling any rangers," Laurel said, biting her thumb. She looked from Ulrike to me. "Maybe she just needs a little more time. Surely the spirits will guide her back to us."

"She no has water," Ulrike pointed out.

I was breathing too fast. *Calm down*, I thought. I sat down in the dirt. I just couldn't stand up anymore. Ulrike patted me on the shoulder.

"I go look. You stay."

"Wonderful, Ulrike," Laurel gushed. "Do you want a blessing before you leave?"

"No, thank you," Ulrike said, and bounded away, her hands holding on to the straps of her backpack.

Laurel didn't sit down. She walked around me in circles, and then started moving back and forth from the edge of the trail to the circle of stones that had contained the fire. She peered into the ring and scanned the ashes there.

"Nothing!" she called back to me, as if that would make me feel better. As if "nothing" didn't already sum up Mom's chances out in the wilderness. Nothing was exactly what she had. Just as I began to wonder if Ulrike had been swallowed up by the vortex, she came crashing into the micro clearing where we waited.

"No prophet," she said. "I think get rangers."

"Ulrike," Laurel began, visibly flustered, "I told you, *nobody* is getting any rangers. Don't *worry*!" She gave a tight, nervous laugh. "It's not like I didn't have a plan for this." She looked around, her head like an owl's, scanning and searching the panorama of the clearing. Her gaze landed on me, like *Aha*. Like an exclamation point. "Van!"

"Yes?"

"Please stand."

I unfolded my legs and pushed myself up, but I didn't walk over to Laurel, which I could tell was what she wanted. Ulrike took a swig of water from her jug and wiped her mouth with the back of her hand.

"I know exactly what we'll do. In times like this, spirit speaks to spirit. Sofia's energy will respond to your energy," Laurel said, in a *like-duh* kind of tone.

"Okay, so you want me to call out to her?"

"Well, yes, that's part of it." Laurel put her palms together like she was praying in a regular church. She pressed her lined-up fingers against her nose and mouth. "I want you to *go out* to her." Because she was talking around her hands, I wasn't sure if I'd heard her correctly.

"You want me to go out to her, like out, out?" I asked. "You mean, like, into the *wilderness* here?"

Laurel nodded contentedly. "That's exactly what I mean! You, our prophet's daughter," and here she put her hands territorially on my arms, "will find the prophet! Why, you're like a Sofia GPS! A homing device."

"I don't think those are the same things," I said, but tried to think as I talked to her. My ideas spun out in parallel lines as I

206

struggled to keep the conversation with Laurel going. "Do you really think I'll be able to do that?"

But I thought, *Maybe this is the best thing that could happen here. I have Marine's cell phone; I'll get reception; I'll call the damn rangers; they'll send some kind of helicopter, or whatever; everything will be okay.*

"I *know* you'll be able to do it!" Laurel said. "And while you look, Ulrike and I will go back to camp and organize a search party."

"She has no woodsmanship," Ulrike interrupted.

Woodsmanship?

"She doesn't need woodsmanship," Laurel said, waving away Ulrike's concern. "She has her spirit guides. Leave her that water, though."

Ulrike dropped the jug in the sand and heaved off her olive-green backpack. "Here," she said, handing over the bag. "You take." I nodded and put the backpack on.

"Always, you back here." Ulrike stamped her foot on the ground, and I stamped mine in reply.

"Okay."

"You go," here Ulrike waggled her pointer and middle fingers back and forth like a tiny pair of legs, "you leave something."

"Um, okay." I didn't know what she meant, but the sooner I got them both out of there, the better.

Ulrike waved her hands in the air like she was wiping something out. "*Nein, nein, nein,*" she said. She looked around the clearing and pulled a fistful of twigs from a low-hanging tree branch. She waved me over and I followed, watching. She mimed walking—taking a few mincing steps—and then stuck a twig in the earth. Then she took a few more steps and planted twig after twig until she arrived at the stone circle. She feigned confusion, throwing her hands in the air, in supplication to the spirits or whatever.

Suddenly, Ulrike smiled and stuck her pointer finger into the air and then tapped at her temple. She shaded her eyes with her hand and pretended to be searching for a contact lens or something. When she discovered the first twig, she shouted "Ah!" and followed the trail back to me. "Yes?" she asked.

"Yes, Hansel and Gretel, I get it."

"*Jawohl! Hansel und Gretel!*" she said. "Okay," Ulrike called to Laurel.

"I think I should do a brief blessing, and then you can be on your way." Laurel scanned the clearing for something, anything she could use in the blessing. A wide smile broke out over her face. "Ah!" she shouted, jumping in the air a little. "The blood of the tree!" She pulled on my arm and we walked to a small pine tree oozing milky sap down one side of its trunk. "Please, close your eyes."

I heard Laurel whisper, and even Ulrike muttered a bit.

"Now you may open them." Laurel's voice was still a whisper. Her hands were smeared with sap. She rubbed the place on my forehead between my eyes and on quarter-sized spots on the back of each hand.

"Spirit," she intoned, "I anoint this child, the daughter of our prophet. May her spirit guides keep watch through the day and the night, through all of her days and all of her nights."

Just get them out of here so I can call for help.

"Thanks a lot, Laurel," I said, trying to whip some sincerity into my voice. "I can feel them guiding me already." I gestured to the sticky, piney places on my hands and forehead.

Laurel beamed. Ulrike did not.

"We'll leave you to it, then. Don't worry." Laurel paused to place a bony hand on my shoulder. "I'll be journeying today, so if you have any questions, or need help, just concentrate on my energy."

"We come back with search party," Ulrike said, running search and party together in a roguish portmanteau.

"Absolutely," I said. "Thanks again. Bye, Laurel! Bye, Ulrike!" I turned away from them and decided to walk up the trail a bit. I listened to their egress, to twigs snapping under their feet and the clatter of pebbles that rolled out of their path. Ulrike's backpack was light, but the jug of water was pulling my arm out of its socket. I figured I'd consolidate the one into the other, but not before I took a drink—*Don't forget, Van,* I told myself, *it's the desert.*

Chapter Twenty-Two

I was feeling optimistic. I didn't know much about cell phone reception, but reaching the highest ground I could get to was probably the best idea. I thought briefly about looking for Mom on my own, but quickly dismissed it. Ulrike was right—I had no woodsmanship and would almost certainly get lost. I aimed to stay as close to the trail as I could. I'd find some kind of marker to tell the park rangers about, and then, once I had a location to give them, I'd climb up—and hopefully only slightly away—from the path to get a signal and make the call. I just wanted to make sure the authorities showed up before Laurel's search party.

The path wasn't well maintained. Piles of brush blocked the way in some places, and the ubiquitous agave plants spiked out into the trail. Every once in a while, I passed a small pile of rocks covered with chicken wire. I figured that they were markers of some kind, but there was no information on them: no numbers, no coordinates, nothing. I was definitely on a trail, so there had to be a beginning or an end, some place I would find a plaque or a name. Maybe I would run into some real hikers. That didn't seem likely though, as Laurel and her group appeared to have selected this particular location in the canyon for its remoteness.

I decided to walk a little more, but if I didn't reach the end, or some other trail soon, I'd make the call. It was getting hot, and I'd already stopped twice for swigs from the water jug. I was covered in sweat, and the plastic was so slippery in my hands that I almost dropped the jug and lost my entire water supply. It was then, I guess, that I realized how vulnerable I was alone on the trail. I had to make that call—I knew I wasn't going to find anything helpful. I struck out from the path in the direction that sloped up.

When I could just barely see the trail, I tripped and fell too close to an agave plant and tore open my hand on the spikes. The blood ran fast at first, and I pressed the wound to my shirt to make it stop.

Jesus, what if there are mountain lions and they smell my blood? My body began to hum with panic. *Just get to a place where you can make the call,* I told myself. I pressed my bloody hand to my chest and climbed up as fast as I could, without tripping or falling down on my face. I could feel the blood seep through the fibers of my shirt and felt the wetness over my heart. I stopped and looked around; I had no idea where I was. *Shit, shit, shit. What if I faint from blood loss?* I wondered. I pulled my hand away from my chest and looked at it carefully.

The bleeding had slowed down, but the wound stung when I held it in the air. The compression definitely helped, but I didn't have anything to bind it with. I grabbed for Marine's phone and switched it on. A dour 4% blinked out at me and a tiny "no service" frowned out from the top right corner of the screen.

I turned off the phone, pressing the power button too hard, so hard I was surprised the plastic rectangle didn't snap under my fingers. Drops of sweat gathered behind my ears and at the back of my neck. I swiped them away with my not-bleeding hand.

Stop being dramatic, I told myself. *You aren't really bleeding anymore.* I wondered if maybe there was some first-aid kit in Ulrike's backpack, or even an extra T-shirt. I unzipped the bag with my good hand and took another drink. I noticed that the level of water in the jug had gone down to almost half. How had I drunk that much? I looked for something, some secret pocket maybe, but there was nothing really: just a pen, a compass, and a protein bar.

I zipped Ulrike's bag closed and kept climbing up. When I let my injured hand swing by my side naturally, it started to drip blood again. Little red drops fell from my fingers and into the dirt. I folded my forearm back over my chest, like I was giving a pledge. It wasn't easy to stay balanced walking like that, with Ulrike's bag banging against my back.

My legs were starting to hurt, too. The muscles in my thighs and calves cramped up almost as soon as I hit an especially steep patch. *Just keep going until you can't go anymore, then turn the phone on again.* The pep talk didn't work. I had to stop right away. I had to try again. I eased off the backpack and stretched my arms. I pulled out Marine's phone and said a prayer into it. *Please God, please anyone, please phone, please satellites, please, please, please.*

I turned the phone on, this time as gently as I could. The battery flashed out 2%, and one, tiny, goddess-blessed, beautiful bar winked out at me. I dialed 911 and pressed the phone to my ear, walking up the grade just a bit more, trying to coax a little more reception out of the phone. After a sickening silence, I heard a stuttering ring.

"Nine one one, what is your emergency?" A woman's voice crackled on the other end.

"Yes!" I shouted. "Thank you, yes!"

"Hello?"

"Yes, hello! I'm lost on a hiking trail!"

"Hello?"

"Hello? Hello! Can you hear me?"

"Hello? I can barely hear you."

"I'm lost on a hiking trail in Sedona, but I don't know where! My mother and I are lost!" I shouted everything, hoping that all of my urgency would make the reception better.

"Hello? Can you repeat that?"

"Yes! I'm lost on a hiking trail in Sedona!" I waited for the woman's voice, but didn't hear it again. "Hello?" The phone was dead in my hand. I screamed out into the canyon. The sound that came out of me didn't sound like something that could come out of a person. It was the sound you would expect from a furious dinosaur. I threw Marine's phone down toward the trail, hoping that if it landed somewhere other humans were, they'd try to figure out where it came from. I knew that the likelihood of anyone finding that phone—or Mom, or me—was practically zero.

I hated Laurel for starting this whole mess, and I hated Marine for bringing Mom into it. I hated Alex for going back to Vegas, and I hated Mom for being so much trouble. I even hated Ida for not being awake. I hated myself most of all for hating the rest of them, for not being smarter or more elevated or whatever. *If you were Mom, in her right mind, you could get out of here. What would Mom do?* I wondered.

Mom didn't have any woodsmanship either, but she was resourceful. I tried to pretend to be Mom. I traced back the way she made decisions. Always, she started with nothing: silence, stillness, darkness. So in the tangle of branches and leaves, and plants that could make a person bleed, I sat down and closed my eyes. Even just not moving anymore felt better. There was something so desperate about my hike up to get reception. Being still was like a bizarre and morbid reconciling, a well-here-we-are-and-this-might-be-it.

Think about what you do have and what you do know.

I had the water at least, which was good, except that I'd been gulping it down like some dehydrated buffalo. I had Ulrike's compass, which was great, except I had no idea where I was or what direction the camp or parking lot or civilization was in. I had a protein bar, which, again, was great, but seemed more like prolonging the inevitable. *Don't worry, you'll die from dehydration before hunger*, said a voice in my head, sounding suspiciously like Ulrike. Had she said that to me? Was I already going crazy from thirst?

Just take a deep breath, I told myself. *There's plenty of air.* I had Alex and Marine—they were going for help. I'd stupidly told them not to call the police, but at this point I would have gotten an I-love-cops tattoo, that's how badly I wanted to see the police. Surely Alex and Marine would understand how things had gotten out of hand when they came back to the camp. They would know better than to listen to me. If they got back to Vegas that night, checked on Ida, rallied the troops or whatever, and left the next morning—*They could be back in Sedona by tomorrow night*, I told myself. *See, it's really not so bad. You won't die here, probably.* But Mom. She was a different story. She'd been fasting for days, and I had no idea how much water she'd had.

Something muddy and powerful pushed up at the backs of my eyes, something that told me to forget about Mom. I could just leave her here; it would be a lot easier. I'd find my way back to the camp, or to a road. I'd go back to Vegas and go on tour with Carol and Joanna. Ida would be fine, fully recovered—Ida would be all the family I needed.

For a minute it felt good, to think like that. Like Mom gets what she deserves. But the truth was, if I left her there, Mom could die. That would make me a murderer. If Mom had any chance of being saved, I was it. Even if Laurel's search party eventually found her, they could be too late. I couldn't just sit in one spot with my water and Ulrike's power bar and wait for help. I'd have to find Mom, get some water to her as quickly as I could.

But how would I do that? I stood up and considered my options. If I climbed up farther, maybe I'd spot Mom. Maybe I'd see her ridiculous robe flapping in the brush.

My other option was to walk down, to try to find the trail again. More wandering and getting lost even worse. I knew, of the two ideas, this was the inferior, but something deep in my blood seemed to push me in that direction with a million little red cell hands.

The way down was steep, but there were incremental, raised waves built into the rock. I looked for places that were more bare to put my feet. I didn't want to fall face-first into any other carnivorous plants. I resolved not to drink more from my dwindling water supply—I would save all that was there for Mom. My route skewed to the left and an open swath of rock and gravel. The trees and bushes had thinned out, and the view that opened up in front of me was really magnificent.

Cliff sides rose up out of the canyon like frozen swells of water, all bubble smooth, all looking like they could reanimate any second and crash down in rusty waves. My mouth was so dry. Even my eyeballs felt dry.

I desperately wanted to drink, but instead filled my lungs with the thin, high-altitude air and rested my good hand in one of my back pockets. I felt a smooth lump in the denim fabric over the curve of my butt. An image of Carapace's crystal flashed behind my eyelids. I pulled out the tiny stone and held it in my palm—a dark, dull ruby.

I didn't know if I was delirious, but I felt a point of pain on my skin where the stone sat. It was dense and hot, like the glowing end of a heated knitting needle pressing down the center of my palm. For some reason, I wasn't alarmed. It calmed me down in a there-is-something-beyond-you-that-is-going-on-right-now way. I closed my fist around it and had a crazy thought. *I'm going to let this crystal guide me.* It was nuts. I knew how nuts it was, but I did it anyway.

I closed my eyes and waited for that blood-pull. But the directions from the stone weren't like the directions from my instincts. There was a feeling in my fist, like a white-hot arrow shooting forward and slightly to the right. It was as clear and tangible as the arrow on Ulrike's compass buried deep in the backpack.

I opened my eyes and followed it—I couldn't see it or anything, it was more like I could feel it, like a magnet. I felt the place where it faded away, too, and closed my eyes, gripping the crystal in my fist again, waiting for the next arrow. This time it pointed down again and only very slightly to the left. I followed that one, too. And when they ran out of charge, or I got to the end of the arrow or whatever, I checked in with the stone and the next one. I had no idea how many of these arrows I followed. It must have been dozens.

I wasn't paying attention to anything around me—I wasn't looking for clues Mom had left behind, or for the trail. All of my attention was on those arrows; they seemed like my only real resource. When I got my last arrow, I knew it would be the last one. It didn't lose charge. If anything, it gained momentum as I followed it. It got stronger, hotter, brighter as it pointed and flashed: *Over here! Over here! Over here!*

The very last arrow didn't lead me to the trail, and it didn't lead me to Mom. It led me to a dead end: a smooth, copper-colored cliff wall. *There must be some mistake,* I thought as I pushed against the stone. There had to be a crevice or secret passage through a cave or something. Waves of nausea coursed through me, and I held myself up by digging my fingertips into the rock.

I pounded my fists against the stone until my hands hurt—especially the bad one. The cuts from the agave plant opened up again, and I watched stamps of my own blood multiply on the coarse gold surface. I threw the blood-red nub of crystal against the wall and sank to the ground. I must have been crazy, I thought, looking for magic from some phony, Laurel-originated thing. I screamed out, one of those grating, back-of-the-throat screams. I was shaking and dizzy. I looked at my hand. It was bad—a hot, throbbing pain spliced between my fingers, and underneath all of the blood my skin was red, like a sunburn.

I had to figure out where I was. Maybe I'd been walking downhill all along. Maybe the trail was nearby. I felt a chilling certainty that it wasn't. I'd led myself to a sandy pool of open space. On one side, a thicket of pine trees created a dense green barrier. The rock face made up the other side. They curled in toward each other to form an empty, shallow oval. I stepped back to get a better look at the rock face, which, funnily, looked like an actual human face.

A square copper chin rose out of the dirt and eased into a thick pair of lips. There were symmetrical dips in the center, where a kind of nose jutted out. I stepped back even farther to see if there were eyes, too, but there weren't. A narrow ridge protruded in the center of the forehead area, like two gathered brows. It was a masculine face, definitely. I got out only one coherent thought: *weird*—before it happened.

A word boomed from those giant stone lips—a single word, like a crack of thunder—VAN.

Holy shit, holy shit, holy shit pulsed through my body with every pump of my heart. I wasn't made up of muscles and bones and blood; I was just atoms of terror, blinking an incredulous, tremulous rhythm.

Was I supposed to answer? I didn't think I could say anything—not even *help*, not even *holy shit*. Instead, I looked up, trying to get the whole face into the lens of my vision. Was

218

I imagining it? I didn't think so. *The mouth was open.* A slice of space between the rock lips had cracked into existence. Or, I was losing my mind. I rubbed a hand over my eyes, too distracted to realize I was using the injured one. I could feel the blood, hot and sticky, where I smeared it over my face.

Other than the opening in the mouth area, the stone face was unchanged. It was quiet for a few minutes, so quiet that I was certain I'd been daydreaming or hallucinating. I wasn't sure what to do. Keep looking for Mom? Take a rest? Was I already dead? I opened Ulrike's backpack and unscrewed the water jug's cap. I swallowed the smallest possible sip, and it felt pretty real. *Okay,* I thought as I replaced the cap.

VAN, again, that otherworldly thunder cracked through the canyon, echoing around me in waves I could feel lap over my skin. GIVE US YOUR HANDS.

What? I figured I was probably dead at that point, so I might as well go along with it. I put my hands up against the face, gently this time. I didn't have a second thought about it. It was like I knew exactly what the face meant.

CLOSE YOUR EYES, it boomed.

My eyes were closed before I made myself close them, like these instructions were the most natural thing in the world. Like I couldn't resist following them. Like breathing.

When you close your eyes in the daytime, it doesn't feel truly dark. The light from the sky, or lamps in your room, will seep through the skin of your lids. Your eyelids will begin to flutter, too, so much so that it gets hard to keep your eyes closed. Neither of these things happened to me. It was like my eyes were sealed over with tar—a heavy, immovable blackness. Opening them again did not feel possible. It all looked and felt black, like there was nothing.

Then these little drops of light started coming at me, bright light, too—like stars dripping out of a clear, black sky. They fell slowly, the consistency of syrup. I couldn't see my body, but I could feel each bright drop as it hit my skin. They didn't burn or hurt. Each drop felt like a fingertip press, about the same pressure you would need to push an elevator button.

I couldn't hear any sounds outside of me, but the running of my own body was deafening. I imagined it was what a baby hears inside of its mother. The double thunk of my heartbeat was much too loud. It was like I'd gone all tiny and was just a speck inside of myself. The sound was heavy, too, the same way the voice from the face seemed to have physical substance.

I almost forgot about the dripping night sky behind my eyes, until one drop grew and swelled as the others fell normally around it. First it was the size of a golf ball, then a watermelon, then a pony, then a house, then a mountain, and it kept coming—not quickly, still at that leisurely syrup pace—until it dropped right onto me. But I wasn't really me anymore. I was just that speck, subsumed by organs and tissue. The giant amoeba-star-glob fell onto and over the shape of my body with a sickening, lurching slurp. I couldn't see anything then, just brightness. I definitely couldn't hear anything. I felt myself opening my mouth to try to make some kind of sound, but nothing came out. Everything came in. All of that syrupy brightness filled my mouth and pushed down my throat. It streamed in through my nostrils. I tried to clamp my mouth closed, but it was too late. The light kept moving in and through.

The outline of different shapes moved through me. It felt like parts of different faces: the hard cartilage of a nose, the jutting bone of a chin, the stiff brush of an eyebrow, a lush, plump cheek. It was like I was swallowing down all of these faces, like some insatiable cannibal. It didn't hurt or feel bad in any way. It felt like drinking water out under the sun. When I'd consumed all of the faces, the letters started to fall, slowly, languidly—enormous, firework-sized letters, one at a time: a code, a message. COULD YOU FIND ME? Color bloomed out and around the letters, the same magenta that had swirled through Laurel's camp and had been painted on Mom's face. I just watched the letters fall and fall.

I don't know how long I stood there like that, but I knew I was still standing somewhere, because eventually my legs collapsed under me and I dropped with a stinging thud.

Everything went dark. The sky, the voice, the faces, the letters, the light behind my eyes—it all flashed up and then contracted into a pinprick of light, and then, turned into nothing. I was alone, completely alone in the silent dark.

I woke up in daylight. I sat up, expecting to feel like a burn victim, or a pedestrian hit by a car. At the very least, I expected my injured hand to be a real mess. I lifted myself as slowly as I could and actually felt okay. I looked at my legs in my jeans—*maybe I'm paralyzed from the waist down*, I thought. But as I experimentally clenched the muscles in my thighs and calves, I realized I was fine.

I rolled to my side and pushed up to standing. Was I taller? I felt taller. I wanted to find a mirror, certain that something about me was different, probably grotesquely so. What if I had the face of a bird or something? I put a hand up to feel around, and there was my regular face. It felt pretty filthy, but it felt the same—no feathers or beaks. What had happened? Was I dead?

Ulrike's olive-green backpack was covered with dust but still there, so I figured she and Laurel and the camp were real. I didn't think I was dead anymore, because it didn't seem likely that you could bring someone else's belongings to the afterlife with you. My mouth was so dry, it felt like the skin on the insides of my cheeks and on my tongue had broken open. *Maybe just a little water*, I thought, *and then I'll keep looking for Mom.* I unzipped

Ulrike's bag and opened the cap. As I brought the jug to my lips I saw in a cloudy reflection a smear of dried blood streaked across my forehead, cheekbones, and the bridge of my nose. It was blood from the day before, where I'd wiped my mauled hand after running into the face. The face.

I turned around, then I turned around again. There was no face, just trees. Only those dense pine trees all around the oval of sand, and me, standing in the middle like the pupil of an eye.

Chapter Twenty-Three

I knew I had to leave that sandy oval, that enormous eye, but I didn't *want* to. Part of me expected that I wouldn't be able to move beyond the golden border. Maybe whatever had happened would hold me there. But when I took my first step onto the gravel outside of the eye, the earth didn't shake and crack open. The sky didn't start raining fire or hail.

I stood, waiting for something to bloom out of that quiet. A direction, a thought, anything. *Think about what you do have and what you do know.* Mom was sure that she'd survive. Everything she'd done, even the most terrible and painful and difficult things, she'd done because she knew she'd survive. It was this same optimistic certainty, I thought, that would guide me to her. I stood up, and decided to follow whatever copy of that certainty Mom had passed down to me. I let the blood in my veins take over, and I moved only where I was certain I should move. If I saw a scuff in the sand, or a spiny plant that listed to one side, that's where I moved. If I saw nothing, then I moved only where I absolutely felt I should go. I drank a few tiny sips of what water I had left—not too much, just enough to keep from falling down.

In the bright daylight, out of the corner of my eye, I saw the overlay of even brighter flashes. White-hot letters at the corners of my vision floated around me as I walked, the same hanging, dissolving C-O-U-L-D-Y-O-U-F-I-N-D-M-E. Ulrike's bag thumped against my back. Some of the twists in the stone looked like letters, and I could swear I was reading them, receiving a reassuring message. I shook my head, trying to clear my vision, but was too dizzy from the heat and thirst to beat away those images.

When I followed a bend in the natural slope of the canyon side, I *knew* Mom would be there, like I'd already been told. And she was.

"Sorry!" I shouted out, stupidly, like I'd just stepped on someone's toe in line at the airport. *MOM-MOM-MOM* thundered through my head. I flung Ulrike's backpack away and knelt down next to her. She was dirty, too, and missing most of her robes. What scraps still clung to her were stained rust colored and black. She looked like she'd just fallen there, the way her arms and legs were splayed. *Check her breathing*, I told myself. *Anyone who's seen even one movie knows that much.*

It felt weird to touch Mom like this, like an intrusion. Also, I was terrified that she was really dead. Her skin was cold and clammy, and her limbs flopped around as I moved them out of the way. They weren't stiff, the way dead things were supposed to be. A faint tingle of relief prickled behind my eyes. I pressed my fingers into the skin at the base of her throat. At first I didn't feel anything, only my own wild pulse, the same rhythm that beat in that spot behind my eyes. *Calm down and pay attention*, I told myself.

"Sorry, Mom," I said as I pressed my fingers even deeper into the side of her neck. The tiniest flicker tapped back out at me, a very weak I'm-here-I'm-here-I'm-here. I wasn't sure if I imagined it, but Mom recoiled just the littlest bit from my fierce poking. I leaned over her, my filthy face just centimeters from her filthy face, and I listened. She was breathing, but it was weak. *Okay,*

I thought. *Now what?* Was I supposed to do CPR? Was I *not* supposed to do CPR? She was probably really dehydrated. Could I make her drink some water? Was that even possible? Could you kill an unconscious person by pouring water in her mouth? I opened Ulrike's backpack and unscrewed the water jug.

I splashed a little water over Mom's lips, but it didn't seem like any actually got in her mouth. I massaged the lower half of Mom's face and pried open her jaw. I poured in some water, just a bit, the same amount that would fill a sewing thimble. I smoothed down the sides of her neck with my free hand, coaxing her to swallow. She coughed or gagged a little, but it looked like she'd drunk most of what I forced her to.

I waited out the morning, every once in a while splashing a little water into Mom's mouth and easing it down her throat. It was hard to stay so still. There wasn't really anything else I could do for her. I tried to compose her body into a more comfortable-looking position, but gave up after every change I made looked more unnatural and painful.

My throat burned with thirst as the hours passed, but I couldn't bring myself to squander the water. The sun beat down on the top of my head and the back of my neck, and I took two micro sips from the jug, but felt pretty bad about it.

Ida, I thought. *What would you do?* The sun moved in the sky, and I felt my skin crisp up under its light. Mom's skin was already sunburned, and I didn't know what a sunburn on top of sunburn would do. It couldn't be helping her dehydration.

I put my hands in her armpits and gently shuffled her body toward the meager shade of a twisted juniper tree. I didn't get very far. Maybe I jostled her too much, or maybe she really did have a broken neck, because she moaned a little. I stopped right away and put my hand on her forehead.

"Mom? Can you hear me? It's Van."

I took another tiny sip of water and topped Mom off, too. Was the moaning a good thing or a bad thing? I couldn't tell. Was she waking up or dying? I rubbed my grubby face and could barely feel the skin underneath all of the grime and dried blood. I kept my eyes mostly on Mom. I even held her hand a little bit, thinking it might help.

I stood up and walked laps around her. Even with the intermittent mini walks, I felt tingling in my fingers and toes. *That can't be good,* I thought. Alex and Marine had to be on their way back. At the very least, Alex and Marine would come looking for us. I wondered if Ulrike would be able to track us. After all, I'd left that trail of blood for her part of the way, so there was that.

Another sound came out of Mom, a faint groan, so faint I thought at first it was the creak of tree limbs. I leaned my ear close to her mouth and focused on her closed eyes. She made a half-gagging, half-choking sound. I sat up and poured a little water in her mouth again. She coughed and nearly all of it ran out, down her chin. I watched, wistfully, as all of the moisture was sucked away into the earth.

"Mom?" I whispered close to her ear. I knelt down so close that my knees knocked into her side.

She coughed again, and this time moved her mouth, opening and closing it. Her lips were so chapped, I knew that if she tried to talk they would bleed.

"More," she grated out. The jug was so light in my hands—it was bad, bad news.

"I don't think you're supposed to drink too much too fast. You might throw up."

Mom nodded: a clear, sentient nod. I felt about a million times better.

"Do you want to try to sit up?" I asked.

She nodded but held a finger up, like she was telling me to wait a second. She opened her eyes. She opened her eyes and she recognized me. I just knew it.

"Oh, Mom," I said, wanting to throw myself down on top of her. But I didn't. I held back—I didn't pounce and I didn't cry. I wiped a dribble of water from the space between her mouth and her chin. She nodded a little and tried to get up by herself. When I saw what she meant to do, I crawled around behind her and lifted her up. I sat in the dirt like a gymnast stretching, with my legs straddled as far apart as I could get them. I pulled Mom against my chest and held her up. My wounded hand throbbed.

"I'm dizzy," she said. Her words came slow and thick. "Where are we?"

"I don't know. Arizona somewhere."

"Is Laurel here?"

"No one's here, Mom. Just us."

"Is Ida here?"

"No, Mom, she's in Vegas. In the hospital. Remember?"

"I don't know." Mom shook her head.

"Bullshit, Mom, you know." I was shocked that I'd said it, but it was true. I could feel the tension in her body when she said Ida's name, when she remembered something was wrong.

"I'm sorry," she said, and leaned back against me. I rested my chin on her dusty shoulder and put my nose in her filthy hair.

"We have to go back for her." A fluid, urgent heat swelled around the words I spoke.

"I know," she said.

• • •

We spent the next few hours figuring out how to get Mom's body to work correctly. I propped her against the juniper tree and slowly fed her the rest of the water. I couldn't trust her to take the nearly empty jug because she just tipped it back and glugged away. Together, we bent her knees up and down, bringing blood back into the muscles of her legs. We needed to find the trail together. Leaving Mom alone while I went for help was out of the question.

I broke off little pieces of Ulrike's protein bar and gave her the crumbs. She ate slowly, and after a few hours the bar and almost every drop of water was gone. Mom made me drink the last small sip. I zipped the empty jug back into Ulrike's bag. If we were going to die, littering wasn't going to be the last thing I did. It was sunset, and that rose-gold of the canyon filtered the air all around us. Mom looked better, but not great. We both knew this was it. Neither of us was going to be any better than we were right that minute.

Mom stood carefully, one arm on me and one arm on the tree she'd been propped against. We rose together with the speed of plants growing out of the ground. We moved so slowly that I got a little woozy watching the earth recede one fraction of a centimeter at a time. When we were up, Mom gripped the side of the tree and I brought over the branch I'd broken down to walking-stick height. She stabbed it into the sandy soil and we began to walk—incredibly slowly, but we walked.

"You don't know the way," Mom said, not like a question.

We shuffled out of the cover of the juniper tree into the fading sunlight.

"Do you want me to try to climb up something? Maybe I'll be able to see the camp."

Mom shook her head. "Do you smell something?" she asked, her head cocked to the side.

I looked at her, and at first thought she meant us, since we were pretty disgusting. But, as I sniffed the air, I definitely smelled smoke. There was a fire within smelling distance.

"Which way do you think it is?" I asked her.

She kept her head tilted and closed her eyes. She leaned her face into the faint breeze that swirled around us. She lifted a hand and pointed: *that way*. I nodded and we walked, slow as ants. Mom stopped a few times to check that the scent was still there.

"It's stronger," she said, and looked to me for confirmation. When I nodded, she started to walk a little faster.

"Careful, Mom, please."

The walking stick dragged along beside us as we struck out into the near-darkness. *Please*, I thought, *please let whoever started this fire be a good person*. We moved around a wide swath of shrubs and saw the glimmer of the fire through a tangle of leaves.

"Hello?" I shouted.

"Hello?" A voice shouted back—an accented voice. A tall, slim shadow approached: Ulrike.

"She is found!" Ulrike beamed and slipped Mom's arm over her shoulder. Which was good, because I was shaking. Ulrike flung Mom's walking stick to the side and we wobbled over, like some hulking three-bodied mutant, to Ulrike's fire. *She's alone*, I realized, grateful there weren't any others. But it made me wonder—*something's happened at the camp*. Mom collapsed on the ground and put her head between her knees.

"Okay?" Ulrike asked.

Mom nodded.

"She needs some more water, I think. And food." I put my hands up to my face and mimed eating a sandwich.

"Yes," Ulrike said. She smacked me on the shoulder and removed her backpack from my arms. I sunk down next to

Mom. Ulrike unzipped a larger trail pack, the kind with a steel frame and dangling, tied-on accessories. She'd only just settled in for the night—none of the neatly packed items in her bag had been removed. She shook out a snail-rolled silver blanket and draped it over Mom's shoulders. Ulrike's mostly full jug of water was already out by the fire, but she rummaged in her pack for a chipped, enameled cup. She filled it halfway with water and passed it to Mom. She handed me a small fabric pouch filled with nuts. I looked up at her, dazed.

Ulrike took the bag back and shook some nuts out into my palm. Mom and I ate and drank while Ulrike set up the camp. She cleaned away the dried blood on my hand with a baby wipe and smeared some ointment on it from a tin jar in her pack. She rested her fleece jacket over my back like a cape and gave Mom and me each a shoulder clasp. Mom and I leaned against each other and breathed in the dark, merciful scent of the fire.

Ulrike took something else from her pack—a phone. My phone. She looked at it and then at me. She pressed it into my hand and put a finger to her lips, puckered in a silent *shh*. I nodded, ready to cry with gratefulness again. "Thanks, Ulrike," I said.

Mom drooped down until her head was in my lap. I wasn't sure when she'd fallen asleep. I smoothed the silver blanket over her. Ulrike nodded in approval, pointed at Mom, and gave me a thumbs-up. I couldn't help smiling at her. She'd really saved our lives.

"Thanks for looking for us," I said.

"Most welcome." She spread a narrow waterproof tarp over the dirt behind me. She smacked the plastic-covered ground, and I stretched out where she pointed. Ulrike practically carried Mom out of my lap and onto the spot beside me, and then spread the silver blanket over us both.

• • •

The fire still smoldered in the morning when I woke up. I wasn't sure if Ulrike had slept at all because she was already doing calisthenics by the fireside. I shook Mom awake. We needed to hurry. Ulrike had already put out some breakfast for us: two protein bars lined up neatly side by side, a small pile of dried mango, and her jug of water. Mom ate more easily than she had the day before. She seemed steadier. Her movements were less wobbly, and even her eyes seemed more clear. Whatever Laurel had given her in the camp had worn off.

I let Mom finish most of the water while Ulrike packed up. The walk back was fast—not the pace, but the distance. Mom held on to my arm even at the most narrow places, where we had to crowd together. She looked over at me a lot, and I couldn't tell if it was because she was confused or because she was sorry.

I heard the camp before I could see it. No drums or music, just a low hum of human sounds—voices and footsteps. Ulrike looked back at us, frowning.

"No," she said, and made a thumbs down with her fist. "Go straight to road, yes?"

"What happened?" I asked.

"No good," Ulrike shook her head. "Police." She pointed to her chest. "No visa. I go back to Sedona, await Laurel."

"Oh," I said, startled that I could feel even more gratitude than I had the night before. "I can't believe you came back to look for us. Thank you."

Ulrike extended an arm and shook my hand.

"I'll never forget this, Ulrike," Mom said. Ulrike gave her a little bow, and then galloped away.

Mom and I continued in a feeble shuffle. My body had started to hurt the night before from all of the walking and dehydration. Maybe it had hurt before then, but I only let myself notice it once we were relatively safe and warm under Ulrike's wing.

When the camp fell into sight, we saw the dark blue figures of the police moving through the crowd. The violence of a raid was missing—their dissembling of the camp seemed more somber and funereal. The decorations that had been strung up to welcome Mom back were mostly destroyed, and rumpled garlands snaked across the red dirt like letters from an alien alphabet. The mangled echo of walkie-talkies bounced back to where we stood.

"Let's try to go around all of this," I told Mom. "Hopefully no one will notice us."

From where we waited, I could see the tepee, the camp's ersatz headquarters. Someone—a woman—inside was screaming. It wasn't a scream of pain. It was the low, guttural scream of frustration.

"What do you have here?" Mom asked, holding on to my hand as we walked. "You have your phone now, yes? Did you bring a car?"

"A car? No." *Awfully demanding for the person who dragged us out here,* I thought. The cops were concentrated most heavily around the tepee, and we slipped by easily.

"Do you want to leave a note or something?" I asked. She was the prophet, after all.

"No," Mom said. "Let's just go. Like I never came here."

"But you did come here, Mom," I said. "And when I came looking for you, to ask for help—for Ida, who could be dying right now—you told me to fuck off."

"Van!"

"Well, you did," I said. "You're so wrong sometimes."

But she was right about getting out of there, immediately. We skirted the camp, and Mom took my hand again, like the mom of a much younger child would. I didn't shake her off, but only because she was still weak. We walked out toward the gap in the canyon wall, out past the abandoned basin camp, out to the patch of grubby parking lot dotted with dusty, shitty cars, out to where we'd find the road.

Chapter Twenty-Four

My throat was scraped dry. It was a long walk for two people who had already been stranded for days in the desert. But Mom, definitely the one in worse shape, was stoic. She didn't break her pace at all. When we reached the ribbon of pavement, it was like Mom had used up all of her struggle to get to the road, and that was it.

"Now what?" I asked her.

"We get a ride to town," she said, sitting down on the ground.

Mom's head lolled to the side and rested on her shoulder. A plume of dust smudged the gray line of road in the distance. I squinted, trying to make out an accompanying vehicle of some kind. A boxy station wagon rumbled toward us.

"There's a car coming," I said.

Mom pushed herself onto her hands and knees and then all the way up. She moved so slowly the car had nearly reached us by the time her back had straightened. She shot out a long, slim arm, the bulge of the robe's torn bell sleeve gathered over her elbow. When her thumb popped up, I coughed out a laugh.

"Seriously?" I asked. "I never thought we'd be doing this again."

"Never say never." Mom didn't smile. I remembered, the last time we'd hitchhiked I was supposed to be in kindergarten. That's what the middle-aged lady driver told Mom. "That child should be in kindergarten," the woman said, a pile of softness behind the wheel. At the time, I didn't even know what it meant—*kindergarten*.

The old station wagon slowed down and then stopped. No power windows, I noted. The driver had to get out to talk to us. It was a man. *Not ideal*, I recalled about getting rides like this, but we were desperate. He was older, at least, and neat looking. He had a full head of white hair that was slicked back in an old-timey style. He looked like James Dean's grandpa or something. A worn, brown leather bomber jacket added to the effect.

"You ladies all right?"

"We'd appreciate a ride into town, if it's not too much trouble." Mom managed to sound demure, even in that ridiculous outfit. I wished I'd had time to at least wash the blood from my face.

"Sure thing." He walked around and opened the door for Mom, and then for me. All the while the driver's side door gaped open, jutting into the road like the fin on a prehistoric fish.

"You sure you're all right?" He asked this question looking right at me in the rearview mirror.

"Yes," I answered, and then, finally understanding what he meant, I said, "We were hiking and I fell."

"All right."

We drove in silence for a while, Mom looking straight ahead the whole time. She didn't betray her exhaustion and weakness for one second. I started to feel pretty guilty when I realized the car was starting to smell because we were in it. There was an old *Time* magazine on the seat next to me and a partly full plastic bottle of water rolling on the floor. I resisted the urge to grab that old, half-used bottle of water and drink it all down.

"Are we almost there?" Mom tried to ask brightly.

The driver turned in his seat a little to look at Mom.

"Almost."

I looked for signs that population density was increasing—other cars, anything. The only sign of life we passed was a boarded-up gas station.

"This doesn't look familiar to me," I ventured.

"It's a shortcut."

Even through the wall of exhaustion I could feel the swell of adrenaline in my chest. *This guy is going to murder us and eat our brains*, I thought.

"Thanks for the ride—I really like your hairstyle," I said, not sure why. Maybe I thought he would kill me more quickly if I was polite.

"Why, thank you, young lady. It's nice to hear some conversation from a gal your age. My neighbor's girl just clicks away at that computer all day long. Conversation is a lost art."

"Isn't that the truth?" Mom said. "You can just drop us here, anywhere. We've been camping, you know, and my daughter fell. And then, lucky us! Our car broke down."

"What a shame," James Dean's grandpa said. "It's no trouble at all. Where would you like me to drop you?"

It was unclear to me whether he meant our living or our dead bodies.

"Perhaps a gas station, or a motel?" Mom said, like she was some kind of ambassadress talking to a local.

"I know just the place," he said.

I held my breath until I felt like I would pass out. A few more cars began to slide down the road, and a strip mall, and then a standalone tire place swam up alongside the pavement. *Okay*, I thought, *maybe we'll make it after all*. But our driver drove on.

The man pointed a wrinkled hand to Mom's side of the windshield.

"It's just ahead," he said. "The King's Ransom."

"What an interesting name," Mom said, turning up the charm. I could hear her relief in the warmth she gave each word.

The King's Ransom had a showy, almost Vegas-inspired neon sign. As soon as Grandpa Dean parked in front, I jumped out. Mom talked to him for a minute or two; about what, I had no idea.

"Thanks!" I shouted cheerfully, waving at the door. *Thanks for not killing us!* I thought. I'd had that thought before, as a little kid, getting out of a stranger's car. It was a long-ago echo of a thought, but it was there.

Mom exited the car and gave a little wave.

I walked up the S-shaped sidewalk and into the King's Ransom. Ahead of Mom, away from Mom. I let her do the talking and inspected the plaques lined up along the wall—documentation of decades-long support of a local girls' softball league. We had been almost dead in the desert, and now we were standing in front of these softball team photos. I had talked to the spirits, or if not the spirits, definitely something not of this earth—had it been an alien? I had maybe talked to an alien, and now I was standing underneath this line of softball team photos.

Had it really happened? Had I been crazy with thirst? Or was I just crazy? I shook my head and pushed away thoughts of aliens and hallucinations. *Just think about the shower you'll take,* I told myself. But I didn't think about my shower; I thought about my ability as a musician. I wondered if it came easily to me, or if I loved it the way I did because I could see things that weren't there.

"Come on," Mom said, and pulled me away. She said it like she'd been talking to me already.

"How did you pay?" I asked.

"My credit card number," she said, like I should have known.

• • •

In our room, Mom flopped down on the bed and closed her eyes for maybe ten seconds before she picked up the clunky phone receiver within her reach. It was an old rotary phone, the kind with no buttons. I went straight to the bathroom and filled one of the plastic-wrapped paper cups at the sink. I drank and refilled it two more times. I filled it back up and brought it over to Mom. She could barely bring it to her lips.

"I'm sorry to ask you this, darling, but can you dial for me? I feel like death warmed over. I asked that man at the front desk to order us some pizza, too."

"Are you going to call Chantal?"

"Yes, next. But first Marine. You said she was coming back for us."

"I did?"

"Didn't you?"

"I don't remember." I really didn't. I wasn't sure if it was because I was hungry and exhausted and dehydrated. Or insane. Talking to aliens.

"Mom," I began, my fingers hovering over the rotary phone's miniature circular craters. "What happened to you out there?"

"What do you mean?"

"I mean when you were 'Getting the message' or whatever." I made air quotes with my free, nondialing hand. "Did you actually, you know, get any messages?"

Mom looked down at the paper cup.

"I'm not really sure. You know how I get when things happen to me that way. Why? Did something happen to *you?*"

I felt her inspection all over me. "I don't know." I shook my head, but couldn't shake out the images of those crystal arrows and drinking down all of those faces. "I'm going to take a shower, okay? Tell me what numbers you want."

• • •

In the cramped stall behind a moldering plastic curtain, I put together a timeline of my search for Mom. But when I tried to focus on it, I only saw that towering, golden face.

I washed the grime off of my body, wearing the miniscule bar of hotel soap down to a thin, white slip. The soap and water stung my sliced-up hand. I washed my hair, breathing in the noxious floral scent of the complimentary shampoo. Smelling anything other than my own rancid sweat was heavenly.

I let the water flow down over my hair and over my face and concentrated on the speaking ripples of stone. It had said my name; I was almost sure of that. Perhaps I had imagined its giant mouth cracking open. People saw mirages in the desert, didn't they? But my name had sounded so real, and the voice had been unlike any sound I'd ever heard—it was more like a natural disaster than a human voice. What would Ida think of all of it?

Had I even told Mom to call the hospital? I couldn't remember. *I'm really losing it,* I thought. Shivering with panic, I twisted the spigot and stopped the water. I leapt out and blotted myself dry with the undersized towel hanging next to the toilet. I wrapped the towel around myself and opened the door, my hair a sopping wet sheet down my back.

Mom was sitting on the edge of the bed, tense and poised to jump, like an aerialist.

"It's Ida," she said.

"What?" I sank down to my knees into the grubby shag carpet beside the bed.

"I spoke with Chantal. She said Ida is not doing well. Your friend is in the hospital with her. You should call him." Mom handed over my cell phone, glowing mysteriously with charge.

"I'm going to take a shower myself. Are there more towels?"

I nodded.

"We're going to need clothes. I'll call Marine's new number when I get out. She should be here soon. Chantal said she left to get us this morning."

I snatched the phone from Mom's hand and called Alex, pressing the phone, too hard, to the side of my head.

Mom disappeared into the steamy bathroom to think her own thoughts.

Alex picked up right away.

"Van?" His voice was undercut with panic.

"Yes?" I said.

"Oh my God, are you okay? Is your mom okay?"

"Yes, yes—how is Ida? You're with her?"

"Yeah," he paused for a long time. "I'm with her."

"How is she?"

"Are you almost back?"

"We're coming—how is she?"

"I'm here at the hospital. Ovid's here, too. And people from the hotel have been coming by a lot, so."

"So is she okay? Is she awake?" I heard my voice going all high and wild.

"She's not awake, no."

"Has she woken up at all?"

"No, she hasn't. These doctors are great, though. Ida's doctor is this lady I think you would really like."

"Alex, just tell me what's going on! Please!" I clamped the sagging towel under my armpits. There was a long pause. I heard the sounds in the hospital on the other end.

"She doesn't have a lot of time left. You guys need to hurry." He was still talking, but I didn't hear anything after that.

"Van? Are you still there? I said, as soon as Marine gets there, turn around and come back, okay?"

"We will."

"Do you have her new number?"

"Mom does."

"Please, please hurry."

"Are you sure it's that bad?" I was crying now. I could hear it.
"I think so."

"Are you sure?"

"It's okay, she's not alone. I've been with her, or Ovid has, the whole time."

"Okay. I just—thank you so much. Call me if there's any news. I have my phone now, so."

"I will. Van?"

"Yeah?"

"Hurry."

• • •

When I hung up, I read all of Alex's texts and listened to the hysterical messages he'd been leaving. Almost all of them sounded like he thought *I* was the one who was nearly dead. *Well, wasn't he right?* I thought. Mom and I and Ida were in the same place in that respect, anyway—all on the edge of death. But there had been a miracle. There had been miracles, plural—Mom's waking up, then Ulrike's surprise rescue. And that face. If all of those things had happened, if all of those things had saved us, then couldn't something equally miraculous happen to Ida? It would only be fair, given the recent symmetry of our lives. Whatever I was feeling about Mom receded when haphazard prayers for Ida swamped over me.

The phone trilled in my hand, and I answered, thinking, for one crazy second, that those prayers had worked. That Ida had woken up and was trying to call me.

"Wow, Van, nice to finally hear from you." It was Carol.

"Oh, hey. Sorry I didn't call you before. My . . ." Nanny? Friend? "friend is in the hospital. And my mom has been, well—"

"Yeah, I heard your mom went off the deep end. Alex told Joanna all about it."

My face tingled with shame. "Yeah, glad he's sharing the news."

"Don't be mad at Alex. I can't believe I just said that. Don't tell him I said that. But he kind of *had* to tell us. I was threatening to hire your replacement."

"What?" I said, dizzy. How stupid was I that I'd never considered that possibility? "You didn't though, right?"

"Relax, Jesus, no, we didn't. When Alex told us what was going on—because *you* never did—"

"Carol, I was in the fucking desert!"

"Whoa, whoa, there's no need to get snippy. All I'm saying is Alex cleared it up. Okay?"

"Okay," I said.

"I *will* say Joanna didn't like you hooking up with Marcos like that."

"What?"

"Marcos said things were getting serious with you two."

"What? No they're not!"

"Whatever, that's between you and Jo to figure out when you get back. So, when *will* you be back? We need to get a couple of practices in, like now."

"I'm not sure," I said, slowly. "It all depends on Ida. I can't go on tour—I can't go anywhere—if Ida needs me."

"Well just *answer your phone*. That's all I ask. See you tomorrow? Probably?"

"I don't know," I said, and hung up.

Maybe when we got to the hospital, Ida would hear our voices and wake up. She could get better. It wasn't impossible. Maybe Ida and I could talk about the tour. I'd let her make the call—if she wanted me to stay and take care of her, I would. If she wanted me to go on tour, I would. Either way, I wouldn't call Carol again until I talked to Ida.

When Mom came out of the bathroom, as clean as me, the air in the motel room steamed up with optimism. We were clean and alive. Ida was going to be okay. A knock at the door: pizza.

"Mom," I began. "Do you really believe Laurel and those people? Did you actually think you were their prophet?"

Mom stared off for a minute before answering. "It's hard to explain. Sometimes it feels like I am, that I am something large like that. But then, you know, sometimes it feels like I am nothing. That I am less than nothing."

"Did you really give them money?"

Mom looked down at the open pizza box between us. "Yes, I did."

"Do you realize the connection between those two things?" I knew it was a harsh thing to say, but I needed to hear Mom say it. I needed to know that we were both understanding at least one thing the same way.

"Yes," she said, slowly. "I see how in some ways they are connected. But I believe I had a true understanding with some of them."

I let my anger simmer and shook my head, even though maybe I had understood. That face in the mountain had come out of *something*.

Mom and I ate while still in our towels and waited for Marine. I paced a little, and Mom scraped all of our filthy clothes into the garbage. When Marine's knocking hammered on the door, it was so loud and forceful that the hinges rattled.

Mom unlatched the door and Marine burst through it, dropping a handful of plastic bags on the floor. I was surprised when she rushed over to me and put her arms around my shoulders, half hugging, half inspecting.

"You're really okay, Van? Sofia?" she asked, reaching an arm out to Mom.

"We're both fine," Mom said.

"I'm so relieved. There's so much I want to say to you both."

Mom drew Marine into a hug while Marine awkwardly kept one hand on my arm.

"We know what you want to say," Mom told her.

What? I thought. *I don't.* But there was no time, and I really didn't care. We had to hurry—I promised Alex.

"Have you seen Ida?" I asked Marine.

She nodded.

"Well?"

"We should leave right now. You both get changed and we'll go." Marine plucked up one of the bags by her feet and handed it over. In the bathroom, I pulled on gray sweatpants and some kind of sweatshirt with a dog on it. I made a last attempt to dry my hair with the damp towel but ended up just throwing it on the floor. The brand new sweatsuit made my skin itch. I looked in the large, chipped mirror, just to see if my hair looked any more dry. I was surprised that I didn't look the way I remembered.

I felt a hot, molten shame in my gut at the thought. So selfish, *Who cares about how you look?* I told myself. *You need to leave now. Ida could be dying.* I kicked the limp towel under the sink and swept out to an empty room. I found Mom and Marine downstairs in the tiny lobby, speaking to a confused clerk.

"But you're not staying?" he asked, his forehead a landscape of creases.

"Something's come up," Mom said. "An emergency. But thanks very much for loaning your charger. Bill my card for the full night, won't you?"

"Are you sure, ma'am?"

"Oh yes, thanks again!"

Mom and Marine gathered me up by the door and the three of us sped out to Marine's dusty red car. The back seat was cluttered with crumpled paper and empty paper cups. I swept all of the debris to the floor and stretched out flat on my back.

• • •

When I woke up, the sky had darkened. I knew I'd been dreaming. I could still catch the scraps of vision and sounds, a booming, gold confetti. I sat up and tried to brush it off, even though I knew it wasn't really there.

"What time is it?" I asked.

"Almost seven," Marine answered.

Mom's head lolled against the window.

"How long has she been asleep?" I asked, and coughed a little, trying to clear the sandy feeling out of my throat.

"A while. Here, we stopped on the way." Marine handed back a plastic bag with a bottle of soda and a waxy-looking donut inside.

"Are we almost there?"

"Yes." Marine kept her voice soft.

"Did my phone ring?"

"Yes." Marine's voice was even softer.

"Did something happen?" Fury and fear washed through me.

"We're almost there now, it's okay."

I wanted to ask Marine if "it's okay" meant Ida was okay, but I couldn't. I think I already knew, somewhere, what had happened. I opened the soda and gulped down nearly the whole bottle and shoved the sickly-looking donut down my throat. My blood boiled with sugar as well as terror, and I bounced and shifted in the back seat, urging Marine to drive faster. The darkness broke up around the car—lights by the side of the road and flashing signs advertising all of Vegas's lewd wares flooded the sky.

I felt my heartbeat thrumming under my breastplate. *It's all the sugar*, I tried to tell myself. *I'm sure everything is fine.* I knew it was a lie. *I knew.* It was like some cord had attached Ida and me, and that hot churning deep in my stomach was what happened when the cord snapped away. *Where did you go, Ida? Where are you?* I pleaded, out at the fluorescent red XXXs and wind-bent cardboard cutouts of curvaceous silhouettes.

I recognized the prelude to the hospital parking lot—a McDonald's, a Burger King, and a Hardee's—a heart-rending ellipsis. Marine stopped the car so gently, I could barely tell we weren't still moving. I stepped out of the car as Marine shook Mom awake. I didn't run—I could only manage the slowest and most sedate pace because my heart beat so violently. Inside, the hospital was glaring white. I walked past the chairs Alex and I had once waited in, past clumps of tired people waiting to be seen. I pushed the elevator button, like I knew exactly where I was going.

When the doors opened, I saw Alex, or the shape of him at least. My vision was blurred and overbright.

"Alex," I whispered.

He didn't see me, though. No one did. There were others there, too. Ovid and Chantal. Their heads hung like heavy globes of large fruit. *Fresh heads*, I thought, hysterically.

"Guys!" I shouted at them, wrestling a histrionic cheer into the word.

They all turned to look up at me at the same time, like a group of Broadway dancers. Alex trotted over to me, halfheartedly, though—there was no real urgency in his movements.

"Van, you're here." He sounded weak, like he'd been the patient this whole time, stuck through with tubes and needles.

"Where is she? Can I see her?"

"Um," Alex began and looked up at Chantal. Chantal moved over to me and put a hand on my back between my shoulder blades.

"I'm so sorry, Van," she said.

I didn't remember much after that: dropping to the floor, the crack of my knees against linoleum, bright light and faces swirling overhead, the ding of the elevator bell, a rattle of wheels rolling by my head. Then Mom, beside me, holding me. Alex on the other side, practically squeezing the bones out of my hand. I tried to push them away, but they were like walls of water, swelling back every time I struck out at them. I hated them all so much. I hated Mom for being so difficult, and I hated Alex for not insisting I go back with him and Marine. *Why didn't he just carry me out of that camp?* I thought. I hated Ovid for keeping Ida up so late, for pushing her beyond her physical limits. I hated Marine for so many things. The only person I didn't hate right then, funnily, was Chantal.

"Chantal?" I called. I could hear the snot and tears in my voice.

I felt the softness of Chantal's body as she lifted me off of the floor and pulled me against her shoulder, smoothing my hair. She didn't say anything. She just kept smoothing my hair and let me cry.

Chapter Twenty-Five

Later, in a small office in the bowels of the hospital, Mom and I sat side by side, still in our matching dog sweatshirts. My newly bandaged hand rested in my lap. The man behind the desk seemed frightened of us and cowered down in his chair. I knew the way I was looking at him was not kind. I was angry and cold from all of the crying. Mom was limp all around—she was still weak. If the circumstances had been different, I'd probably have tried to convince her to get checked out, but there wasn't room for any of that, because we sat in the cowering man's office to discuss Ida's remains.

"I understand our patient didn't have any additional family in the state."

"That's correct," Mom said. Her hands were folded in her lap and her legs were crossed at the ankle. The juxtaposition of her classic chairwoman position and the droopy-eyed canine emblazoned on her chest surely wasn't lost on the hospital administrator. He cleared his throat and looked up at the ceiling.

"That's unfortunate, since we usually require a next of kin to claim the remains. Although, as her employer, Mrs. Lowell, it's possible we can make an exception for you. If no next of kin is available. You're sure there's no one?"

"Quite sure."

"I see. Well, I'll speak to my supervisor, if you ladies will give me a moment."

"Of course," Mom said.

The administrator stepped out of the room, all paunch and wrinkled suit, leaving us alone.

"Is that true? Does she really not have anybody? I thought there was somebody in Canada she used to talk about."

"No, it's not true. I just don't want to leave Ida here, alone in this—place." Mom felt guilty, I could tell.

A rustle at the door made us turn at the same time, matching movements and expressions directed at the sagging administrator.

"Thank you so much for your patience, ladies. If you'll sign these, Mrs. Lowell, you can be on your way. We'll have the body shipped wherever you decide. There's a list, just there, of reputable funeral directors."

"Ida wanted to be cremated," I said, and Mom nodded.

Ida had always said it was what she wanted. "When my time comes," she'd start. Mom and I followed up her repeated cremation requests with oh-Ida-you're-going-to-live-forevers. But here we were.

"Certainly, I'll just make a note on that list, if you'll give me a moment." The administrator jotted down a line at the bottom of the page. His handwriting scribbled underneath the neatly printed list looked like a dead spider.

"Thank you." Mom snapped the paper away from him and handed it over to me, where I rested it on my lap. "Where did you need me to sign?"

I unfocused my eyes and listened to Mom scrawl away.

"We'll transport the remains to the . . . chosen facility . . . and you'll be able to pick them up there. You'll just need this information." He swooped a pile of paper together and slid it into a somber navy blue folder. "I'm so very sorry for your loss," he said, standing again.

"Thank you," Mom clipped. "Would you mind giving us a moment?"

"Of course not," he said, confusion stippling his forehead. Only Mom could make someone feel like their office was really hers.

The door closed, sealing us in. Mom looked down at her hands, not at me, which is how I knew it was going to be bad. I didn't know if my body could feel any more angry.

"Van." She said my name like it was half a question and half an answer. Mom looked around the room, her eyes finally settling on the wall beside my left ear. "I lied to that man."

"What? Yeah, I know." Maybe the exposure and coming down from wherever she'd been still clung to Mom. Maybe she was still shaking something off.

She shook her head, snapping her neck back and forth with a kind of self-flagellating violence.

"This should never have come from me," she said. "But you need to know." Mom looked down into her lap, at the two stacked palms she had composed there. "I lied to that man just now. Ida does have next of kin here."

"What?" How had her cousins already arrived? I thought no one knew how to get in touch with them.

"She has only one next of kin." She looked up at me. "And it's you."

What? Obviously Mom had gone back around the bend. *Great.* I started to stand up. "Mom, maybe we should get you checked out."

"No, Van. No." Mom pulled me back into my seat and tried to hold my hand this time. "Ida was Michael's mother."

"Michael? Who the fuck is *Michael*? *Mom?*" I yanked my hand out of Mom's and stood up, retreating to one of the small room's corners. I knew what Mom was going to say before she said it—I *knew* it. When I finally understood, I hurt with the thunder of it. Like I was clamped in the mouth of that giant stone face in the canyon, being crunched to smithereens. Like what was happening in the hospital administrator's office and what had happened out in the canyon were consuming me, black-holing me into some other creature.

"Michael was your father."

"What?" It was only a whisper, but I managed it. I was dizzy, struck. Like the air all around my head was filled with bees.

"I'm sorry, sweetheart," Mom said. "I'm so sorry it's happening this way." Mom shook her head. "Ida was just never ready to tell you."

Mom dropped her head into her hands. Her cheeks were flushed, and I could see her trying to subdue her anger. *At who? Ida? Michael? Herself?*

"Then *you* tell me." I wanted Mom to answer me, but in the same instant, I realized that I'd always been Ida's. All of Ida's affection and attention, all of her jokes and the secret language between our four eyes, that was not something that came from a stranger. "Oh my God," I said. A rush of relief and anger—but not just at Mom this time, at Ida, too—pressed through me. "What the fuck, Ida?" I whispered into the sloppily patched wall I leaned against. "What the fuck?"

"She didn't want you to know."

I tilted my head to the side and could see Mom worrying the hem of her sweatshirt. "*I* didn't want you to know. Ida wanted to get to know you. She didn't want to force you to like her. And I didn't want you to be disappointed."

"What do you mean?"

"When Ida found us, you were already big enough to make up your mind about things. She thought you would push her away if she told you." A long pause. "She thought you would hate her for missing all of that time with you. She thought that you would hate her for not helping us when you were a baby." Mom's accent quivered out into the room, clotted with the hospital administrator's lonely artifacts.

"What do you mean, when Ida found us? Why *didn't* she help us?" My chest stung with a sharp, bright swirl of feeling. I remembered another time, far away, when Mom and I slept like tigers in the wild, curled around each other in the cold, on the grass, under the sky. Where *had* Ida been then?

The lights of the city twinkled through the room's only window and Mom's silence.

"Mom?"

"When I told you your dad was sick and died—"

"He overdosed, you mean."

"Yes. I went to Ida for help. You were so little, I think she'd only met you once before that. Ida didn't come around to our place much. She and Michael . . . they weren't good with each other."

I wasn't used to Mom talking like this about anything, all open and afraid. Afraid of me.

"When he died, Ida was very angry." I turned to watch Mom's face, but I could only make out the shape of her body through my blurred vision. *Was I crying?* I didn't even know.

"If you can believe it, she threatened me."

"I believe it," I said.

"Yes, well. She came to the apartment and threatened to have me deported, accusing me of murder, that kind of thing. She said she was going to take you."

In a warm flash I formed a picture of what my life with Ida would have been, without Mom, without the adventures and travelling. I imagined my childhood, going to school, making friends, eating the lunches Ida packed, getting a learner's permit, waking up every day in the same place. What would have happened to me?

"I was afraid, Van." It was unusual for Mom to admit something like that. "And maybe I did the wrong thing—I don't know."

"We ran away," I said.

"Yes. *I* ran away." I saw Mom's hands smooth down the front of her sweatpants. "We're all she had, Van. We have to do the right thing for her."

"Mom," I said, soft and terrible, "why didn't *you* want me to know?" I lurched toward her as I said it, wanting to push her off of her chair.

"I'm not as good as I want to be," she whispered.

I'd never felt such a mixture of loathing and surprise. I think it was the first real thing Mom ever said to me.

"I'd like to bury her next to Michael, if you're all right with that."

Was I all right with that? Was I all right with *anything*? I did want to do the right thing for Ida—still, always. I turned so that my back was flat against the wall, so that the wall was holding me up. I nodded at Mom. She stood up and we left the hospital, sweeping past the hospital administrator pacing outside of his office.

• • •

Usually, on a Thursday night at the Silver Saddle, the staff crackled with the possibility of the weekend—so much money to be made, the disappointments of the last weekend forgotten. But that night, when we returned from the hospital with a slip of paper instead of Ida, the mood in the lobby was dour. Even the lights looked dimmer, like they hadn't been turned up all of the way. The Silver Saddle knew we were coming, and everyone who had a free minute waited for us: in clusters outside, and in hushed conversations at reception.

Each person or group we passed spoke out softly, or pressed our arms and shoulders. I knew it was nice of them to be sorry, but every time I tried to look one of those people in the eye, all I could think was, *You have no idea.* You have no idea what she meant to me; you have no idea who she was; you have no idea what a gaping shithole my life will be without her.

Mom held me in the elevator, and I let her, our sweatshirts pressing their doggie faces against one another. It didn't feel any better. Mom knew I was angry. I think that she knew, before I knew, that I would never look at her the same way again. I wanted to really hate Mom, but she was all I had left, and I didn't want to hate my only person.

Our suite looked exactly the same as I'd left it. The little things I'd knocked askew getting my backpack together for the bus trip to Sedona, those things were still crooked: a vase scooted too close to a shelf edge, a chair pulled out when Ida would have pushed it back in. Ida was everywhere, even her old-lady smell. Every time I blinked I thought *Ida*. It was crazy and messed up and I needed to stop it. The inside of my head was like a swamp, all soggy and dismal.

I got down on the sofa and drew up the blanket Ida had slept under. I lay there and pretended that I was a mummy in ancient Egypt, entombed in the casino's night sounds. All of the darkness and fear that rasped at the pyramid wall wouldn't get in to where I rested, not then at least.

I knew that I cried, and I knew that I slept, but I didn't know how much. I thought back to the massive golden face that knew my name. I had these little flashes of wanting to be dead myself, but then equal and opposite flashes of desperately taking it back.

All I knew was that Mom left me alone. Everyone left me alone until late-late, when Alex knocked. I knew it was him. I didn't know what time it was or if I would let him in, but I knew, with that knock, that it was definitely him. The door to Mom's room was closed, and I was sure she was asleep.

I walked over to the door and I almost opened it. I realized, before I touched the handle, that this was no place for Alex. I was in some other dimension, some other fold of space-time that wasn't safe for people like him. I stood by the door for a long time, listening. *Maybe he's still waiting out there for me,* I thought. But I never checked. I couldn't bear to check. Some raw, dark thing lumbered in me, and it needed to stay where it was. Alex, if he was still waiting, was safe on the other side of the door.

• • •

Mom was good at tying up loose ends. The next morning, by the time I got dressed, she was talking to Marine at the glass dining table. They were quiet, their voices muted by the hum of the air conditioner. Two room service trays sat on the counter. Mom and Marine held mugs of coffee in their hands. They stopped talking when they saw me, and Marine looked over toward the living room. Someone had picked up Ida, because there she was, on the coffee table. It was just a box, a plain, white cardboard box. It looked light. No heavier than a houseplant.

"Good morning, dear Van," Marine said to me, sweet but with no smile.

"How is it today, honey?" Mom asked.

"Shitty," I said as I moved to sit across from them. It was too absurd, that we just sat there like it was any morning.

Marine nodded and stood to pour me a coffee from the tray. "Did you talk to Alex? He's been calling me, trying to get in touch with you."

How chummy, I thought, distantly. Their relationship had obviously warmed on the ride from the camp to Vegas.

"Not yet," I said.

"You should find him. Say goodbye. He's a nice boy."

"Go ahead," Mom said, her voice still soft.

"Yeah," I said. "My stuff is there, Mom." We were leaving soon—just Mom and me and Ida's remains. My suitcase was packed—the same one I'd brought to Vegas. I'd nestled Ida's guitar into its case and set it by the door, too.

"I'll meet you downstairs in half an hour," she said.

I nodded. I felt like she was trying to explain something to me. So many of the conversations and discussions between Mom and me, about important things, about real, life-altering things, were conducted in silence. It was like one of us would suggest something, or ask a question, and we'd just stare at the air between us until it got figured out. Like the genetic similarity of our brains would make the synapses fire in the same direction and domino to the same conclusion. *We're not coming back here, right?* she was trying to say.

I saw Marine's bags by the door—the same ones she'd brought to the same door, the ones Ida had called the size of Delaware. I knew it would be the last time we saw her. I expected Mom to be miserable, but it was Marine who seemed sadder. She stood and snuffled into my shoulder as she hugged me goodbye.

"I'm going to sort out a few things at home," she said. "If you're ever in Cleveland, Van, come find me. You are an extraordinary young person!" Marine shook me a little on each word as though trying to emphasize their meaning—extraordinary—young—person. She finally released me and wiped at the crescents under her eyes.

After everything, I was actually surprised to find that I was a little bit fond of her. Most of my anger had shunted off onto Mom. Marine looked over my shoulder, where Mom stood, fresh tears streaming down her long face. I looked back at Mom and left, closing them both away.

I loved Mom, of course, and I felt the same relief I'd felt when I'd found her, when she woke up, when I held her next to Ulrike's campfire. I felt that relief like some animal's tongue, warm and rough, surprising and constant, sometimes pleasant, sometimes not. Of course I'd love Mom forever, with that fierce marsupial clinging, but knowing the truth—with Ida, my grandmother, dead on the glass-topped coffee table—well, it made me want to kick her. To know that my connection with Mom was so powerful, that I could be this angry and still love her, made me furious. All I wanted was to close her out, and I loved and hated that I never could. I probably wouldn't be able to even when Mom was dead on a glass-topped table somewhere.

I went looking for Alex, not sure what I was going to say or do. *Thanks for coming last night? Sorry I couldn't get it together to open the door for you? Oh, did you know, Ida was actually my grandma? Also, I'm pretty sure there's something seriously wrong with me—while you were gone, a giant face in the desert talked to me.*

I took the elevator to the lobby and turned down one of the employees-only hallways

"Hey, Van." Someone caught my elbow and shuffled me over against the wall. It was Joanna.

"Oh, hey," I said.

"I'm really sorry about Ida. She was a really nice lady."

"Yeah, she was," I said. I could hear how flat my voice sounded. I remembered that she was supposed to be mad at me, about Marcos. Whatever fear that should have inspired in me was subsumed by the greater darkness in my mind. Joanna looked up at me and squinted a little.

"I'm on break. Come outside with me." She pulled me along behind her before I could say no. I knew I had to find Alex, to say goodbye, but it was so much easier to stumble after Joanna. She led me to a little alcove beside the employee parking lot—a low wall separated it from a row of dumpsters and drunkenly parked laundry carts. She hopped onto the wall, her slender body like a vine in a garden. She offered me a hand, but I scooted up on my own. Joanna pulled a cigarette from her pack and held another one out to me.

I shook my head. She smoked and we kicked our legs. I actually felt all right sitting with Joanna under the sun like that. I liked that she let the quiet spool out between us. It was settling. I could almost believe everything was fine, that Ida was cracking jokes upstairs and that I'd never taken that bus to Sedona. I tried to pretend it was the day after the show.

"Thanks for letting me play with you guys. You're really amazing," I finally said.

"*You* are amazing." Joanna blew smoke out to the side, away from our faces and grinned at me. "So, you're going to call Carol back, right? She really, really wants you to call and set up practice and say you'll do the tour. You're going to do it, right?"

"I'm not sure if I can," I said, clutching the rim of the filthy peach-painted half wall. "Do *you* want me to?"

"I know it's probably not the best time to say this. I mean, I'm really sorry for your loss." Joanna squinted out at the place where the desert pushed itself against the sky. "But this is something— *you* are something. I mean, even Carol's impressed, and *nobody* impresses Carol. I don't want to push you at the wrong time, but you're perfect, and I'm dying for you to say you'll come with us." Joanna looked me in the eye as she spoke.

I smiled down at my legs.

"I'm not just saying that. This tour will be incredible for us. If we can get it together—I mean, you'll still need new gear, thanks to fucking Marcos," she muttered.

"I'm really sorry about that. That you thought that. About me and Marcos. Nothing happened," I said. I felt like I had to say it, to acknowledge Joanna's difficulty, too.

"Please, do you think I believe everything Marcos says?"

I raised my eyebrows a little, surprised at how calm she was. "What? Carol said you were really upset. Again, not that anything actually happened."

"Don't take Carol so literally. She lives to mess with people. And even if you were with Marcos for some reason, I really think everything would be okay. I'd rather have you for a guitarist than him for a boyfriend."

I brimmed with shy delight at that, at the way Joanna knew exactly what to say to pull the weight of everything that had happened the day before up and off, even just a little. I was genuinely comforted on that half wall by the dumpsters, next to Joanna, in the sunshine.

"But," she shrugged as she flicked her cigarette into the lot. "If you decide you want to do this, let Carol know. As soon as you can, okay?"

I nodded.

"I really hope you will." Her voice was gravelly and gentle. "I have to go back in, but, about Ida—let me know if I can do anything." She put an arm around my shoulders.

"Thanks," I said.

I reminded myself that I was about to get on a plane with my lying mom, to lay my lying Ida to rest. I stumbled away from the alcove by the dumpsters, away from Joanna, and retreated into the noisy coolness of the Silver Saddle. In the lobby, I vaguely noticed Chantal's arms around me and some handshakes from the daytime desk staff, but mostly, I noticed Alex.

I walked past Mom, who was waiting by the door, and took Alex's hand. I led him outside into the dry, dust-filled morning.

"You're coming back, right?" It was the first thing he'd said to me since the corrosively terrible night at the hospital.

"It depends on my mom," I said. What I didn't say was, *It depends on me, too*. I wanted to be alone. I had to figure out what had happened—or was happening—to me.

"I don't understand how you can give her that kind of consideration. After what she put you through." Alex's jaw wobbled a little.

"She's my mom. She's the only person I have."

"I'm a person," he said. "You have me." And then he hugged me for a long time, and I hugged him, too. "Will you come back?"

"I want to," I told him. It was the truth.

• • •

All of the goodbyes had made us late. We almost didn't make it to the airport in time. I was used to feeling a certain way in airports—calm, focused. Maybe it was because Mom and I always set off feeling like we were on the same page, moving on to the next thing like it was a decision we had made together—even if, especially if, it wasn't.

That afternoon at McCarran International, it was clearer than ever that the world of Mom-and-me had changed. I felt the difference, the way you feel a loss of weight on your body. It's still your body, but the familiar, comforting swells and dips have disappeared.

She stayed close, keeping a hand on me through the long security line and in the restaurant where we bought lunch. We didn't talk, which, in itself, wasn't especially foreign. Mom often wandered away on one of her thinking jags, leaving me behind. This time, though—I was leaving *her* behind. I felt like she was looking at me, trying to talk, and not able to do it.

On the plane she tried to sit next to me, but in the row of three seats, I set Ida's box in the middle. The rental car, too, was filled with dense silence under the rain and the rhythmic sweep of the windshield wipers. The white box wobbled on my lap. I could barely look at Mom. I could barely look at my own watery reflection in the window.

I was quiet in Seattle. I was quiet in the overly clean business hotel Mom checked us in to. The only noise I made, I made with my hands. I couldn't put Ida's guitar down. I played all the Neil Young songs I could remember. My injured hand made my strumming clumsy and broken, but somehow it sounded more right that way. I thought, again, about what I'd seen in the desert, about that face, and tried to make sense of it across the frets of my grandmother's guitar. I didn't speak at the funeral home, where Mom picked out an urn and a set of yellow flower arrangements. Mom decided—and I nodded in agreement—that if it was only going to be us at the burial, to keep it short, like Ida would have wanted. I was quiet while Mom signed a bunch of checks under the carefully arranged, sympathetic gaze of the funeral director.

In the morning, we would drive out to the cemetery and Ida would be buried in the same ground as her son. I was curious about where he was buried. I wondered if there were any trees nearby, and what his tombstone looked like. I wondered if it would be one of those ornate ones with angel statues lounging on top. By the time we left, it was raining.

Inside of the floral-scented rental car, I finally spoke. "Mom, I love you. You're wrong a lot, and sometimes I can't stand you, but I really love you."

She looked at me like I'd just punched her.

"I'm not going to go with you, wherever you're going next. I'm going to do my own thing, okay? A girl from the Silver Saddle has a band that's going on tour, and she asked me to be in it. I'm going to tell her yes." I felt proud and guilty all at the same time.

It was Mom's turn to be quiet. She shook as she shifted the car in reverse and drove out of sight of the funeral home. But once we were out onto the road, she had to pull over, she was crying so much. I put a hand on her back, I couldn't help it, and we let the bland radio station music wash over us as the rain trickled down the windshield and windows of the car. I turned my face into the little rivulets, one hand on Mom, and one cheek pressed to the glass.

Chapter Twenty-Six

The cemetery was enormous. Morning gloom swallowed the dark funeral-home car ahead of us. The signal light beat through the opaque mist and Mom turned onto a narrow paved road. A pool of leaves to our right nearly covered the sign, but I could see as we drove by three large black words: Evergreen Hills Cemetery. I hadn't ever been to a cemetery. I was unprepared for how large Evergreen Hills was. I couldn't help but imagine how many bodies were encased in the earth we drove over. Thousands, probably. I shivered in my navy blue cotton dress. Mom hadn't slept at all the night before. She was showered and dressed, drinking out of a paper cup from some coffee shop chain nearby, by the time I woke up. I could always tell when she hadn't slept by the sharpness of her morning conversation and too-wide eyes. She was watching me, watching to see what I'd do next.

I knew she wanted me to take back what I'd said, but I wouldn't.

The cemetery grounds were drenched in green. Enormous maple trees soared over the drive, and the gray-white monuments hovered in the mist in jagged rows. There were lots of American flags, and clusters of flowers mobbed the well-tended graves. Some of the stones looked pretty derelict, though, seamed with cracks and nestled in organic debris—piles of leaves and moldering grass clippings. I wondered what my dad's would look like—probably the latter. The black car pulled to a stop in front of us. The funeral director had sent an underling, Thad, along to deal with us. Thad leapt from the dark car and scurried over, opening the door eagerly for Mom.

She kept her head low and strode to where a dark figure waited by a bend in one of the sand-colored footpaths that wound through Evergreen Hills. I could see Thad rushing over to my side, so I quickly slid out, opening and closing my own door. He gave a comic *oh-darn* snap, but shook it off right away, a little shocked by the inappropriate gesture. I smiled at him, which surprised me. It seemed like maybe Ida would have liked his goofing around.

When I caught up, Mom was already in conversation with the reverend, a stocky Asian woman with a crop of short, black hair. She was dressed in black robes and held a plastic binder in her hands. Mom waved me over.

"Van, this is Reverend Cindy. Reverend, this is Ida's granddaughter."

"I'm very sorry for your loss," Reverend Cindy said as she shook my hand, squeezing it very tightly at the same time.

"Is there anything you'd like her to say, specifically? Do *you* want to say anything, honey?" Mom asked. I could feel her wanting to do and say the right Mom things.

I shook my head.

"Let's begin, then."

"Of course," Reverend Cindy replied with a somber nod.

A small hole in the muddy earth gaped out at us, partly covered by a thin strip of Astroturf. Two workmen in coveralls stood to the side. It was obvious why they were there. Thad had disappeared into the dark car to retrieve Ida's ashes. He emerged, holding the polished brass urn. He offered it to Mom, who shook her head, and then he offered it to me. I shook my head, too.

There was something about the urn—so formal and final. When it had been just the white cardboard box, I'd felt Ida pulsing through, somehow. The golden urn looked just as dead as Ida—it wasn't something I wanted to touch.

Thad moved so that he was positioned between the hole in the ground and Reverend Cindy. Mom and I stood, so close we were almost touching, on the reverend's other side.

"Family, friends," Cindy's voice boomed out over Evergreen Hills, impressive in its volume and maple-syrup cadence. "We are here to celebrate the life of Ida Bouchard, beloved mother, friend, mother-in-law," Cindy looked meaningfully at Mom, "and grandmother." She clutched the white plastic binder in front of her. "Beloved Ida was a woman full of spirit and strength, yes, and love, too." Reverend Cindy spoke like she was trying to reach each pair of deceased ears underground.

The flower arrangements we'd chosen the day before stood on either side of the open grave, splotches of yellow in the green, green grass.

"We beseech you, ruler of the universe, to ease beloved Ida's transition into the next world. Her path on earth has been righteous, may her path beyond also be." Here, Reverend Cindy opened the binder in her hands and looked out, at Mom and me, at Thad, even at the duo of workmen slouched in their coveralls like old sacks of bones.

"Sofia has kindly provided me with a piece to read this morning. This was a piece near and dear to Ida, and, as I understand, to her son, Michael. It is also, I'm happy to say, near and dear to me. If you're familiar, please feel free to join." Cindy held the binder lightly in one hand and smoothed a palm over the single page of paper nestled inside. And then she began to speak, her magnificent voice looping through the air like some mystical lightning bug. She half recited, half sang "Astral Weeks."

It should have been so terrible, this too enthusiastic, possibly Wiccan priestess half singing and half chanting my dead father's favorite Van Morrison song, but it wasn't. Cindy's voice rose and broke through the song like some ancient lament, reaching down into all of us who stood around the tiny gravesite. Mom and I wept, and so did Thad. He had to readjust his hold on the urn, and the two workmen, who didn't cry, seemed to slump even more. I wiped my eyes and nose on my cardigan sleeve, and Thad handed the urn to the workmen. They lowered Ida down into the hole using the narrow strip of Astroturf. Thad fished a handful of yellow flowers from a green bucket behind his legs and handed them out. Everyone dropped a flower onto the urn, even the workmen, before they filled the hole with dirt.

We shook hands all around, Mom and I, our eyes still oozing tears from Cindy's performance. I hugged her before she left, that's how great it was.

"Do you need anything else, ladies? Can I escort you back?" Thad asked.

"No, thank you," Mom answered. "There's someone else we need to see here."

We left the pair of men shoveling dirt over Ida, sealing her inside of Evergreen Hills for all eternity. Mom took my hand and led me onto the winding footpath.

"I think it's over here," she said, pointing to a row of headstones about twenty feet away. We stepped off of the path and into the grass. The muddy ground yielded and sucked at the soles of my shoes. Mom pulled a square of paper out of her pocket and unfolded it.

"Right there," she said, striding over to the row abutting a low, verdant hedge. Mom walked ahead, looking down at the names. I stood back. I didn't want to stumble onto Dad's grave—I wanted to walk up to it knowing what it was. The gravestones in that row were nearly identical: white marble and low, the size of briefcases. Mom stopped in front of the eighth one over. She bent her head and crossed her arms. Her Burberry raincoat pulled tight across her back. I let Mom take a minute—I wasn't going to ask her what she was thinking, because I knew she'd never tell me. But I'd lived alongside her long enough to understand—she didn't love and miss him, but she felt guilty. She felt guilty about me, and now, she felt guilty about Ida. A cruel flicker unfurled in my chest as I realized a great way to hurt Mom's feelings would be to bring up how she couldn't even get a spot for Ida next to Michael.

And Mom, like always—like her brain could always go where my brain went—turned and spoke to me.

"I'm sorry I couldn't get them closer to each other," she said, shaking her head. "There was just no room. Nobody was thinking ahead when Michael died, I guess."

I felt a swell of anger—certainly *she* wasn't thinking ahead. I tried to push it back. I wanted to be neutral meeting my dad for the first time. It seemed disrespectful, and too late, to bring any of these other twisted feelings I had to the foot of his grave. I took a deep breath and then another one and put my hand on my chest. I felt my body and my mind settling down.

I clasped my hands in front, with the decorum of a choir singer, and walked over to Mom. I looked down at the worn, white marble, at the words there: MICHAEL BOUCHARD MAY 29 1970—DEC 11 1998. A lacey spray of flowers umbrellaed the text. Michael Bouchard. *Van Bouchard*, I thought. I thought about the ordinary life I could have had with Ida, if she'd taken me in as a baby. I thought about all of the faces I'd swallowed down in Sedona in front of that booming stone god, and I wondered if one of them had been Michael Bouchard. I wondered if all of them had been Michael Bouchard, different faces for all of the different things he would have said to me, different faces for all of the ways he would have looked at me.

If I hadn't known it before, I surely knew it now—we were all imperfect weirdos: Mom, Ida, Michael Bouchard. All of us, even—*especially*—me. But I was still here, and I could make something from all of it. The band was a beginning, an opening into a world where I could understand and explain all of these entrances, exists, and absences.

I looked down at Michael Bouchard, and then across at Mom. *This is what you have to work with*, I told myself. It was a lot. It was so much—a continuum from raw darkness to soaring crystal arrows. Even a month ago, the thought would have terrified me. It didn't, though, not anymore. I had my own place to go, and my own things to do. I could figure it out.